W9-AJU-452

Michaels, Grant.
Love you to death.

4

$18.95

DATE			

RENEWABLE

CONCORD FREE
CONCORD
MA
PUBLIC LIBRARY

BAKER & TAYLOR BOOKS

LOVE
YOU
TO
DEATH

Also by Grant Michaels

A Body to Dye For

LOVE YOU TO DEATH

Grant Michaels

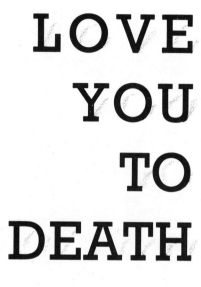

St. Martin's Press New York

LOVE YOU TO DEATH. Copyright © 1992 by Grant Michaels. All rights reserved. Printed in the United States of America. No part of this book may be used or reproduced in any manner whatsoever without written permission except in the case of brief quotations embodied in critical articles or reviews. For information, address St. Martin's Press, 175 Fifth Avenue, New York, N.Y. 10010.

Design by DAWN NILES

Library of Congress Cataloging-in-Publication Data

Michaels, Grant.
    Love you to death / Grant Michaels.
      p. cm.
    ISBN 0-312-07027-6
    I. Title.
    PS3563.I3317L68   1992
     813'.54—dc20   91-40473
                                                 CIP

First Edition: March 1992

10 9 8 7 6 5 4 3 2 1

for Wayne and for Crystal

Again and always,
thanks to my friends.

Contents

LOVE
YOU
TO
DEATH

1

THE PARTY'S OVER

Have you ever tried to diet?

    I don't mean the prefab kind, with the cans of Trim-U-Lax and the frozen entrees. I mean The Regime, with the yum-yum veggie sticks and the high-fiber crackers and the water. Water, water, water—the inexorable ten eight-ounce glasses (or is it eight ten-ounce glasses?) of *agua* every day. Drink and chew. Chew and drink. When you're not doing that, you're peeing. And through it all, you still want real food. You even dream about it—recurrent visions of Reuben sandwiches, French fries (with a side of bleu cheese dressing, just for dipping), or something lighter, like a slab of chocolate amaretto cheesecake with a Brandy Alexander chaser. Awake or asleep, you can almost taste the fat-filled, flavorful fantasies, only to be dashed by the reality of carrot sticks, bran wafers, and the goddam water.

    And then what? The ultimate challenge: You're invited out. That's right. After resigning yourself to dietary deprivation, after nights of noshing alone in front of the television, after your thumbs are callused from pressing the channel-scan button, and your gums are raw from all the air-popped, unbuttered popcorn—after all that, people now want you at their posh dinners or their fabulously catered parties. Suddenly you're the Most Popular Boy in the City.

So, what do you do?

I'll tell you. First you find the darkest togs in your wardrobe that you can still get over your hips without rending the fabric, or else you go out and *buy* a new outfit—all pleats and over-blouse to conceal the lard. Then you get your hair cut in a style that brings out the angles and planes of your face, wherever they're hiding. And then you Step Out.

You promise yourself you're going to be good at the party. You mutter those absurd affirmations—I *am* a slender person, I am *lithe*, I *will* be satisfied with blanched broccoli and sodium-free seltzer. But temptation wins, as it usually does, and you end up eating yourself into a coma, diving repeatedly into that roving platter of hot puff-pastry appetizers, nabbing two or three with one graceful swoop of the wrist, while nary a butter-soaked crumb falls into the plush-pile carpet cushioning the kidskin pumps on your feet.

Got the picture?

The gala reception was for Le Jardin Chocolatier, an exclusive candy store about to open its portals in Boston's Copley Place. Their timing was perfect, since Valentine's Day was less than two weeks away. There'd be just enough time for a frenzy of sweet holiday purchases in the new shop, and another boutique enterprise would be launched. The big party was Sunday night, not the best time for the working class to be out carousing, but then, these weren't exactly working-class folk. Besides, I could pretend to be just like them, since tomorrow morning I wouldn't have a care in the world either. As a hair stylist, Monday is my day off.

Three hundred highbrow guests milled tastefully about in a large ballroom at the Copley Plaza Hotel, entertained by a salon orchestra, superb food, and one another's dull wit. I was feeling like a proud yenta at a wedding reception, since I had introduced the two young professionals who were launching the new business. They were both clients at Snips Salon, where I create my grand designs, on Newbury Street, just around the corner from Boston's Ritz Carlton Hotel.

Liz Carlini, whose wild raven hair I cut so expertly, was the business savvy behind the venture, and Dan Doherty, whose dark, springy curls I simply like to get my hands into, was the imaginative designer who'd set their products and image far beyond anything in existence. The theme of Le Jardin was flowers, and Danny had taken it to the dimensions of grand opera. One specialty item: liquor-drenched, chocolate-covered rose petals, arranged in a glorious blossom atop a slender candy stem complete with sugar crystal thorns and marzipan leaves. They are divine, and they cost a king's ransom. But the bread-and-butter of the business is the *truffe au chocolat*, known to us plebes as a chocolate truffle—a gob of dark chocolate, sweet butter, heavy cream, and pure flavoring all mixed together, then dusted with cocoa or dipped in more chocolate. It's the kind of stuff that keeps cardiologists booked.

For me, though, the party was a perfect way to relax after a hectic week at the shop. There were no late appointments, no whining customers, no chemical surprises. All I had to do was stand around with a tumbler of good bourbon and a napkin full of fattening snacks and watch the fashionable crowd—study the women's hair work and size up the good-looking men. Alas, the pleasant moments were interrupted by a familiar voice accusing me of some heinous crime.

"Stanley, that is *not* on your allowed list."

The voice was Nicole Albright's. Nikki owns Snips Salon, but she plays the resident manicurist. That way she can easily indulge her passion for gossip.

I quickly popped the last of three crab-stuffed bouchées into my mouth, chewed the luscious morsel, and swallowed. A gulp of hundred-proof bourbon helped it home.

"Nikki," I replied, "I left my allowed list at the door, along with yours. We can both pick them up on our way out."

Nicole gave me a cool stare. Tonight her bottled-auburn hair was swept tightly back into a classic chignon. "Don't include me in your idle weight-loss experiments," she muttered. "I eat what I want."

I glanced at her thickened waistline, luxuriously draped with a ruby-red silk cocktail dress. "It shows, doll."

An arched eyebrow—more pencil than hair—was her response to that, though in fact Nicole's svelte figure was long gone, left in Paris years ago with her modeling career, way before I knew her.

Just then a handsome young waiter paused before us with a tray of drinks. Nicole exchanged her empty champagne glass for a full one, and I requested another double bourbon. The waiter rendered a fawning smile, then sauntered off.

Nicole sipped her champagne while she scanned the crowd for appealing men. Her eyes stopped on a distinguished gentleman in his fifties, impeccably groomed and endowed with a full head of thick salt-and-pepper hair. The silvery crown was a perfect complement to his suit, a double-breasted jacket and pleated trousers of gorgeous Prussian blue wool. He was talking pleasantly with Liz Carlini and Dan Doherty, and I could sense Nikki's pleasure over the man's appearance.

"I wonder who he is," she said, her machinations noisily at work already.

"Don't you recognize him? He's been to the shop once or twice."

"I wouldn't have missed him."

"I wouldn't think so. That's Prentiss Kingsley."

"*The* Prentiss Kingsley? Of Gladys Gardner chocolates?"

I nodded. "Serious wealth, doll."

"Island home?"

"Many. He's also Liz Carlini's husband."

"They're married?" she asked with disappointment and disbelief.

I nodded.

Nicole continued, "But she's half his age."

"Not quite. But look who's calling the kettle black, with you and that man-child from Harvard Business School. What's his name? Rod Love?"

"He's finished *law* school, Stanley, and his name is not Rod Love."

"It might as well be, for all the use you get out of him."

Nicole glowered. "You never know when you're going to need a smart young lawyer, which Chaz certainly is. Besides, I'm not married to him."

"You couldn't be, with any discretion, doll. You're old enough to be his mother."

"That's *not* why I'm not married. But I wonder why Liz Carlini didn't take her husband's name. Isn't the Kingsley tag an asset in Boston society?"

"Maybe if you spend a lot of time in the Athenaeum. My guess is that Liz just doesn't like having to sign all those dividend checks Elizabeth Anne Carlini-Kingsley."

"It is quite a mouthful," said Nicole.

Which is exactly what I had in mind when a salver of smoked seafood drifted by, carried in the long dark arms of a beautiful Jamaican woman. It was Laurett Cole, the former receptionist at Snips, now about to manage Le Jardin's new store. Though we already missed her at the shop, Laurett's new job was a kind of step ahead for her, with more responsibilities and more money. For tonight's celebration, I'd styled her long black tresses into a shimmering cascade of perfectly sculpted finger waves. Nicole took credit for the lacquered nails, with crescent moons just peeking out near the cuticle line. And finally, Laurett's makeup glow was courtesy of Ramon, Snips's sexy shampoo boy, who'd given up his waning career in faux-finishing to pursue esthetics.

Through a broad smile Laurett exclaimed happily, "I am hoping to find you two!" Laurett had two speech patterns. One was an appealing combination of perfect British diction combined with faulty and inconsistent grammar, which she used when she was relaxed and with people she trusted. The other version was what she called her "good speech," which she used in business or with strangers. Laurett also had amber-colored catlike eyes, which could disarm you with their direct and intent gaze. She shifted the large tray onto one arm, then she ran her free hand over my newly shorn red hair. "This is being short like a brush."

"It's the new definition of butch," I said. "A crew cut in the middle of winter in Boston."

Nicole asked, "Why are *you* serving food, Laurett?"

Laurett smiled politely—too politely, as though mocking her subservient role—then explained, "Miss Lisa want me to wait on them tonight, so they know me in the store, where I will wait on them again tomorrow."

I said, "Laurett, her name is Liz, not Lisa."

"I know, Vannos" she replied, addressing me by my salon name with a broad grin. "But didn't I explain once who Miss Lisa is? I mean, for me?"

She had. Miss Lisa was Laurett's pet name for her . . . well, for her feminine parts. Don't your nether regions have a nickname?

Laurett continued, "That's why I'm always saying to her Miss-Lisa-this and Miss-Lisa-that." A delicate laugh trickled out after her words, then she thrust the platter of smoked seafood toward me, pretending to serve one of the snooty guests. "Would you like some fish, sir?" Then she laughed more heartily, knowing my intimate predilections lay elsewhere. But foodwise I'm less particular, and I eagerly took one sizeable morsel of each—salmon, oyster, and eel.

Nicole clucked, "Diet."

"It's all protein," I replied as I gobbled the oyster.

Laurett offered the seafood more politely to Nicole, who shook her head and said she'd wait for the pâté. Laurett said, "I send it by here," then she departed and moved on through the crowd.

"It's a lousy turn for her to have to work the party tonight," said Nicole.

"Not from Liz Carlini's business point of view," I replied.

Nicole returned her gaze to the three guests of honor—Prentiss Kingsley, his wife Liz Carlini, and their friend Dan Doherty. Liz was now conversing seriously with another guest who'd joined them, a crusty old gent who looked as if he'd been dusted off and rolled down from a Beacon Hill attic just for the occasion. "Look at her go," Nicole remarked. "She's almost attacking that poor old man."

"It's called networking, doll, and Liz does it with religious fervor."

Nicole watched as Liz Carlini insinuated herself onto the older man, who was cowering under her social assault. With one eyebrow slightly raised, she said, "This might be a good time for me to introduce myself to the distinguished, wealthy, and handsome Mr. Kingsley."

"Ah, now *that's* called schmoozing, which is more to your taste, Nikki, with all its effluvial connotations. Just remember, they're married."

"Stanley, don't project your parochial school morality onto me. I'm simply going to introduce myself to the man and congratulate him on his lovely wife's success."

"Nikki, you don't do anything simply."

She set off toward the trio of honored guests, while my eyes followed her distinctive strut across the room. Nicole's posture and gait was like that of a high-strung show horse prancing before the judges' stand, a holdover from her days on the Paris runways.

At that moment though, at least for my eyes, she was outdone by someone else—a dark-haired and dark-eyed stranger emerging from the kitchen. Except for the nose, he could have been movie-star material from the days of romance and mystique, when a smoldering glance stirred the heart more than an exposed crotch ever could. He'd slicked back his hair, but I could still discern a natural, barbaric curl under the gel. And there was nothing shy about the nose either, reminiscent of an eagle in profile. He'd just let go of the swinging door when he looked my way and caught my admiring glance. He smiled openly, then waved to me, as though he recognized me. He motioned for me to join him as he made his way toward Danny and Prentiss and the others. I headed that way too, and saw him get there just when Nicole did, still in her pursuit of Prentiss Kingsley. The handsome stranger and Nicole actually bumped, but he smiled and nodded politely to her. Then he took firm hold of Danny's shoulders and pulled him away from the small group toward another part of the hall. Nicole, meanwhile, sidled up to Prentiss Kingsley, while Liz Carlini seemed a bit distracted by all the sudden intrusions. Seeing his chance, Liz's elderly victim took advantage of the lapse in her attention and quietly escaped. With Danny and the handsome stranger out of reach for the moment, I decided to go talk with Liz and steer her attention away from Nicole, whom I knew would flirt brazenly with Prentiss Kingsley. Nothing was intended by it, except perhaps to upset Liz, the cool, ambitious, asexual businesswoman, the very kind Nicole detests.

Liz seemed almost relieved to see me. It probably comforted her to have someone to latch onto and overpower. She threw a cold glance toward Nicole, who was already maneuvering Prentiss Kingsley toward a large table where the entire Le Jardin product line was lavishly displayed.

Liz said to me, "I'm surprised that manicurist from your salon is here tonight."

I answered frankly. "When you and Danny invited me, you said I could bring a guest. I didn't think it was conditional."

She blinked nervously as Nicole and Prentiss disappeared into the crowd. She seemed worried that Nicole might corner her husband and expose herself, or something equally outrageous. Then again, knowing Nikki . . .

I said quickly, "Nicole loves to meet new people." I should have added honestly, "especially men," but I already noticed a defensive tone creeping into my voice.

Liz sipped nervously at her drink—undoubtedly pure imported mineral water—and spoke again before she'd completely swallowed the last bit, which caused her to cough and sputter a moment. It seemed to embarrass her, as though *real* professional people didn't have the same visceral functions as ordinary mortals. Even simple things like coughing or sneezing were undesirable. She looked out over the crowd as she tried to explain the coughing away. "Excuse me, please. I seem to be so excited by this whole event, I'm afraid I'm forgetting myself."

Whoever that is, I thought.

The errant droplets lingered in her throat, teetering between trachea and esophagus, while Liz waited impatiently for their decision. I wanted to tell her to relax her throat, which would help the water go where it belonged. Instead, I remained silent and watched the tears well up in her eyes as she resisted the urge to cough. Finally, after a hyper-controlled clearing of her throat, she spoke again.

"Vannos, there were moments in the past year when I wondered if this business would ever get off the ground. You have no idea of some of the difficulties." She sipped at her water again, as if to prove that she was unafraid of another cough. Meanwhile, I prepared myself to administer the Heimlich Remover, just in case her swallowing reflex was still faulty. But she merely smiled and continued talking. "Now we're finally home free, and we can start making some money."

"I didn't know you had any problems at all, Liz," I said, thinking of the relative ease with which a new business can be launched when money is an unlimited resource. "Was it labor trouble then?" I asked.

Liz turned her head sharply toward me. "Did Danny say anything to you?"

"No, I was just curious."

She looked at me suspiciously.

I continued, "I didn't mean to pry."

I was always a bit hurt by Liz Carlini's haughtiness. Most clients want to share at least one deep, dark, serious secret with their hair stylist, especially after they've known each other a while. Liz was strange that way. I'd been doing her hair for two years, and I still didn't know much about the woman under the head of lustrous, dense black hair.

Liz shook her head forcefully, as though trying to cancel our exchange, as though our words were on a computer screen and she could push the "clear" button to make the conversation go away, as though the past had never happened.

From within the crowd, Laurett reappeared before us with the seafood platter, which was less than half full now. Liz spoke sharply to her. "Finish with that, Laurett, then make sure everything is ready in the kitchen for the final presentation."

"Already?" said Laurett. "Miss Lisa, there is much more food to serve." Her good speech had been activated.

"Don't talk back," said Liz. "Just finish that platter and get back to the kitchen."

I leapt to action and rescued the platter from Laurett's arms. "I can help with that," I said. I nudged her with my shoulder, aiming her back into the crowd where I wanted to be too, away from Liz Carlini. I turned my head back toward Liz and called out, "See you later!" I was surprised to see her look forlorn. Had my sudden desertion caused it?

As I pushed Laurett along through the crowd, she asked, "What are you doing? You want to feed these hungry rats too?"

"This platter gives me a good excuse to walk around and meet people." I cocked my head toward Danny and his handsome friend. "Especially him," I said.

Laurett shook her head and wagged a finger at me. "You bad, Vannos," she said, and headed back toward the kitchen.

I continued on my way toward Dan Doherty and the exotic young man who had waved to me earlier. The two of them were standing in a quiet alcove, and they seemed to be arguing. Nothing like a good fight to show a person's mettle, I say; so I strolled over to them with the platter of smoked seafood, as though they were exactly in my intended path. They both looked up as I approached. Danny frowned, but the other man, my obscure object of desire, smiled that charming smile again.

"Hey, Christian!" he called out to me with a heavy accent. French, I thought, and no wonder he's so friendly—he thinks I'm someone else, probably somebody influential. I saw Danny say something to him, but the handsome stranger didn't respond. He was too busy smiling at me.

When I got to them, I offered the platter. "This is the last of the seafood."

Danny seemed surprised. "The food is gone already?"

"No, but Liz wants to stop serving now and start the dessert soon."

Danny said, "It's too early for that. I'll go talk to her." He turned to leave, then said curtly to his friend, "We'll finish with this later." Then he walked brusquely away back into the crowd in search of Liz Carlini, leaving me alone with the handsome stranger. I couldn't have choreographed it better.

"How you been, Christian?" he asked with suave broken English.

"My name is Stan," I answered. "I think you have me confused with someone else."

"Mebbee. But I see your hair. Is short and copper, just like Christian." He pronounced the word "copair."

"I had it cut yesterday."

He gave a blasé shrug. "So, you are not Christian, but you are nice." His dark eyes danced and flirted, taking in me, the party, and the world all at once.

"Well, you seem nice too," I said.

"I am Rafik," he said, and extended his hand. His name rhymed with technique.

I juggled the platter onto my left arm, and shook his hand. He held onto mine even after I released the pressure of the handshake. He squeezed it strongly a few times. Then, as he let go, he pressed his fingers against my palm. I felt a little shiver of pleasure, since his message was clear. Hell, Valentine's Day was in two weeks, and I was, as usual, single. My last romance with a young Balinese had ended abruptly when he returned to California to pursue a degree in Fashion Administration. And since most of my friends own wash-and-wear bridal gowns, I often wonder when it will be my turn for romance, with the flowers and candy and kisses, and whatever physical gymnastics might follow the sweet, sloppy, sentimental part of courtship. In fact, I was ready for some deep and dirty loving.

"Are you French?" I asked.

"Yes, *non*," he said with that killer smile. "I am born in Paris, but I grow up in Montreal. My parents . . . is very complicated."

"But you live here now?"

"Oh yes," he said with a nod—a sexy, inviting nod.

A brief silence followed, and I became slightly flustered, as I often do when a desirable man has touched me. He asked, "How you know Danny?" He pronounced it "Dunny."

"I do his hair."

"You are hairdresser?"

"Yes."

"But you are so *masculeen!*"

Why did the word sound more convincing with a French accent? And what was causing this unlikely admiration? Was it my coppery hair, freshly cut in a faux-butch style? Perhaps it was the reddish mustache hovering over my full lips, which tend to grin easily. Or the green eyes? My guess is that it's my big square jaw that appeals to people. Though my face is a bit fleshy, it's also blessed with the strong, angular kind of bones usually reserved for television sports reporters or lumberjacks, though rumor has it that some of those he-men trip rather lightly too. So, okay, my jaw is big and manly. Once you know me, though, you'll find it's just a home for tongue and teeth and sass.

"I'm one of the new breed," I replied. "No more limp wrists. We're all brawny brutes now, yanking hair out by the roots."

He chuckled and said, "You are funny man."

I let the remark slip and asked, "How do *you* know Danny?" in my turn of tit-for-tat.

His eyes looked down for a moment, as if to recall a poignant memory. Then he said, "We meet at the cafe."

"Here in Boston?"

"En Montreal."

"So, you're lovers?"

Rafik shifted slightly on his long legs. "We are friends. I help with business."

"Then you have a job?" Always important to know, especially with charming, good-looking men.

He hesitated. "Yes . . ." Then he switched on the bedroom gaze. "I like to see you."

"Already? You must need a green card."

"Eh?" he replied, puzzled.

"Are you a U.S. citizen?"

"No . . ." he answered cautiously.

"You must want to get married then."

"Go to bed?"

"That too, probably," I said with a shrug.

"I like that," he said, showing all his white teeth.

"I'm not sure Danny would, though."

From behind me I heard, "Not sure I'd like what?"

It was Danny. Of course he'd overhear. This is me and my timing we're talking about. I explained sheepishly that Rafik and I were just kidding around.

"Take him, Vannos. I've had enough. No deposit, no return. He's all yours."

"Danny, I didn't mean—"

"We were just breaking up when you came over with that tray, Vannos, so your timing was perfect."

I let out a heavy sigh. My playfulness had been misconstrued, and now Danny was having a queen attack. Why didn't Rafik say something to clear the air, to calm Danny down?

I gave a resigned sigh and looked down at the tray. "I guess I'll finish serving this stuff." But as I turned to go, Rafik held my arm.

"Excuse me?" he said, asking it like a question.

I looked across my shoulder into his eyes.

He said, "Your name is Stan, or Vannos?"

"In the shop it's Vannos, in real life it's Stan."

"So," he said with that ever-inviting gleam in his eye, "I am real life for you, eh?"

Danny interrupted our lingering tango. "You'd better hurry up with that fish. Liz is in the kitchen burning her rotors to get the dessert served. I couldn't change her mind about it."

On the way back to the kitchen, I noticed Prentiss Kingsley being corralled by another man—a stocky, broad-shouldered guy in his forties, wearing a plain brown suit. He looked like a former preppy jock gone slightly paunchy. The man was annoyed about something, as though the refined Prentiss Kingsley had just snatched an overnight parking space from him. Neither Liz nor

Nicole was anywhere near them. The guy was pushing Prentiss Kingsley into a narrow, empty service pantry that was remote from the main part of the floor. I skirted around the crowd and went to stand near the opening to the pantry. I trained my ears on their conversation, and I caught a good part of it.

"Prentiss, this party is decadent. You have no right—"

"I have every right, John. I always have."

"You got your mother's money on a fluke, not a right."

"But I did get it, John."

"And now you're squandering it on frivolities."

"This business venture is not frivolous. In fact, Van Gumpfe of Switzerland has already made a generous bid for Le Jardin. I don't meddle in your sordid affairs, *dear brother*, so please keep your petty complaints and your tiresome envy in check."

"Half brother, Prentiss. We're half brothers."

"That's right, John. You've finally accepted the fact that the Kingsley name and fortune are mine and mine alone. You can keep the Lough surname all to yourself, along with everything and everyone connected to it."

The name rhymed with tough . . . or fluff. At the moment I couldn't tell which.

"You and your dead mother's name," said John Lough. "Don't forget your young wife and her young friends, Prentiss. They seem to be enjoying the Kingsley money too."

"I will not have you insult Elizabeth and Daniel."

Their argument seemed to be getting out of hand, and the next thing I knew, Prentiss Kingsley and John Lough came out from the service pantry and were facing me directly. I was caught. I looked down at the tray I was carrying. The seafood was beginning to look a little tired, but it still looked worthy to offer to Prentiss Kingsley and his sparring partner. With my best service-industry persona, I asked, "Would either of you two gentlemen like some seafood?"

Mr. Lough's eyes narrowed in rage. "Leave us alone."

Mr. Kingsley said, "I must find my wife now," and he walked away without even acknowledging me.

But John Lough said, "Get back to work."

Thoroughly humiliated by the ruling class, I wandered back into the party crowd, where Nicole intercepted me. "What was that all about?"

"You saw?"

She nodded. "Everything."

"The estimable Mr. Kingsley seems to have family problems. He was arguing with his brother about money and property—the usual party banter."

"But you also struck paydirt, Stanley. Who was that dark-eyed beauty hanging around Danny?"

"You don't miss much, Nikki."

"Not men like him."

"Dark-eyes is Danny's lover, and he's got a great pair of round heels too."

"Are you going to spin him then?"

"Nikki, the next time my ovaries start clacking over a handsome man, just hog-tie me and throw me into the ice bin."

"With pleasure, darling. But I must insist that you be gagged first."

"Sure, have your way with me. Anything for a pal."

She put her arm around me and hugged me, slightly upsetting the serving platter.

"Stani," she said, using the nickname that my Czech grandmother liked, "why don't you go dump that in the kitchen? You're the only one out here still holding food."

It was true. In the time since I'd taken the platter from Laurett, all the other servers had long since left the floor of the party hall. I snaked my way through the crowd back toward the kitchen. Along the way, hands appeared from behind bodies and snatched the last pieces of smoked seafood from the salver. By the time I got to the kitchen door, the platter had been picked clean by the starving rich.

As I was entering the kitchen, Liz Carlini was coming out. "Are you still serving food?" she asked curtly.

"Just returning the empty platter, Liz. Feeling a bit testy tonight?" I thought perhaps some light humor might loosen her up. It didn't.

"The guests need time before dessert," she said flatly. "The floor should be devoid of food for at least a half-hour."

"That doesn't seem hospitable."

"We are not here to be hospitable. We are promoting a new business venture."

It was interesting to see one of my clients in real-world action, outside the salon. I'd already guessed that Liz Carlini was ambitious, but now I saw that she was unpleasantly quick-tempered under pressure. It seemed an unsuitable trait for working with the public, especially with a company whose product was ultraluxe chocolates.

In the kitchen I got rid of my tray and was about to return to the party when I heard Laurett's voice arguing with someone else. It seemed to be a night full of social conflict. I followed the sound of the voices until I found her. She was trying to supervise the preparation of dessert—chocolate truffles and more champagne, along with coffee or tea for those of us with more pedestrian needs. But another woman was alongside her, yelling at her and interrupting her work. She was in her early sixties, small and wrinkly like an irritable old terrier. And she had a henna rinse in her hair that could have only been done in a bathroom . . . or a garage.

"Keep your fingerprints off them," she yelled at Laurett, who was trying to rearrange a large platter of truffles that had been upset.

"Don't tell me what to do. I don't work for you."

"You don't deserve to work for anybody here. You island people should go back where you came from."

"Just leave me!" wailed Laurett. I saw tears in her eyes.

"And you get *him* out of here too," yelled the older woman, pointing to a stranger standing partly concealed in a dark corner a few yards from the work table. Then she turned away from Laurett and stormed past me on her way toward the kitchen door. Her angry footsteps seemed too heavy for such a small person.

When she was gone, I asked Laurett, "Is everything all right?"

Laurett nodded silently.

"Who was that?" I asked.

"That is Mary Phinney," she said, trying to control a sniff. "She hates me because I'm being the manager in the new store, and she wants that job." Then, after a moment of calming herself down, Laurett resumed working on the chocolates in front of her. I watched her carefully apply a miniature candy blossom to the top of a plain truffle. I noticed two other truffles already decorated with flowers, each one on its own small sterling silver plate.

"Are those for the guests of honor?" I asked.

"Sure-you're-right," answered Laurett, saying the phrase as one word. She finished the job with a small flourish. "There," she said with a tiny sniffle. She spoke to the chocolate as she placed it on the third silver plate. "Now you be perfect too."

It was then that the stranger who'd been lurking in a nearby corner came into the light and slouched against the wall. He stared at Laurett and me. He was young, mid-twenties, good-looking, and muscular, like a spoiled pretty-boy from the suburbs. But he also had the cold, manipulative look of an opportunist. He spoke with a weak, raspy voice, as though he needed water badly. "What about a piece for me, babe?" he said, then snickered vacantly at his own words, as though he was drunk or drugged.

"Not now," answered Laurett.

"Who's that?" I asked quietly.

Laurett frowned and didn't answer me. She obviously knew the man, but didn't want to introduce him. It seemed that the approach of Valentine's Day was causing more friction than affection among the loving couples I'd met that evening.

Sensing trouble, I asked, "Do you want me to stay around?"

She shook her head no. "You go back out and enjoy yourself." But I could tell she was forcing her voice to sound steady and controlled.

"There's no fun, Laurett, now that the food's gone."

"Vannos, there were being some nice-looking men out there. Don't put all your mind on the food."

I wanted to protest that I wasn't one of those people who

satisfy their sexual frustration with food, but it would be futile. I fully realized that the only time that night when I'd neglected my alimentary canal was during the brief and vain pursuit of Rafik.

The tough stranger standing in the corner of the kitchen spoke up again. "Hey, babe, who is this twink? Can't you get rid of him?"

On a closer look at the man, he seemed familiar, but I couldn't place him. Had he been to the shop?

Laurett scowled at him again, then spoke quietly to me. "Vannos, please go now. I have work to do."

Uneasy, I left the kitchen and returned to the party floor. As I came through the doorway, though, many people looked my way, as though I might be bearing a new course of snacks for them. Contrary to Liz Carlini's belief, these folks still wanted chow. And since many of them appeared to be couples, and presumably were sexually satisfied, I wondered what their craving for unneeded food meant for them.

I saw Nicole talking, or rather arguing, with Liz Carlini. I approached them, and when Liz saw me, she turned abruptly and walked away.

"Liz seems edgy tonight," I said.

"Stanley, that woman is rude."

"What happened now?"

"She's making accusations."

"You mean the same ones women usually make after you've met their husbands?"

"Stanley, that remark is uncalled for."

"Aw, Nikki, even if you do prefer grad students and married men, I still love you. Besides, Prentiss Kingsley has troubles of his own, even without you breaking up his marriage."

Nicole replied, "From what I've seen tonight, no one is too happy to be here, as though the whole event is an obligation and not a party."

"Amen, doll."

Just then the kitchen doors swung open and a long line of servers filed out into the crowd.

"Uh-oh," I said. "The grand finale. Dessert time."

Each server carried a tray, some with chocolate truffles piled into pyramids, some with champagne flutes full of bubbly, others with hot coffee or complete tea services. Laurett Cole was with them, but she went to Dan Doherty, Liz Carlini, and Prentiss Kingsley and presented each of them one of the specially decorated truffles on a small silver plate. She was extra careful about who got which plate. After a few more minutes, every guest in the party hall was holding a chocolate truffle in one hand and a champagne glass or hot beverage in the other. The lights were lowered except around the three special guests, who now stood apart from the crowd, as though they were receiving Olympic medals. The salon orchestra played a little fanfare before each one of the three made a little speech. Prentiss Kingsley went first.

"By helping my young wife Elizabeth start Le Jardin, we are continuing the fine tradition of quality and service begun by my great-grandmother, Gladys Kingsley, and which has continued through the family line until my dear late mother, Helen Kingsley. We are proud of this moment. . . ." He went on like that, rather too regally, and I thought his words were in bad taste, referring as they did to all the old dead Kingsley ladies. However, the quiet appearance of Rafik behind me, covertly squeezing my nether cheeks during the spiel, was not in bad taste at all.

When it was Liz Carlini's turn to speak, she said—and I'll give the woman credit for bragging so blatantly in public—"Le Jardin is a new concept in chocolate. We have gone beyond tradition to create new pathways in the art of chocolate-making. The days of old-fashioned boxed chocolates are ending." As I said, empty, but in complementary taste to her husband's words. Meanwhile, Rafik continued his good taste in seduction tactics by whispering into my ear, grazing the lobe softly with his lips.

"Mebbee you like to ride my truck?"

It sounded like kinky fun until I found out he was the driver for Le Jardin's spiffy new delivery van.

Then Danny took the floor, and after glaring at Rafik and

me, said, "I'm grateful for the opportunity to have my ideas seen by the world. I owe a lot to Prentiss and Liz. Enjoy the chocolate, folks." Did I mention that Danny was young and idealistic? His words may have been trite, but at least they were brief and honest. At Danny's words, Rafik had disappeared, the coward.

Then, simultaneously, all three speakers took a bite of their truffle. Liz Carlini bit into hers, but watched Danny and her husband intently, waiting for their reactions. For his part, Danny barely had one. I think to him it was just another hunk of chocolate. The better reaction was Prentiss Kingsley's. Though he is a handsome gent, his refinement borders on blandness, except for what he did at that moment. He bent his head over the silver plate in his hand and spit out his mouthful of truffle onto it. He looked like an obtuse child who couldn't bear the taste of grilled eggplant. The audience gasped at the seeming impropriety of the act.

Then we all heard a long, loud scream from the kitchen.

At once I recognized Laurett Cole's voice and ran to help her. She was standing at one of the long stainless steel counters, screaming at a man lying on the floor, who was writhing in pain and making loud, dry, gasping sounds. It was the same person who'd been in the kitchen earlier, the one who'd been bothering her and insulting me. I went to him to try to help. In my mind I pressed "Play" to start the mental cassette of the CPR class I'd taken months ago. The man's shirt collar was already open, but I went through the motions of loosening it further. There was melted chocolate in and around his mouth. I put my fingers in there and felt around for any blockage in his throat, but came out with nothing. Besides, through the gasping and grunting, I could hear the air going in and out, so I figured the airway wasn't blocked.

"Where does it hurt?" I yelled stupidly, as though he couldn't hear me.

But the man didn't answer. Instead, he squirmed violently on the floor, then he lapsed into spasms. I cleared the space around him so he wouldn't hurt himself. Perhaps he's epileptic, I thought. But within minutes he'd turned as red as a cooked lobster, and then he stopped moving. Everything stopped—his arms, his legs, his head, his breathing. I felt for a pulse, first at his wrist, then at his jugular. Nothing.

Quickly I tilted his head back, pinched his nostrils, and administered cardiopulmonary resuscitation. Giving the breath of life had seemed so easy in CPR class, kind of like kissing from the diaphragm. But I can tell you, it's not pleasant when you do it for real, when you're trying to revive through a filthy mouth what you know in your head and heart to be a corpse.

I continued puffing him up for five minutes, then surrendered to the facts of life. The guy was dead.

I looked up from where I was kneeling on the floor. Nicole was standing above me, along with two of the party's security guards. Behind them the crowd of guests was gathering and craning their necks in morbid curiosity. I said to the guards, "You'd better lock the doors until the police get here." One of them radioed his crew to seal off the party room and the rest of the building immediately. Meanwhile, I stood up, found a telephone, and called the Boston Police Department to report a dead man.

2

MY OLD FLAME

While we waited in the main hall for the police to arrive, I got to watch how the unexpected arrival of death was affecting some of the party guests. Prentiss Kingsley was holding his wife, Liz Carlini, close to him, almost tenderly. I'd never figure a Brahmin capable of such warmth, especially in public. Then again, perhaps the lovey-dovey bit was only because they *were* in public. For her part, Liz Carlini was pale and shaky. I guess among all the details of her grand scheme that night, she hadn't counted on death appearing as an uninvited guest at her party.

Near them, and also standing together, were Dan Doherty and Rafik. They looked confused and lost, as though the drama of their rocky romance had been rudely interrupted by sudden death. The curtain had come down on them mid-scene.

Farther away I saw John Lough with Mary Phinney. I recalled that earlier he'd been arguing with Prentiss Kingsley, and she had yelled at Laurett in the kitchen. The unlikely twosome—a growling brown bear and a yappy yellow lapdog—looked around the crowd suspiciously while they exchanged words through tightly held lips. I couldn't quite make out their relationship. Were they husband and wife, brother and sister, or just corporate colleagues? Whichever it was, they looked personally bothered by the turn of events, as though the inconvenience was solely theirs.

Nicole, Laurett, and I were together too. Nikki was comforting Laurett, who was weeping quietly.

Meanwhile, the security guards had their hands full trying to keep order through the rest of the crowd. A few bloodthirsty souls wanted to get into the kitchen to see the dead man first-hand, but most of the guests wanted to leave the premises entirely. Their clean, insulated lives rarely had to face death so directly, and they wanted no part of it. For them, death was probably an antiseptic, secondhand experience by telegram or telephone, some sorrowful words describing the merciful passing of a favorite aunt, along with the bitter news that *you* now own the property in Martha's Vineyard or Belvedere. "Isn't it sad?" they utter mournfully; but mentally they're jumping dikes and thinking, "How swell!"

The noisy arrival of the police only roused them all to the kind of emotional chaos usually reserved for a Dow-Jones plummeting. For their part, the cops entered with their inimitable style—all heavy feet and loud voices and squawking radios. Their particular kind of intrusion can push anyone's latent hysteria over the edge. They probably plan it that way.

The leader of tonight's gang turned out to be a familiar face, one Detective Lieutenant Vito Branco. I'd met him previously, and we . . . well, let's just say we spent a lot of energy trying to get along with each other.

On the positive side, Branco is a Mediterranean dreamboat—tall, proportioned and muscled like an athlete, with olive-toned skin and black curly hair, and those glittering blue-gray eyes. He's also straight, which makes him good fantasy material. His greeting?

"Christ, not you again." The lover spaeketh to his beloved.

"Hello, Lieutenant," I said with a fey wave of my left wrist. "It's been a while."

Branco responded with a grunt, which was his version of a quick retort. "Not long enough," he muttered. Then he asked, "What happened here?"

I explained the events as clearly and as calmly as I could. "I was with the others out here in the party hall. We all heard a scream, and I recognized Laurett's voice, so I ran into the kitchen to see what was wrong."

"Which way is the kitchen?"

I pointed the way, and Branco ordered some cops to go there. Then he turned back to me. "Who's Laurett?"

"She's my friend." But when I went to point her out, she'd vanished from Nicole's side. "She was here a minute ago," I began to explain, but Branco turned to one of his assistants and barked an order.

"Find her!"

Then, as if to win a round of an ongoing but unstated contest between us, he said to me, "We've got the place surrounded. She won't get away."

"Lieutenant, she's not trying to escape. She had nothing to do with this."

"We'll decide that. Go on with your story."

"Sure," I said, and looked directly at his face—a brief look that required me to reconcile, yet again, that this handsome creature who seemed to exude an intoxicating scent of wild balsam was, technically speaking, the enemy. After a moment of visual and olfactory pleasure, I continued. "Laurett was trying to help the man, but he wasn't responding." It wasn't exactly what I'd seen happening earlier—she hadn't tried to help him at all. But I wanted her to appear blameless, so I enhanced the facts a bit.

"Then what?" asked Branco.

"Then I got down to help him. I thought maybe he was choking, and I know CPR. But I couldn't do anything for him. He was gone within minutes."

Branco turned and addressed the crowd of restive party-goers. "You'd better get comfortable, folks. We're going to be here a while."

One of the crowd spoke up. It was John Lough. "Can't this be done another time?" he said. "It's inconvenient for some of us to wait around here at your leisure."

Leisure is not a word I'd use with Branco, who replied coldly, as if reciting from his rule book, "We'll question you all here, now, one at a time."

Of course, that kind of arrangement wouldn't go down with

these people. Mortal upsets didn't play any part in their pastel-ordered lives. But as it dawned on them that they couldn't delegate this unpleasant task to some minion, they began muttering and grumbling among themselves. Branco raised his big right-hand palm to silence them, and damn if it didn't work—they all shut up. Then he gave orders to his sergeant to organize them for questioning. He turned back to me and said, "You stay here. I want your story first."

"So, I'm head of the class?"

Branco sneered and pointed a scolding finger at my face. "Kraychik, don't start that wise-mouth stuff again. I got a belly-ful last time and that was enough."

"*Mea culpa,* Lieutenant," I replied, but I'd barely heard his harsh words. No, I was in bliss—for Branco had remembered my name. It was like high-school days with the gym teacher, a seedy but muscular ex-Marine with a military haircut much like my own recent clip-job. He had acknowledged by name only the most athletic jocks and me, the class sissy. My distinction? I'd gloriously failed every one of the tests ordered by the President's Council on Fitness. But I redeemed myself when it came time to transform the coach's gym for the annual spring cotillion. No mere crepe paper decorations for my grand designs. Under my direction, the double basketball court became mise-en-scène.

"Lieutenant," I continued, "I was only trying to help the guy. There's not much more I can tell you about it."

"I'll help you remember. And if your friend shows up, you tell her to stay put too." Then Branco went off to arrange for an interrogation room, where he'd probe and press and get personal, but all in the quest for facts, facts, facts.

Nicole, who'd been watching Branco and me, lingered behind the crowd. I asked her secretively, "Where the hell is Laurett?"

"Ladies' room."

I shook my head. "Not good timing."

"Nerves, darling."

"It looks suspect."

Then, with a sudden lilt in her voice, Nicole asked, "Does hope spring eternal?"

"What?"

"Were you happy to see the lieutenant again?"

"Nikki, you know as well as I do the man is straight. Pathologically straight."

"So is spaghetti until it gets wet."

"Doll, he'd die before he'd face another man intimately."

"Now, Stani . . ." There it was again, the diminutive of my full name, Stanislav. Nikki really wanted to win this round of Big-Sis-Little-Brother. "You can tell me, darling. Don't you harbor a secret dream of exchanging vows with the lieutenant at a nice ethnic wedding, with both families showering you with money and gifts?"

"Along with a vine-covered cottage? Nicole, your imagination has no connection to reality."

"That's the best kind of dream, darling."

Another officer appeared to take me to the questioning room, which turned out to be a large storage closet just off the kitchen. Once Branco and I were alone in there, amidst the steel shelving and the industrial-sized canned goods, the real fun began . . . fun for me anyway. Personally, one of my pleasures is enjoying absurd situations—situations like hearing your mother's voice on the answering machine while you're having tantric sex with the UPS man on the living-room rug; or like finding that your cat has fastidiously picked out all the fresh crab, only the crab, from a platter of appetizers you've laid out just as your guests arrive for cocktails; or like sharing a six-foot-square cubicle with a mega-macho cop. Whatever the absurdity, I try to make the most of it and have some fun. Alas, Branco wasn't cooperating that night. Some examples of his imaginative interrogation: "Did you know the victim? Why were you in the kitchen? Tell me again exactly what happened. Do you know anyone who wanted to hurt or kill the victim?"

There he was, pounding away with inane questions, looking for an answer that I certainly didn't possess. It reminded me of the annoying questions a mistrustful lover might ask when you return from the grocery shopping. Your arms are full of bundles, the food you bought for *him*. You stagger and stumble and juggle with them, while he sits at the kitchen table enjoying fresh coffee and Danish pastry. Then he has the nerve to ask, "What took so long?" or "How many stops did you make?" and "Was the market cruisy?" It's curious how similar police interrogations are to lover's trysts . . . and quarrels.

When Branco was content for the time being that squeezing this fairy wasn't going to produce any more facts, he finally relented and said, "You can go now, but I want you to stay in town."

"Yes, sir," I said with a salute. "I guess I'll have to cancel that vacation in Sitges. But, Lieutenant," I said as I stood up to leave, "if you'd question Nicole next, I'll wait for her and we can leave here together."

Without looking up, Branco flipped his notebook open to a new blank page and said, "I'll take things in my own order." Then he called his assisting sergeant to take me out of the room. It was all done with fascist detachment.

As I was escorted from the interrogation chamber, two other police officers appeared, grappling Laurett Cole between them. She was struggling to pull free, and I was embarrassed for her, especially since one of the officers restraining her was a woman. I stepped up to Laurett and said quietly, "Don't resist. Just surrender."

"Surrender what, Vannos? I did nothing!"

"I didn't mean it that way. But you have to be questioned like everyone else."

"I did not give him any chocolate. He took it."

"Don't talk now, Laurett. Wait until they question you. You're only making it worse."

"Vannos, they will send me back. And my boy too. What about my boy?"

"Laurett, listen to me." It was clear that she needed to relax, so I tried to help her breathe deeply. She resisted, but I kept on. Holding her close with my lips near her ear, I murmured a soothing mantra—not my own personal mantra, of course, but something simple and quieting. But it was hopeless. My cop escorts were tugging me away from Laurett, while the officers holding her were doing the same from her side, only more violently. Meanwhile Branco came out from the questioning room just in time to hear one of the cops say to me, "Keep to yourself, mister. There's no secrets now."

"I'm just trying to calm her down."

"She's got plenty of time. She'll get her chance."

Branco stepped up to the two officers holding Laurett. "You got her," he said to the sergeant. "Good. I'll deal with her later, after we're finished here."

"Lieutenant," I said, "she's upset."

Branco gave me a cold, blank stare.

I went on, "She'll say things she doesn't mean. That's entrapment."

Branco ignored me and ordered the officers to take Laurett outside to a cruiser. "We'll handle this now, Kraychik." His voice had no feeling in it, just calculated power.

Laurett looked back toward me as the police dragged her away. "Vannos, tell my boy! Stay with him. He is waiting for me."

I nodded to her. "I'll take care of it, Laurett."

Laurett's son was a precocious four-year-old named Tobias. When Laurett worked at Snips, I saw a lot of Tobias, sometimes too much. I suppose technically I was his godfather—make that fairy godfather—if you believe in such things. Sitting out the night with Tobias wasn't exactly what I had in mind, but then, what are friends for? I wanted to tell Nicole what had happened and where I'd be, but the party crowd was locked away in the main hall, and the door was guarded. I'd have to call her later, from Laurett's place, since my own cop escorts were shoving me roughly toward a nearby exit.

Outside, in the painfully cold February night air, the street was full of people and police cruisers. It was all flashing lights and cawing radios—the epitome of the ordered chaos the police are so good at creating. I loitered a few minutes, hoping to sneak back inside to Nicole, but the outside cops let me know that I was not welcome anywhere near the crime site. Here I'd been a good citizen and called them in and tried to cooperate with them, and what did I get for it? Booted out and sent off like a bum.

3

A SUDDEN STORK

I could have taken a cab to Laurett's place, but I decided to walk instead. I could feel tension building in my body, and I've learned that the best way for me to dissipate it is to give my long legs some motion and give my scalp some outdoor space around it. So despite my usual gripings about New England winters, which usurp about five months of the year in Boston, tonight I found the subfreezing air refreshing. My face and newly shorn head tingled from the gusts of dry, cold wind; and the crunch-crunch of my shoes over the grimy, snow-crusted sidewalks yanked me back to mental and physical alertness.

Fifteen minutes later I was at Laurett's place in the ungentrified part of Boston's South End—the neighborhood I call the panty line of downtown Boston, since it marks the divide between the so-called clean and dirty neighborhoods. My hike ended in front of a large, blocky brick building that was part of a low-income housing project, euphemistically dubbed "affordable." At almost ten o'clock on a Sunday night the street was dark and deserted, lit only by the stray light from some of the apartment windows. I rang Laurett's apartment, hoping her son's baby-sitter would let me in, but it didn't work. So I rang every other apartment in the building. The notion of security long gone in that neighborhood, someone did buzz me into the building, even though I was unknown and unidentified. Good thing I was on a do-gooder's mission.

Once inside, I climbed the four flights of stairs to Laurett's apartment. Like me, Laurett lived on the top floor of a five-story building. Ironically, her place even had an elevator, but it never worked.

I knocked on her apartment door, and after a few minutes I heard a young girl's voice through the door.

"Hello?" she said, sounding like a shy, bleating lamb.

I told her who I was, and that I was there to see Tobias.

The girl replied, "Missus Cole told me don't open the door for anyone 'cept her or my daddy."

"That's good, but you can trust me. Tobias knows me."

I heard soft murmurings behind the door. Then I heard a familiar boy's voice. "Uncle Stan?"

"Tobias, open the door."

"Why you here?"

"Your mom asked me to stay with you until she gets home. Just let me in, please."

More quiet murmurings between the two of them, then the girl's voice rose slightly. "No, Toby, don't!"

The doorknob twisted, but the door didn't open. I heard Tobias say, "It's Uncle Stan. He can come in."

More arguing behind the closed door, then finally I heard the dead bolt being released. The door opened a crack, held with the safety chain. Tobias's brown face appeared.

"Uncle Stan?" he said with squinting, sleepy eyes.

"Hi, Tobias."

The baby-sitter's darker face appeared above his. She was barely a teenager, and she sure didn't trust me. Her eyes were wide open and wary.

Tobias said, "It's okay. It's him."

The safety chain was released. I'd earned my way in. The first thing I saw was the young girl running to the telephone. "Who are you calling?" I asked.

"My daddy."

I felt a tugging at my pant leg. I looked down to see Tobias there. Though he's only four years old, with his tawny complexion and blond curls and bright green eyes, I knew that he was already turning heads. As an adult, he'd probably be a knockout and a perpetual heartbreaker.

He was in a flannel nightie, and I saw that the sofa bed was open. Tobias had been asleep, and I reminded myself to be cautious about telling him too much about his mother's situation. I didn't want this nighttime intrusion to scar his young psyche.

"Where's my ma?" he asked, as though reading my mind.

"She'll be home later, Tobias."

"Did the police take her?"

How can a four-year-old boy know so much?

I nodded. "There was some trouble. Your mom's with the police now." I purposely avoided telling him about the death of a strange man. "She asked me to stay with you until she comes home."

"Okay," he said, then climbed sleepily back onto the sofa bed and crawled under the covers. He dozed back to sleep almost instantly. Perhaps by tomorrow morning he'd remember our brief exchange as a harmless dream.

Meanwhile, the baby-sitter had put her coat on, and she still looked frightened of me. She seemed too gentle, too innocent, to be caring for a young boy in a rough neighborhood at night, but then, Laurett Cole probably had little choice in trustworthy baby-sitters.

"It's all right," I said to the timid youth. "You can go home soon."

"I am," she said, "as soon as my daddy comes." Then, tentatively, her chin still quivering, she asked, "Is she dead?"

"Who?"

"Missus Cole."

"No," I said sharply. Then I realized my error. I'd purposely censored what I'd said so far, and without all the facts, the girl was assuming the worst. "No," I said again, more gently. "Laurett's okay. There was some trouble at the party tonight, so she had to go with the police."

We heard a car blasting its horn loudly and insistently outside. I looked out the window and saw it double-parked near the plowed-up snowdrift down on the street. "Is that your car?" I asked the baby-sitter.

She came to the window and peered downward. "Yes," she said, then nervously buttoned her coat and ran out of the apartment.

"Wait," I called out. "What about your pay?"

The girl stopped halfway down the first flight of stairs and came back. "I forgot," she said. "Missus Cole pays me when she comes home."

"How much?"

She told me, and I paid her double. "That's for the extra time and for staying calm and for trusting me."

She took the money. "Thank you," she said with a voice like snowflakes settling on soft wool.

"Thank *you*," I replied.

She departed, leaving just me and a sleeping Tobias in the apartment. I'd been there a few times before, sometimes visiting Laurett, sometimes taking Tobias out for an afternoon. But tonight felt different. I uneasily sensed that Tobias and I might be spending more time together than either of us was expecting, or perhaps even wanting.

I called Nikki, just to see if she'd got home yet. Her answering service took the call—no machines for that woman. I left a message that I was at Laurett's place, along with the number there. Then I sat back and began the vigil, waiting for Laurett to get home. Since it was too late to phone any of my friends for a little chat, I turned on the television, the electro-narcotic.

The telephone woke me with a start. I fumbled to pick it up and expected to hear Nicole, but it was Laurett. She was upset and angry. "Vannos?" she asked anxiously, using my shop name again. She never could accept that my real name was Stan. "Vannos, how is Tobias?"

"He's fine, Laurett. Sleeping." Like my brain.

"Vannos, I'm in trouble. They are keeping me here."

"Why?"

"They say I tell lies."

"Laurett, they can't hold you without a charge."

"Oh, they charge me too. Then they say I can call one person, so I call you. Vannos, I need a lawyer."

"Now?"

"Sure now! That's why I call you. I need help."

I hedged. "Well, I'll try, Laurett. I don't know who'd be available now. It's late already."

"I'm going no place."

As my mind became clearer and more awake, I realized there was nothing to do but help her. "I'll make some calls, Laurett, then I'll call you back with the news."

"Vannos, you can't call me. You have to come in person. They don't give you a secretary here."

Stupid of me. Since when do the police provide private telephones for their prisoners?

I said, "Then I guess someone will be coming by the station later."

"Vannos, you have to do something right now. You have to take my boy away from there."

"Why?"

"Because they might come and take him. He be safe with you at your house."

"But Laurett—"

"You want them to put him in a home?"

"No, of course not."

"Then promise me."

I hesitated. What was I about to agree to? "Okay," I said reluctantly. "I'll take him home with me."

"And Vannos," she added, "Take him some clothes with you, and take my money. It's under my kitchen sink, in the can of Drano."

"I don't think I'll need money."

"You take it, or else the police will."

"Okay, Laurett, okay, but we'll probably get this all straightened out tonight." Big words, easy to say, but could I make good on them? What fresh hell was my goddam sense of duty and obligation getting me into this time?

Suddenly Laurett was speaking secretively, in a low voice. "Can you still hear me?"

"Yeah," I answered, in a similar hushed tone.

"There be some chocolate there, too, hiding near the telephone. Take it out."

"Chocolate?"

"Truffles. Take it all."

"Sure, Laurett, but—"

"Just do it. And *don't* be giving any to my boy."

"But—"

"Hurry, Vannos, before the police are getting there."

"Okay, Laurett, I'll do it."

Then we hung up.

So much for the popular delusion that hair stylists see only glamor and high life.

Within seconds the phone rang again. When I picked it up, an angry voiced buzzed from the handset.

"Who the bloody hell have you been talking to?" It was Nicole, yelling at me and neglecting to use *whom*.

"It was Laurett. Besides, I was just about to call *you* again."

"Well, I'm finally home, and I can tell you, it's been no party."

"Nor here, either."

"Stanley, after you left, Lieutenant Branco became as dull-witted and clumsy as a bureaucrat."

"Nikki, he *is* a bureaucrat."

"I think he needs you to provoke him. You seem to bring out the best in him."

I ignored her taunt. "Doll, listen. Laurett's in trouble. They're holding her on bail, and she needs a lawyer. Can Charles help her out?"

I heard Nicole lighting a cigarette and I envied her. She always seemed to find the perfect moment for a smoke, then light one up and actually enjoy it. "Darling," she said, and I could almost see the smoke streaming from her lips, "Chaz does corporate law, not those criminal cases."

"I'm not sure there's much difference."

Silence. Another exhalation.

"He does owe me a big favor," she said.

"Good. Get some practical use out of that aristocratic law degree. Can you call him?"

"Now?"

"Perry Mason wouldn't hesitate."

"I'm not sure I want to use my favor yet, Stanley."

"Nikki, there'll be other times you can harness your catamite for your own devices. Right now Laurett needs help."

"What part are you playing in this domestic drama?"

"I promised her I'd look after Tobias until she gets out, which I hope will be tonight. I'm taking him to my place now."

"Why don't you both wait here instead? That way, when Chaz gets Laurett released, he can bring her along and pick up Tobias here. We'll all be together, at least."

"So, you'll call him?"

"For your sake, yes."

"And you think he'll spring her tonight?"

"Darling, I have complete confidence in him."

"Thanks, doll."

Then, in her usual manner, Nicole hung up without saying good-bye.

I called a cab, which was a fifty-fifty proposition in Laurett's neighborhood. Fifty-percent chance they won't stop when they see where the address is, fifty-percent chance they won't show up at all.

I woke Tobias up and calmly explained that we were going to wait at Nikki's place until his mother came to get him, kind of like a late-night adventure. I left him to put on his clothes—he's already that independent—while I went to the kitchen to find the money Laurett had mentioned. I didn't intend to use it, but I figured it would be better to take anything valuable—or suspicious—out of Laurett's place before the police arrived and searched the premises. Being a Gemini, my hands are pretty

clever, but I couldn't figure out how to get the damn cabinet door
open. After a brief but noisy battle with the childproof locks, I
heard Tobias say behind me, "You want Ma's money can?"

"Uh, yeah, Tobias."

"I'll do it." In a simple grip and twist motion, supposedly
possible only by adult hands, Tobias flicked the latch and opened
the cupboard door. He crawled in and got the can of Drano.

"Be careful, Tobias. That's poison."

"Not this one." He opened the can—another so-called
childproof container—and shook out a fat roll of twenty-dollar
bills. "It's Ma's money," he said with a self-satisfied grin.

I took the money and jammed it into my pocket. Then I
went to the telephone table and searched for where the chocolate might be hidden, the stuff Laurett had mentioned. After a
few minutes of futile searching, Tobias asked what I was looking
for. When I hesitated to tell him, he exclaimed, "I know! I bet
I know! The chocolate!" Then he showed me a small, concealed
hatchway in the floor under the telephone stand. I'd have never
found it on my own so quickly. As he pulled two boxes of chocolate truffles out from the cache underneath, he explained, "Ma's
afraid they'll find out she took it and didn't pay for it. She thinks
I don't know."

I asked him, "Did you eat any?"

"No. Ma keeps count."

I felt those facts clink and tumble their way into my Slavic
data bank.

The last thing was to pack some clothes for him. If Charles
was as good as Nicole predicted, none of this preparation would
be needed, since Laurett would be released that night. But I
reminded myself to expect nothing and be surprised.

I bundled Tobias up warmly, and we waited for the cab to
honk its horn for us. Mercifully, it arrived shortly.

Nicole's penthouse suite at Harbor Towers has a panoramic
view of Boston Harbor and the best angle of the downtown
skyline. How she affords such a place is one of Nikki's unshared

confidences, even with me. Perhaps someday I'll earn the right to know.

It was after eleven o'clock when I got there. She opened the door to greet me, but was taken aback by my burden, arms heavy-laden with a sleeping Tobias along with two boxes of chocolate truffles and a small suitcase with Tobias's clothes. As I struggled through the doorway, she placed her glass of champagne on a small Hepplewhite table in the foyer.

"What a lot of stuff!" she exclaimed. "Give him to me, Stani."

As she tried to lift the sleepy four-year-old from my arms, Tobias stirred lightly and said, "Ma?"

Nicole grimaced at his choice of words. "No, dear. It's Nicole. You remember me, don't you? From the shop."

"Ma?" repeated Tobias.

Nicole let go of him and took the chocolate from me instead. "Maybe I'm better off with these," she said, as she opened one of the boxes.

"No!" I yelped. "Don't touch them." My voice caused Tobias to stir in my arms. With exaggerated caution, Nicole closed the box she'd opened, then she replaced both of them back on top of Tobias in my full arms.

"Fine, darling," she said sulkily. "You take care of everything yourself." She picked up her glass of champagne and sauntered back to her place on the huge, custom-made sofa, a perfect hexagon upholstered in pink shantung and sized to fill most of the sunken living room. After a quick sip she added, "If you want coffee or a drink, you know where everything is."

"Nikki, please don't get contrary. I'll explain why in a minute. Can you just take the boxes so I can put this boy to bed?"

She reluctantly got up again and did what I asked.

"And while I dump the kid, you can dump some Irish whiskey in a mug and add a splash of that fresh-brewed coffee I smell in the kitchen. Please?"

Nicole nodded.

I took Tobias to the guest bedroom and put him under the covers. I didn't bother undressing him since I still assumed that

Laurett would be picking him up later. I went to the kitchen where Nicole had prepared my strong Irish coffee.

She handed me the hot mug and said, "I called Chaz right after I talked with you. He said he'd go to the station and find out what Laurett needed."

"The only thing she needs is *out*," I said, then took a big gulp of the coffee and burned my mouth. "Yow!"

"Too hot, darling?"

"Unlike the last man I dated—six months ago."

"Darling, for once can you forget about your barren love life? I doubt Laurett is thinking about hers tonight."

"She may be, Nikki. I think that was her lover who was poisoned. I'm almost sure he was the same guy who used to bother her off and on for the whole two years she worked in the shop."

Nicole thought a moment, then frowned. "I remember the one you mean, and he was quite a pest. Things got very unpleasant between them."

"Unpleasant, yes, but would Laurett have killed the guy?"

"Never underestimate a woman's survival instinct."

"I can't believe she'd kill anyone. Though if I think about my great love and how it went wrong, and how I used to ponder ways to kill him . . ."

"Stani, we've all had thoughts like that."

"I know, and some people act on them. Which reminds me—those chocolates."

"The sacred ones I couldn't touch?"

"Right. They were hidden at Laurett's apartment. She asked me to get rid of them, since she knew the police would be searching her place."

"What's the big deal?"

"They look like truffles from Le Jardin. According to Tobias, she took them without paying."

"So? I should think any chocolate company would at least let its employees eat the goods."

"I agree, which is what makes her wanting to hide them suspicious."

"Stanley, you make it sound as though Laurett might actually be guilty of something."

"Nikki, that guy *was* dead," I said and gulped some more coffee. My scalded mouth felt no further pain now. "What does Charles think?"

Nicole paused. Then she made a pronouncement. "Darling, he prefers Chaz."

"I know what he prefers, but he is not a Chaz. He's a Charles—a Char-rulls, to be exact."

Nicole ignored my opinion, as she usually did. "As I predicted, Chaz thinks there'll be no trouble in getting Laurett released tonight. In fact, he's certain."

"He always is."

"He's a Harvard graduate."

"They're programmed to be certain."

"Just accept help when it's given. I told him to bring her here directly from the police station."

"Let's hope he can deliver what he promises, and that I packed Tobias's clothes in vain."

"You'll be eating humble pie when Chaz brings Laurett here later. I guarantee she'll be home with her boy tonight."

As if on cue, the doorbell sounded. Nicole went to answer it, and I followed. It was Charles. And no Laurett.

Nicole stood with him in the foyer while I retreated quietly back into the living room, out of sight. Charles doesn't like me much and the feeling is mutual, but I didn't want to jeopardize any help he might be to Laurett. Charles was, at that moment, Laurett's savior, so I kept myself invisible and eavesdropped on them from the living room. After some sexy sweet talk that implied he'd done Nicole's bidding and wasn't he a good boy, Charles explained callously that Laurett had been charged with voluntary manslaughter, that she'd deliberately given the strange man some poisoned chocolate, if not to kill him, then at least to make him violently ill. She was being held at the WDU, the Women's Detention Unit. Bail was set at two-hundred-fifty-thousand dollars.

"What!" I said.

When Charles heard me, he murmured something unintelligible to Nicole, who giggled in response. Then I heard kissing sounds coming from the foyer. More murmurs, more giggles now from both of them. Then they walked into the living room. Foreplay interruptus.

Charles was tall, sandy-haired, blue-eyed, clean-shaven, tanned, toned, and trim. In fact, I hated him for being so attractive and so self-assured. Wasn't there a single molecule of doubt lingering anywhere within his arrogant body? And what did Nikki see in him? Was it purely physical?

He nodded toward me, but gave no verbal greeting. I didn't deserve any in his eyes, being an invert. We'd met before, at the shop, where Charles had come in for a manicure. That's also when he met Nicole. The rest is recent history.

Nicole asked him, "Chaz, darling, what's to be done next?"

He replied brusquely, "Investigation, indictment, trial, and verdict." How simple life was for a smart young attorney, where everything could be put into order with four words. Nothing like the world of, say, the hair stylist, who has to deal with variables like color, texture, moisture content, growth pattern, and curl line, along with the two most unpredictable ones of all: the client's obscure self-image combined with the fickleness of fashion.

Nicole told Charles that Tobias was there with us, that he was fine, and that I would take care of him until Laurett was released.

"Not good," said Charles. "He should be in court custody unless someone else is named legal guardian."

"Laurett's a friend," I said.

"And the law's the law," he replied, reminding me of Branco's kind of logic and also proving that cops and lawyers come from the same factory, the lawyers playing the CEO's and the cops working the assembly line.

Charles said to Nicole, "I thought I might stay a while, but since you have company . . ."

Was that a sneer on his face?

Nicole led him back out to the door, explaining, *apologizing,* that she and I had things to talk about, and she'd call him later. I wondered, Later when?

He finally left, and I felt something was amiss. Laurett couldn't have killed another person. It was that simple, in spite of Nicole's theory about the female survival instinct. More urgent, however, was that Tobias needed care and a place to stay until his mother was cleared of the absurd accusation.

"I guess he was wrong, eh, doll?"

"Explain yourself, Stanley."

"Earlier tonight both you and he were certain that Laurett would be released. Now they've booked her. And what's to be done with Tobias until she's acquitted?"

"You heard him. Chaz thinks he should be placed in the custody of the court."

"And I think that's betraying a friend. Nikki, it's for Laurett. She's in trouble. She worked with us for over two years. Doesn't that mean anything?"

"It means she did her job well and I paid her. Technically the arrangement doesn't go beyond that. I'm not running that salon to bestow gifts on the troubled and needy."

"But doesn't all that time spent together—"

"All in the past, Stanley. Besides, it was all time spent on the job. Unlike you, I don't become personally involved with anyone I work with. Sentimentality and business don't mix."

"You got friendly with me."

"You are the notable exception to my rule."

"Any regrets?"

"Daily."

"Friendships can end too."

"Not ours, Stanley. We're star-crossed. If you'd been straight or I a man—"

"We'd probably have a split-level home somewhere with a beauty shop attached, along with two dogs, a cat, a station wagon, two VCRs, a satellite antenna—"

"We'd probably be divorced by now too."

"I'd have contested," I said. Then I raised my coffee mug in a toast. "Here's to fairies and fag-hags," I said, "and may their friendships endure."

Nicole replied, "I'd prefer different labels, but I'll drink to the thought."

We sat quietly a moment, allowing the alcohol to work.

I thought of Nicole and Charles and their romance, and about my arid love life and about being alone so much. I said, "Perhaps Tobias and I should stay here tonight. He's been through quite a bit already, and you have lots of room."

Nicole cocked her head. "Yes, I do, Stanley." She usually used my full name to imply seriousness. She sipped champagne and continued coolly, "But there's no need to make sleeping arrangements with it."

"But aren't we kind of obligated to take care of him? Think of the times he used to be in the shop and would pick up rollers and combs that fell from my station."

"From *your* station, dear. He was always in the way for me."

"But this is different. His mother's in jail."

"Stanley, I'm afraid this is your decision."

"But I can't do it alone. Couldn't we set up a schedule so that you get him sometimes too?"

"I have no desire for a child."

"But it's only temporary, and you'll get to savor the thrill of parenthood for a brief time."

"But, but, but, Stanley. What is it about the word 'no' you don't understand? I'm not interested."

"But think of how it will help with the customers."

That remark caught her attention. With the mention of the business, I sensed her resistance drop a notch, so I pursued it. "Nikki, when they talk about *their* kids, now you'll have first-hand experience to counter with."

"You're wrong there. The competition among professional parents regarding their children is fierce, not the homespun cottage industry you make it out to be."

"Doll, the only serious competition left in this city is the orchid exhibition at Horticultural Hall."

"I maintain the boy is yours and yours alone."

"Please . . . ?" I whined.

"Don't whine. You know I detest that."

"Okay, okay. No whining." So I pouted.

"And don't pout."

"Nikki, I'll use whatever works. I'm desperate."

"You're not desperate. You're manipulative."

"I'm charming."

"On second thought, maybe you are desperate."

"Nikki, what if you just take Tobias some of the time? How about every other day?"

She sighed in exasperation. Then she finished her champagne and said, "All right, here is what I will agree to." She paused to light a new cigarette before stating her terms. Big moment. Light change. "On the days you work at the shop, Tobias can be there as well, for both of us to look after. Two evenings a week I will entertain him, though not overnight. For the remaining time he's yours."

"But then I get no nights without him."

"That's true, but what else would you be doing anyway?"

"That's low, doll. Just because you have a hot young lover doesn't mean the rest of the world is sitting around tatting shade pulls."

"Caring for Tobias wasn't my idea, Stanley. My offer stands. Take it or leave it."

I groaned. "It's as conditional as a limited warranty, but I guess it's a deal. You don't much like kids, do you?"

She answered, "You'll soon discover why." Then she extinguished her cigarette with meticulous precision and stood up. "I think we've done just about all we can tonight."

"Is that my cue to take Tobias and go?"

"If you wouldn't mind. Chaz did want to come by for a while. I'll pay your cab fare home."

"I accept the bribe. Far be it for me to encroach on a friend's sex life."

Nikki called a cab while I once again donned my winter garb and wrapped the sleeping Tobias up warmly. Arms full again, I left her place. In one night, without warning, during what had started out as a party, I'd become a single parent. And I sensed the beginnings of a rift with my best friend.

Home is a fifth-floor walk-up on Marlborough Street in the Back Bay. It's a spacious one-bedroom apartment with a bay window facing the street, a working fireplace, a huge bathroom with the original marble tiles intact, a sliver of the Charles River from my bedroom window, and rent control. The place has been slated for mondo-condo conversion for years, but we tenants are no fools. We've exercised our renter's rights and retained our homesteads. So what if I have to walk up four long flights of stairs every night? I've got good legs anyway. And that night I needed them, with all I had to carry.

When I opened the door, I expected the usual greeting by my roommate, Sugar Baby, a taupe-colored Burmese cat almost the same caramel color as her candy namesake. Instead of a trill and a chirp, though, she bristled and ran away when she saw Tobias in my arms.

"Sorry, baby," I said. It had been a long night, and my poor cat was probably feeling abandoned. And now, instead of coming home and giving her all my attention, I was arriving late and bringing a strange person in with me. Did she at least realize Tobias wasn't a trick?

I tucked him into my bed, then I gave Sugar Baby her supper. After that, there was just one more thing to do before setting up the sofa and collapsing onto it. I took the two boxes of chocolate truffles to the kitchen table and opened them. Without touching the candy inside, I carefully examined each piece as it rested in its ruffled paper cup. I searched for some clue that the stuff had been tampered with, but none showed any finger-prints—which didn't surprise me, since chocolate makers usually wear plastic gloves. However, many of the truffles did have decorations that had either been clumsily applied or else clum-sily altered. I wondered why Laurett had wanted me to dispose of them. Had she done anything to them? Was there a chance that some of these truffles were loaded with cyanide? Is that why she'd tried to hide them from Tobias? And the worst question for me was, Should I turn this stuff over to the cops as possible evidence against my friend, to help that handsome, hunky foil, Lieutenant Vito Branco?

4

BABYCAKES

I was awakened from a heavy sleep by the sound of Sugar Baby yowling from the kitchen. I knew something was wrong, since that girl usually sleeps in, buried under the blankets, until five minutes before I have to leave for the shop. That's when she deigns to leave my unmade bed, wrap herself around my legs—leaving her scent and strands of taupe-colored fur on my black chinos—and look up at me with big, sad eyes that imply that the portion of premium quality cat food just placed into her Limoges porcelain bowl might not be to her liking today, and would I please remain close by in case she desires something else? Yes, my cat is pampered and lives in a higher social stratum than I do. Why else would I work so hard?

So when I heard her making unrefined noises from the kitchen in what seemed the middle of the night, I knew something was wrong. I jumped out of bed, naked as usual, but it wasn't the bed, it was the sofa. No time to think or remember why. I stumbled toward the kitchen, where a light was on. Burglar? I thought drowsily. But instead of a dark-clothed stranger in the kitchen, I saw through my squinting eyelids a young boy on his hands and knees. It was Tobias. What was *he* doing in my kitchen? Was I dreaming? Then the facts rushed in all at once, and I remembered last night's events.

Tobias had cornered Sugar Baby and was tying a piece of cotton twine around one of her hind paws. Though his *modus tormenti* with the cat was harmless, I was still mortified at his pleasure in making her life a piece of hell.

"Stop that!" I yelled.

He turned and looked at me calmly, giving Sugar Baby a chance to scamper away, the long string trailing behind her.

"Just leave the cat alone."

"She woke me up, sniffing in my face."

"You were in her bed."

"Where's my ma?" he demanded.

Last night I'd planned to tell Tobias the bad news in the morning, over a nice family-style breakfast—kind of set the scene warm and homey and secure, then calmly slip him the fact that his mother had been booked for manslaughter last night. "She's still with the police," I explained quickly.

"Was it Trek?"

"Trek?" Perhaps it was a new street drug. "What's trek, Tobias?"

"He's my pa."

"Trek is a man?"

"You need a man to be your pa, don't you?"

"That's a fact," I said, wondering again where Tobias had learned so much in four short years. But with a chill I then surmised that the Caucasian stranger who had been poisoned last night was possibly Tobias's father. The bad news had just got worse.

Tobias stared at me. "Did he hurt my ma?"

"No, Tobias." How could I tell him that the opposite was more likely?

"Where is she, then?"

"I told you, she's with the police."

"In jail?"

"Tobias, why don't I make us some breakfast and we'll talk about it, okay?"

His eyes remained glued on me, quiet but defiant. Then, out

of nowhere, he remarked, "Uncle Stan, you got a nice ding-dong."

All too late I realized that I'd forgotten to put on a robe. Hell, I was at home, wasn't I? Why should I have to be modest and demure in my own apartment? Why? Because I had a four-year-old house guest who perhaps didn't realize the trouble such a scene might cause if it ever went public. Trouble for me, that is. And with Tobias's yapper, I knew anyone within earshot today would hear about his Uncle Stan flying into the kitchen this morning, wagging his unit in the innocent boy's face. I grabbed a dishtowel and held it over the happy handful in my crotch. "Tobias, look, I just forgot to cover myself. It's nothing. It was an accident. I didn't mean for you to see me like this."

Tobias looked at me and shrugged nonchalantly. "Trek is always naked too." He pronounced the word "nake-it." "He likes to show sex, just like you, Uncle Stan."

I wanted to gag the little brat with a chastity belt. It was unnerving to hear him spouting off so casually about the very stuff on which my Roman Catholic upbringing had left its holy scars. Tobias had not yet been brainwashed about the sacredness of sex, lucky boy. Then I had a troubled thought: What if this Trek guy, supposedly Tobias's father, had ever been a bit too intimate with Tobias under the guise of sex education? Where did a parent draw the line? Biologically speaking, it shouldn't matter. But we poor humans have to contend with the baggage of psychology and theology and just plain old consciousness too.

I got my robe from the bedroom, where Sugar Baby had dispatched the demon twine from her hind leg and had reinstated herself properly under the covers. Then I returned to the kitchen to make breakfast. It was six-thirty, but at that hour during a Boston winter the sun is nowhere near the horizon. I put on some coffee, heated milk for cocoa, popped in some toast, and set the small table in the dining nook. When I called Tobias, he didn't answer. I went into the living room and called again. In response I heard a muffled groan from the sofa. The little monster had crept under the blankets there and had gone back to sleep. So much for his breakfast and our heart-to-heart talk. But for me, once awake, it's hopeless to try to get back to sleep. So I stopped the toast, then showered quickly and returned to the kitchen to have my breakfast alone. The radio was tuned to a public station at the low end of the dial, the one that begins its broadcast day with the gentle forest sounds of twittering birds, a sound of nature rarely heard in downtown Boston. After that, an overeducated but groggy voice announces the news. Though that station is fastidiously adverse to sensational reporting, the feature story that morning was the killing last night of a man who'd crashed the glamorous reception for Le Jardin chocolates. Names were named, and Laurett Cole was being held for the killing of Trek Delorean. His name sounded like a European road race.

I was glad that Tobias had gone back to sleep. I'd hoped to tell him less bluntly what had really happened between his mother and his father. But then, did I really know? As it turned out, though, Tobias was standing in the doorway and had overheard the newscast.

"Did Ma kill Pa?"

"No, Tobias." Was it still a lie if you didn't know all the facts?

"That radio said he's dead."

"He is."

He stared sullenly at the floor, then looked around aimlessly, as though searching for Sugar Baby. "How long do I have to stay here, Uncle Stan?"

"Until the police release your mother."

"When?"

"Tobias . . ." I sighed heavily. "It might be a while."

"Will they send me to a home again?"

"I won't let them. You can stay here with me."

"But Ma said you can't have children."

"Hydraulically speaking, Tobias, that's not true. But the urge to procreate isn't too strong either."

"What's that mean?"

"It means if I ever have children, I'll probably adopt them."

"Will you adopt me?"

His frankness surprised me. "You'd be at the top of the list."

He seemed content with that answer, and climbed up to sit at the table with me. He took a piece of toast from the warm plate and clumsily spread butter on it. The he took a huge bite from it and chewed it all with his mouth agape. I watched the browned bread transform into grey mush within the small pink cavity of his mouth.

"Close your mouth when you chew, Tobias."

"Why?"

"It's impolite and unattractive."

"Ma doesn't make me."

"That's because she's witnessed all your other bodily functions so far, which makes her more tolerant. When you eat with me, it's mouth closed."

He then pressed his lips tightly together and jammed the slice of toast against them, mashing it onto his face.

"What are you doing?"

He mimicked someone talking, but kept his lips sealed, then smashed the toast against his face again, crumbling more of it onto the table and the floor.

"Tobias, stop that."

He opened his lips a hairline crack and spoke through the buttery crumbs and goop around his mouth. "Yr shed kip muh mth sht."

"When you chew."

He broke into laughter, then took a bite of what was left of the toast and let it sit on his tongue, mouth open, jaw slack. I glared at him, and he said, "I'm not chewing, so I can leave my mouth open."

I was about to scold him again, then realized that, more than likely, his terror tactics at breakfast were his way of expressing fear over what was to become of him without his mother or his father. So instead of further instruction in dining etiquette, I asked him if he was hungry for more toast. He said nothing, but shook his head no. I knelt near his chair and faced him directly.

"Tobias, your ma's going to be all right. She'll want you to be strong while she's gone." Then I hugged him. A little brainwashing and Pavlovian conditioning sometimes work better than a round of cat and mouse. Sometimes. At least I felt victorious for the moment, having restrained myself from applying the remainder of the toast onto his head, à la Clifton Webb and the projectile oatmeal in *Sitting Pretty*.

Breakfast finished, I prepared Tobias for a quick sponge bath, under loud protest. "Ma don't do this," he wailed.

"I know, Tobias," I said, sniffing the air around me. "And my nose knows too. But if you're going to stay with me, you wash every day. It would be real nice if you'd learn to do it yourself."

"I'm not washing."

"Then it comes down to this: I'm bigger, I'm stronger, and I'll do it." Perhaps the sweet-talk, negotiating school of parenting *was* less efficient than the bullyish, power-wielding approach. I wondered, Is this how Branco thinks? Then I wondered, horrified, if bathing a screaming child qualified as molestation.

Through all the morning's antics, I was still planning my day's itinerary. It's another advantage of being a Gemini: One of your personalities can be doing one thing while another is somewhere else entirely. My first stop that morning would be at Snips, even though it was my day off. I intended to leave Tobias there while I did some legwork. Nicole didn't yet realize that she and Snips Salon had a sideline in the day-care business.

Tobias and I walked to the shop together, which is only about six blocks from my apartment. Once out in the world, Tobias adopted the personality that made him so lovable. He was a frisky, inquisitive, humor-filled young boy, with blond curly hair and burnished bronze skin, a natural performer, with the world as his stage and the adult population his audience. Too bad some of us had to experience Tobias's backstage foibles as well. Then again, who would have thought that this boy's mother was now in jail for the possible killing of his father?

We arrived at the shop around eight-thirty. Nicole had already opened the place, proving that when necessary, she could be out and about with the rest of the clock-conscious world. She greeted us warmly, as though we were loved ones arriving after

defiant. Her first remark was, "How is my boy?" Her voice came over a small speaker mounted in the wooden counter under the window.

I yelled back, "He's fine!"

With her index finger to her lips, she gave me the sign to shush. Then she pointed to the chipped black button near the speaker, and I heard her voice over the speaker again. "Push the button, Vannos."

I pressed it and heard a slight pop over the speaker. "Better?" I asked.

Laurett nodded. I wondered why she knew how to use the intercom so well. Who else had visited her? Or had she been in here before? I realized unhappily that I was already doubting my own friend.

"Where is he now?" she asked.

"At the shop with Nicole."

"Why didn't you bring him here?"

"I didn't think he should see you like this."

"Like what? Vannos, my boy will learn how the world turns. You bring him here next time, let him see what they do to his ma. Promise?"

Reluctantly, I nodded.

The social niceties over, I launched directly into why I'd come to see her. "Laurett, that man who died last night—was he the same one who used to see you at the salon?"

Laurett sat up defensively. "Who?"

"Trek Delorean."

"Who?" she said again, and already I sensed that she was playing stupid.

"I recall you had a boyfriend—"

"So what? Is that against the law?"

"Was Trek Delorean Tobias's father?"

"That what my boy say?"

I nodded.

Laurett's eyes narrowed and hardened. "For a baby man, he have a wild mind and a big yapper."

"He mentioned a guy named Trek, which was the dead

man's name, so I figured it was the same person. He said Trek was at your place a lot."

Laurett studied my face warily. "What else Tobias tell you?"

I felt my face flush. "That Trek liked to walk around naked a lot."

Laurett burst into raucous laughter, which she kept up long after the joke had passed, whatever it was. Finally she said, "You a grown man believing what a four-year-old brat telling you?"

"You deny it?"

"That boy's pa be back in Jamaica where I left him."

"But—"

"I should know my own boy's pa, shouldn't I?"

"Yes, Laurett," I admitted sheepishly. "But Tobias has obviously got white blood in him, and Trek was white. . . ."

Laurett grinned. "Mr. Vannos, there be white men plenty in Jamaica." She was on the verge of another laughing fit, but this time the joke was on me, who'd jumped to a stupid racist conclusion based on circumstantial evidence.

"But Laurett, the chocolate you gave that guy was loaded with cyanide."

Her face stiffened instantly. "Vannos, I give him nothing. He took it."

"But I saw you decorating them."

"Sure I was, but I didn't give him that, and I sure didn't put poison inside."

"Then how did the poison get into it?"

"I don't know. Someone put it inside there before I took the flower off. Then Trek ate it when I leave the kitchen."

"Wait a minute," I said. "You took the decoration *off* the truffle?"

"Sure I did. That candy was all covered with fingerprints. I couldn't put that on a silver plate. So I fixed a new one with the same flower."

"So the truffle that killed Trek was supposed to go to someone else, one of the three special guests?"

"Sure-you're-right."

"So, whose was it?"

Laurett looked at me with absolute blankness.

I pressed her. "Well?"

She maintained her stoney stare.

"Laurett," I entreated as quietly as I could over the microphone, "who was supposed to get that truffle?"

Finally, after long moments of silence, her face softened into sadness, and she said, "It was for Mr. Kingsley."

This was the key then. Someone had wanted to kill Prentiss Kingsley.

Laurett repeated herself. "That truffle, the almond one, was for Mr. Kingsley, but it looked bad, so I changed it for another one. That's what I was fixing in the kitchen when you come in. When I took them other ones out to the party, Trek ate that one. But it was all an accident."

"No, Laurett. It wasn't an accident. It was a mistake. The deadly truffle just went to the wrong person."

"But I didn't do it, Vannos."

I had to believe her, didn't I? What else could I do? Laurett's natural dark beauty gave her that advantage, the one that made you want to believe her. It was the same with good-looking men. Beautiful people can lie to you point-blank, but their face is such a marvel of surface and shadow that you tend to believe anything that comes from its lips, even the lovely lies.

"Laurett, who's in charge of making those truffles?"

"That's Old Misery herself, Mary Phinney. She's the boss lady at the factory."

I thought a moment and remembered hearing the name. "Wasn't that the older woman you were arguing with last night in the kitchen?"

She hardened her face again. "Before you ask any more, Mr. District Attorney, I will explain. Mary Phinney is with Gladys Gardner for a hundred years or more." Laurett cackled lightly at her own joke. "She was not too happy with the new store."

"But why pick on you?"

"Because Mr. Kingsley and Miss Lisa and that young

Danny, they all hire *me*, and Mary Phinney want that job herself."

"To manage Le Jardin?"

"Mm-hmm," replied Laurett with a Buddha-like grin and a curlicue inflection in her voice that mocked the likelihood of a henna-haired crone managing an upscale boutique.

"Laurett, since you were in charge of presenting the special truffles, you must know what flavors the other two guests of honor had, right?"

Laurett nodded with a sly grin. "Even the police didn't ask me about that, Vannos. Young Danny had orange—Grand Marnier, it's called—and Miss Lisa . . ." Laurett smiled at the intentional misnomer. "Miss Lisa have plain, just like herself. Heh-heh."

"What else did you tell the police?"

"Only what they ask me. But did they believe one word? No, they think I'm just trying to put the blame on someone else. Now, why would I do that? You tell me."

Seeing no graceful way to continue on that tack, I changed the subject. "Nicole's lawyer friend said he'll represent you at the inquest."

Laurett grinned broadly. "His eyes got a big surprise to see a beautiful black woman waiting for him here last night."

"Don't look a gift horse in the mouth, Laurett," I said. But I was thinking that horse's ass was more appropriate for Charles. I started getting my coat on. "I'm going now, Laurett. I've got some new leads, thanks to you."

"And I'm thanking you, Vannos, for taking care of Tobias. I make it up to you when I'm out of here, I promise that."

"Don't worry about it."

I got up and left the visiting room. On my way out, I went over the new facts Laurett had laid out. Branco must have known them too. I wondered if he was following up on any of it, especially the fact that Prentiss Kingsley was the actual intended victim. Or was the mighty Branco content to let the case roll along to a hearing with the evidence as he saw it?—just a mixed-race domestic argument that had culminated in the ultimate violence.

I phoned Nicole from the WDU to tell her I'd be back to pick up Tobias after my next stop, the Gladys Gardner Chocolate Company, where I wanted to talk with Prentiss Kingsley and warn him that someone might be trying to hunt him down. It wouldn't hurt to meet Mary Phinney there either, since she'd presumably been in charge of making the candy. When Nicole found out my destination, though, she said, "I think a field trip to a chocolate factory would be a delightful way for a young boy to spend some time with his Uncle Stanley."

"But Nikki, I've got to talk to people. How am I supposed to do that with a kid in tow?"

"You should have thought of that earlier."

"What if something happens to him? It will be on your conscience for not baby-sitting him."

"What's going to happen, Stanley?"

"I don't think they make bulletproof vests small enough for him."

"Your arguments are futile. I'm running a salon, not a day-care center."

"I can just see the little tyke, wounded by a stray bullet. . . ."

"Stanley, stop this cops-and-robbers nonsense. You get back here and take the boy with you."

"Yes, Ma'am," I said.

She hung up.

Back outside, the bright morning sun was trying to warm up the snow-frozen ground, but to no avail. February in Boston means cold, period. I headed back to the shop, troubled by my growing doubt over Laurett's innocence. Perhaps her story about Prentiss Kingsley was true, but the truffles I'd taken from her apartment still rankled me. Had she brought them home just to practice loading them with poison? But then, whom would she be trying to kill, and why?

6

DOWN THE GARDNER

PATH

I got back to the shop around ten-thirty. Tobias wanted lunch already. True, he hadn't had much of a breakfast with me, but I wasn't hungry yet, at least for food. Last night's rich party fare was still sticking to my ribs and hips. But I *was* hungry for more facts related to the killing. And I wanted to warn Prentiss Kingsley that the deadly truffle from last night had really been intended for him. If Laurett was telling the truth, then Prentiss Kingsley was in mortal danger; and if she wasn't, well I wanted to find that out too. So for the moment I promised Tobias we'd have lunch sometime during our outing to the Gladys Gardner factory. In my mind I'd already decided we'd eat on our way home from candyland, after my part of the mission was accomplished.

We took a cab to the factory. For some reason, the driver assumed that Tobias and I were tourists, and he recommended that we stop in at the outlet store, where we could buy the famous Gladys Gardner chocolates at half price. My heart and tummy trembled at the opportunity, but my new dietary restrictions didn't allow such wantonness. Tobias, however, bounced up and down on the car seat, insisting that we go in. So only to appease him did I sacrifice my nutritional self-discipline. Besides, a bit of chocolate might satisfy him until later. After all, it worked for robust Alpine skiers.

The cab left us at the small store, which was half a block away from the factory's main entrance. The inside of the store reflected a half-hearted attempt to reproduce the romantic ideal of an old New England kitchen, a place that somebody's grandmother in colonial Vermont once cooked in, supposedly. But the Formica pine tables and the plastic brick fireplace—filled with empty cartons instead of a welcoming blaze—provided insufficient ambience to counter the grimy acoustic tile ceiling, the flickering fluorescent lights, and a dusty, painted cement floor. Only the showcase glass sparkled amidst the general drabness of the place. And the air was heavy with chocolate, which at that hour was almost disturbing. It wasn't the pleasant kind of aroma that eased you into the day, the same way coffee and toast or fresh muffins do. Rather, the concentrated smell of chocolate was disquieting, almost sexual. The visit to the store would probably only re-energize Tobias, rather than calm him, as I was hoping.

The woman behind the counter might have been the model for the fake oil portrait of old Dame Gardner, or whoever she was, that hung high up behind the counter, strategically placed to be the visual focus of the store. It wasn't sweets these folks were selling so much as the idea, the fond remembrance of a doting, loving grandmother figure in everyone's past. Even if you never had one, you could pretend you did. I wondered if Dame Gladys would ever be modernized the way Betty Crocker had been, transformed into an urbane superwoman, the kind who does, rather who *delegates* the vaccuuming while wearing pastel eyeshadow and stiletto pumps.

Gladys's flesh-and-blood facsimile smiled at us benignly, but I sensed that her contrived courtesy began and ended at the threshold, during business hours and for customers only. She expected us to buy some candy, and to do it quickly. She stared at us for a while, expectantly, and when we didn't order right away, she turned her back on us and knelt down behind the counter. I gazed longingly at the contents of the display case. One inner voice was saying, "Go on, you deserve it," while another one parried, "Straight to the hips, lard-ass." From behind the counter I heard the sounds of heavy boxes being pushed and yanked and scraped along the gritty cement floor. After a few minutes the woman rose back up again and faced me, a little flushed from her exertions.

"Is there something you want here?" she asked gruffly.

Her look was cool and indifferent, then suddenly it changed to absolute horror at the sight of something going on behind me. I turned around and saw Tobias reaching for a gigantic, red-flocked, heart-shaped candy box. The thing must have been two feet wide with five pounds of chocolate inside. He was pulling at it from the bottom, where it rested on a display shelf.

The woman yelled, "Don't touch that!"

But the big box was already slipping from its Lucite stand. It all seemed to happen in slow motion, reminding me of those horrible school days, of having to play softball during "phys-ed" class, when I was always assigned to the outfield. Whenever a batter swung and hit the ball, I would follow its airborne flight, then casually but methodically move myself *away* from its path. It didn't take the class bullies long to figure out my technique, so they'd purposely hit the ball toward my side of the field. Hell, it was a guaranteed base hit, if not a home run. I suppose, in a way, I was doing my part to cultivate their goodwill toward sissies.

But the imminent threat of paying even half-price for a five-pound gift box of Valentine's chocolates spurred me on to more heroic feats. For a few seconds, I imagined myself a professional ballplayer whose life depended on this single catch— Creative Visualization, it's called. Me, who's never once caught a ball, I dove and lunged and slid and . . . yes! . . . caught that baby with nary a scuff on its faux-velvet covering.

Lying on the hard floor with the big heart safely in my grasp, I saw the film of my life resume its normal speed. I got up and replaced the box on its stand, then pushed it far back from the edge of the shelf. I did the same for all the other boxes within Tobias's reach.

"Curiosity killed the cat," said the woman with a warning tone.

"And almost killed half a day's tips too," I added.

Oblivious to the microcrisis he'd just caused, Tobias re-marked, "I want some candy, Uncle Stan."

The woman asked with sudden interest, "He's your nephew?"

I nodded cautiously. "Kind of."

"In that case," she said, "I'm sure we have something for the little man." She'd switched back again from crabby shop-keeper to generous granny, a role that strained her limited acting talents. She handed Tobias a single piece of chocolate over the counter. He took it without a verbal response, so I prompted him.

"What do you say, Tobias?"

He studied the piece of chocolate without a word.

I nudged him. "Say thank-you, Tobias."

Instead he poked his finger into the bottom of the candy. When a pale orange-colored cream oozed out, Tobias said, "I don't like this," and handed the goopy mess back to the woman. "I want those," he demanded, pressing his now sticky fingers onto the spotless glass of the counter's showcase and pointing to an arrangement of dark chocolate caramels, and then to a pyra-mid of solid chocolate cubes.

I said meekly, "I guess I'll take a quarter pound of dark caramels."

From behind the counter, the woman grabbed a handful of chocolates from a box, rather than upset the display case. Then instead of ringing up the sale on the register, she slapped the bag on the counter top. "We don't want the boy to leave here disap-pointed, do we?" she said. But her face had a look that meant, Here's your hat, what's your hurry?

I reached for my wallet, but the woman shook her head. "You've got your chocolate. Now have a nice day," she said brusquely, and folded her hands together on top of the counter. The beneficent matriarch had changed back into a nasty nanny whose patience we'd pushed too far. Tobias and I left the shop. Within seconds, he had the bag open and had jammed four of the chocolates into his mouth. His cheeks bulged like a greedy little hamster's. I snatched the bag away from him and said, "No more for now." Chocolate wasn't the best thing for his empty stomach.

I led him by the hand toward the factory entrance, two massive oak doors set under a huge granite archway a short distance from where we were. As we started walking toward the doorway, a gleaming lavender-colored delivery van appeared out of nowhere and screeched to a halt at the curb beside us. The side of the van was hand-painted with vivid purple irises arranged over the name Le Jardin Chocolatier spelled out in elaborate cursive script. Even in midwinter the van's lustrous paint seemed immune to road grime. The driver's window opened and a familiar head emerged. It was Rafik, the handsome French-Canadian man from last night's party.

"Stani!" he called out with a broad smile. How did he know the diminutive form of my name? Only Nikki and my maternal grandmother could use it with impunity. Well, and perhaps Rafik now.

"What are you doing here?" I asked with a happy hop in my nether regions.

"I am working."

"But don't you work for Le Jardin?"

"Is all the same company." He pointed to the Gladys Gardner factory.

"It is?"

"Oh, sure. But mebbee now Le Jardin will close."

"You mean after last night?"

"Is big scandal, no?" Then, gesturing toward Tobias, Rafik asked, "Is this your boy?"

I shook my head. "I like men. Remember?"

Rafik shrugged. "Many gay men have children."

The proof that sexuality and logic are unrelated.

"Why are you coming here?" he asked.

I explained that I wanted to see Prentiss Kingsley. In response Rafik raised one eyebrow, much the way Nikki often does. Was it a Parisian hallmark?

Rafik said, "Is too bad. Mr. Kingsley—he's not here today."

Damn! A wasted trip. "Do you know where he is?"

"I think mebbee at his summer house."

"In the middle of winter?"

"Is very beautiful there."

"Where?"

"Is called Abbey-gail, I think."

"Abigail," I said. "Abigail-by-the-Sea."

Rafik nodded, and he was right, too. It is very beautiful there.

Then Rafik winked mischievously. "Mebbee you like to see how they make the chocolate now?"

I shrugged. "Why not? We're here."

"I take you."

"But it's just down the street."

"Get in," he ordered.

I opened the passenger door and shoved Tobias up onto the seat, then squeezed myself in behind him. Rafik slammed the accelerator to the floor, and we departed in the style of the best gangsters, tires squawling on the pavement.

"Where's the fire?" I asked.

"No fire," he said with a grin. "I like to drive."

Rafik raced the van around to the back of the building and swerved sharply into the truck entrance. The sudden turn threw Tobias and me off balance and sent us tumbling toward Rafik. At the loading dock, he backed the van up, rubber tires squealing, and banged it against the rubber guardrail on the dock. Nothing like a hard-driving man. He told us to wait while he went inside to make arrangements for our tour of the factory. After a few minutes he emerged from the building and galloped to the van. "Is all set," he said energetically as he opened the van door. "Go in there." He pointed the way through a doorway on the loading dock. "Ask for Mary." Then he added, "Is good you have the boy here. Looks okay to the boss."

That devious logic had escaped me, but now I saw its value, especially when investigating at a chocolate factory. I silently thanked Nicole for insisting I bring Tobias along with me.

"Are you coming too?" I asked.

"I have to work now. You can get back yourself?"

I nodded. "I'm a big boy, Rafik."

He replied with a wink. "I hope so."

I took Tobias by the hand and led him into the factory. Rafik waved good-bye and disappeared through another door.

Once inside, I was struck by the honest industrialness of the factory. It was a place where things were made, work was done—a contrast to the candy store, where money and merchandise and lies were exchanged. The air inside was cool and carried a bitter, though not unpleasant smell. I'd expected something sweeter, but I'd later learn that I'd been anticipating the smell of sugar cooking rather than the pungent aroma of chocolate being tempered.

I stood near the door with Tobias for a few minutes, trying to get my bearings. I felt a little lost, and I'm sure it was obvious that we didn't belong there. A small electric-powered forklift, its chipped yellow paint streaked and speckled with chocolate, beeped at us and swerved too close as it buzzed by. I jumped back, pulling Tobias with me, and I saw the young driver smile self-contentedly at the success of his show-off scare tactics. Perhaps that was how he enlivened his dull life, pretending the forklift was a sports car, or a skateboard.

While we waited for the woman named Mary who was supposed to take us on a tour of the plant, I looked around, trying to guess what was going on. From where we stood I could see through a large window five women of varied ethnic origins (none Caucasian, however) packing chocolates into boxes. They stood while they worked, and I was mesmerized by the blurred motion of their hands, guided by the same fantasmic force that inspires the best haircutters in their swift but deliberate work. A conveyor belt moved an interminable line of empty boxes unhaltingly past each woman while she urgently added her portion of candy to each box. It was the exact opposite of the famous skit where Lucille Ball picks chocolates off a conveyor belt in a growing frenzy. In real life it's the boxes that move on the packing line, not the chocolates. I guessed that the last woman in line had the most difficult job, fitting those final pieces into whatever space was left and doing it exactly within the allotted time.

Perhaps she had some dubious title to reflect her talents, like
Senior Last Packer.

When our guide finally appeared, I recognized her instantly.
It was Mary Phinney, who'd been at the reception last night.
Small and wiry, trotting like a nervous animal, she approached
us warily, as though we were intruders on a top-secret project.

"Are you the ones here for the tour?" she demanded.

I nodded and noticed her laminated name tag, which had
her photo—obviously taken years ago, before the crepey skin
and wattled neck had appeared—along with a number, a low
number, a kind of status symbol that implied a long term of
dedicated service to the company. Mary Phinney wore her employee badge proudly.

"Who are you with?" she asked with a high, raspy bark.

I felt compelled to correct her grammar but restrained myself. She stood facing me, hands on her hips, defiant.

"It's just we two," I answered.

"You're supposed to be with a group."

"We are the group," I said.

She gave Tobias a disapproving glance and said, "Is he
yours?"

Tobias interjected proudly, "That's my Uncle Stan."

Mary Phinney's eyes bugged out momentarily. "Why you
people ever want to mix together, I'll never understand."

"I'm his godfather."

Mary Phinney said nothing. Maybe it was the god word that
shut her up. I could see it was going to be a challenge to keep my
temper with this woman, but I reminded myself that I wanted to
find out who had made the truffles for the party the other night.
In particular, I wanted to know who'd made the three specially
decorated ones. I could already tell I wasn't going to get too far
with her. My first impressions had been wrong: Mary Phinney
was no feisty terrier, she was a pugnacious pit bull.

Already five yards ahead of us, she motioned for Tobias and
me to follow her. "Come on," she yelled back at us. "And tell
your boy to keep his hands in his pockets. These aren't free
samples."

I waved the small bag of chocolate we'd extorted from the outlet store earlier. "We came in with this," I said, holding up the bag, "so don't accuse us of pilfering."

"Hmph!" went Mary Phinney as she led us through a set of airtight doors into the factory. The air in there was cool, around fifty degrees Fahrenheit, but still relatively warm for us, since we'd come in from outside. We walked by racks of plastic jugs that looked exactly like gallon-sized containers of automobile antifreeze. The labels said things like "natural rum flavor" and "raspberry concentrate" but the lists of chemicals that followed looked like antifreeze too.

We continued walking toward a large open area. On the way we passed by long rows of tall metal racks on wheels. All the shelves were empty, and I asked our grumpy guide why.

"That was all Valentine's stock, went out months ago. We're finishing with Easter now."

It sounded like the fashion industry, where everything behind the scenes is many months ahead of what the public buys. And in the big work area ahead of us, I found out exactly what "behind the scenes" meant in the chocolate trade. The first noticeable change was that it was a few degrees warmer in there, though still not warm. Perhaps the change in temperature was caused by all the machinery and motion in that area, which resembled a scaled-down amusement park with belts and wheels and turntables and platforms all twisting, turning, tilting, and whirling thousands of chocolatey objects.

One extra-nasty machine caught Tobias's attention. It resembled the revolving drum of a monstrous music box, but in place of delicate pins plucking dulcet tones from a metal harp, the drum housed a collection of plastic molds—bunnies and ducks and chicks—impaled helplessly all around its surface. The rotation and revolution and vibration inflicted upon the poor chocolate creatures reminded me of the laboratory torture that astronauts must endure to overcome their sense of gravity.

"What's that one for?" I asked Mary Phinney.

"Spinners," she barked back. "Keeps the chocolate even in

the mold. They're all automatic. Each one puts out two hundred pieces an hour."

It sounded impressive. Then we came upon a conveyor belt carrying ranks and files of bleached white coconut creams on their fateful way into a mysterious machine. Just before entering the dark chamber, each row of creams was transferred to another conveyor belt of coarse screening. As I peeked inside to watch, I felt Tobias tugging at my pants leg.

"I wanna see."

I lifted him up and we looked inside the machine together. First, the conveyor belt dipped down into a shallow trough of melted chocolate, which coated the bottom portion of each row of coconut candy. Then, the quarry was dragged directly through a curtain of melted chocolate, which completely enrobed each piece. All excess chocolate ran off through the porous conveyor belt, just as the chocolate-covered creams were transferred to another belt to be carried into a cooling tunnel. I caught hold of Tobias's little arm just as it was snaking its way into the dark chamber, eager to snare a freshly-coated coconut egg.

Mary Phinney saw him and snapped, "I told you, keep his hands in his pockets."

The next pieces we saw were specialty items for a local Roman Catholic girl's school, part of next springtime's fundraising drive, according to the message on the wrappings. The items were solid milk chocolate crosses with a white chocolate Jesus attached. I asked Mary Phinney, "Does this come with a white cross and a dark Jesus?"

She didn't answer me.

Against one wall I noticed a row of large metal drums, like the ones crude oil comes in, with big block-stenciled letters on each one spelling out PURE CANDELA.

"What's that?" I asked.

Mary Phinney answered. "Wax."

"For the floor?"

"For the chocolate."

"You put wax in the chocolate?"

"You have to," she said, shaking her head in annoyance. It

was obvious that she didn't enjoy conducting tours, and I wondered why she did it at all. She explained about the wax. "You know how hard it is to make a good product? One or two degrees off, and it gets dull and grainy, no sheen, no smoothness. You'd need a laboratory to do it right. You know how much that would cost? But with a little wax, you don't have to worry, and you still get good product."

"But you end up eating wax."

"Don't even taste it."

"I'll bet it's a lot cheaper than cocoa butter too."

Mary Phinney was about to agree, but caught herself. Meanwhile, I wondered how much wax you'd need to make champagne truffles over a campfire. I was quickly learning that chocolate-making could be just another heavy industry, one that occasionally produced an edible product.

"Excuse me, Ms. Phinney, but I was wondering—"

"It's Mrs. Phinney. My husband is dead."

"Sorry," I said, then continued. "I'd like to see where the truffles are made."

She set herself stiffly on her little legs and said, "Those aren't ours."

"I thought Le Jardin made their truffles here."

"They rent space and equipment, that's all."

"I know the people who own the business," I said.

"Then get them to show you around."

"I just want to find out who made those truffles for last night's big party."

She aimed her nasty litle eyes at me. "Why?"

"Because one of them was full of poison, and it might have happened here."

"I don't know anything about it," she said.

"Don't you supervise all the work here?"

"Who told you that?"

"Laurett Cole."

"Then why don't you ask her about it?" she said with a snarl. "She's the one who made them."

"No, she just arranged them. I want to know who made them."

Mary Phinney suddenly turned and faced me. "What are you doing here? If you're trying to help her, it's too late. She got all the special treatment she'll get from this place."

"Who put the poison in that truffle?"

The woman flinched. "I told you, it was Laurett Cole. Her kind don't know any other way to fix the problems they get into. It figures she'd get caught, stupid woman."

"That's my ma," exclaimed Tobias, and in a second he was at her, punching and kicking with all his little strength.

Mary Phinney screamed loudly for help, then yelled at me, "Get that little bastard off me!"

I didn't think good Irish Catholic women said things like that, but then, I've lived a cloistered life. I pulled Tobias away from her, but I didn't use much strength. I wanted him to get in a few more good punches and kicks before I stopped him. Meanwhile, some of the factory workers had gathered around us, curious about the sudden outbreak of violence. I noticed that none of them offered to help Mary Phinney either. They just stood by and watched as I disentangled Tobias from the older woman.

Just then a man emerged from a glass-enclosed office that overlooked the entire production floor. I recognized him as John Lough, whom I'd also seen at the reception last night. Again I sensed bearlike strength, not sluggish fat, under his economy-grade business suit. He approached the place where we were standing, the arena where the hag had been mauled by the wild young boy.

"John!" gasped Mary Phinney. "Call the police! That boy attacked me!"

The man said nothing for a moment, but quietly surveyed the situation with keen eyes. "There's no need for that, Mary," he said with the disinterest of a judge. He rested his gaze on Tobias for a while, then he turned to me. "What seems to be the problem?" he asked calmly.

His badge said Senior Vice-President of Operations, and I wondered who he was when he wasn't wearing the badge.

"I'm Stan Kraychik," I said. "This is Tobias Cole, my, er, nephew. We were on a tour of the plant when this woman insulted Tobias's mother. She provoked him, and he reacted."

"Liar!" exclaimed Mary Phinney. "He attacked me."

John Lough addressed the crowd of workers who'd gathered around us. "Everything's under control now. Go back to your stations and resume your work." He gave orders comfortably, more easily than Branco did, without the brittle edge. Maybe John Lough was naturally better suited for supervising people. Or maybe being a cop required a constant level of repressed anger, something Branco had in abundance.

John looked at the three of us—Mary Phinney, Tobias, and me—then he gently but firmly guided Tobias and me away to his glass-walled office. "Please wait here," he said, and left us alone inside the crystal cube.

He went back out to talk with Mary Phinney. Through the glass walls of his office I watched them exchange words and gestures, but I couldn't hear a word. Mary Phinney's mouth wouldn't stop moving, and sometimes her jaw flapped so hard that her whole head jumped and shook about in reaction. John Lough stood quietly while she railed at him. Then he said something to her that stopped her mid-sentence. Just like that. She pressed her lips tightly together, then she turned and walked away from him. I wondered what magic phrase he'd used on her, which psycho-button he'd pressed to turn her off so easily.

He headed back toward his office, where Tobias and I were waiting. When he entered, he flashed one brief, insincere smile at us. "Everything's been settled. Now, in way of apology to both of you, I'd like to show you something that few people get to experience."

He led us out of his office and away from the production floor to another part of the building, through doorways, up elevators, down crooked corridors, far removed from the chocolate-making machinery we'd just seen. We passed through a set of heavy doors and I heard a strange, raucous crackling noise from somewhere within. When we pushed our way through a second set of heavy doors, we were at once immersed in the source of the sound, inside a long, narrow cavern that resembled a steamship's boiler room. But was sound the word for what was happening to our ears in there? Lined up along two sides of the dark chamber were twenty huge machines that looked like frontloading clothes washers, but Paul-Bunyan-size. All twenty copper drums were rotating slowly, and they rattled as though they were full of pebbles, tons of them. The racket was horrible and actually painful. John Lough handed Tobias and me some earshielding headsets to dampen the sound. We put them on and felt instant relief. Thus protected, we could walk past the two rows of machines. I lifted Tobias up so that he could look inside them, and what we both saw was . . . jellybeans. There must have been thousands, no, millions of them. Each giant machine was coating and glazing a single color of jellybean. One copper drum contained red, another pink, then yellow, white, orange, green, purple—twenty colors in all, like a big set of crayons. Gosh, I thought, more wax.

We departed from the other end of that long room, descended a few long flights of stairs, and eventually came into another cool area where more of the molded Easter items were being wrapped and packaged for storage before shipment. I said to John Lough, "I was hoping to see where the Le Jardin truffles were made."

He replied quickly, but politely. "I'm afraid I don't have any more time today, but I can arrange for some samples to take with you now."

Tobias said, "She told us no samples."

"I can make exceptions," said John Lough with authoritative confidence. From the shelves of Easter merchandise he picked a huge chocolate rabbit and a large basket full of smaller items—bunnies, chicks, and eggs. "I'm sure it was all a mistake," he said. "Please accept my apology for the misunderstanding."

Tobias took the chocolate goods and thanked him, but I added, "We do not waive our right to lodge a formal complaint against that woman. She harassed this boy. Who knows the trauma she may have caused him? I doubt a little chocolate is going to set things straight. It's not so simple."

Tobias poked me and said, "Shut up, Uncle Stan."

"Good," said John Lough. "The boy is sensible. I hope you are too." Then he escorted us to a nearby exit, and we were suddenly back outside facing the parking lot of the Gladys Gardner Chocolate Company.

"C'mon, Tobias," I said and tugged him over the wet asphalt toward the MTA station, where we'd catch the subway back downtown. He was already tearing into the basket of chocolate novelties. Here it was, not even Valentine's Day yet and the boy was unwrapping foil-covered chocolate Easter eggs. I took one, bit into it, then spit it out. Shinola came to mind.

While we waited on the platform for the train to arrive, Tobias asked me, "Is my ma dead too?"

Nothing like direct examination. "No, Tobias," I replied. "Why do you think that?"

"The way they talk about her."

"I promise you, she's all right, Tobias."

"Can I see her?"

"We'll go there soon."

My answers must have satisfied him for the moment, because he stopped talking and focused on his quarry. He peeled off some of the cellophane wrapping from the chocolate bunny and munched contentedly on the ears. As for me, I was becoming mentally distracted by a confusion of questions and recent observations. My mind was beginning to resemble the convoluted candy-making machinery we'd just seen.

When we got back to my place, I found outside my door a big, flat, plain cardboard box without identification. No words, no labels, no nothing. Nothing except the faint aroma of chocolate from inside. I took it into my apartment. Sugar Baby was waiting to greet me, but then scampered away at the sight of Tobias. Smart girl, she hadn't forgotten his recent terrorism that morning. I shook the mysterious box, but the heavy contents didn't move or make a sound. I sniffed at it again. Definitely chocolate and possibly alcohol too. Not a bomb, I thought, unless they're making them out of food these days. I opened the box and found inside a large velvet-covered heart. It was real velvet, finely napped, possibly even real silk, not like the dusty, fake flocking on the box Tobias had almost destroyed in the discount chocolate store earlier. I lifted the top of the heart and saw nestled inside two dozen large chocolate truffles from Le Jardin. Who'd sent them? Did I finally have a secret admirer? Or was someone perhaps wooing me with poisoned delicacies?

I called Nicole at Snips and tried to convince her to watch over Tobias while I went to see Lieutenant Branco. I wanted to bring him up-to-date on what I'd found out, and on what had just appeared on my doorstep. But Nicole refused to help me. So before bundling Tobias up again to face the great outdoors with me, I made some tea—cocoa for Tobias—to prepare us for another wintry foray. It was then that I heard strange sounds coming from the living room. I looked in to see Tobias sitting on the sofa, gagging and coughing, with melted chocolate all around his mouth. He began to cry too when his little body went into quick, jumpy spasms. My first panic-stricken thought was that he'd eaten a truffle from the mysterious box that had just arrived. Had he accidentally poisoned himself? Then, just as quickly, I realized that what he'd actually eaten was almost an entire two-pound chocolate bunny on an empty stomach, and now was about to upchuck the near-toxic product. I grabbed him up into my arms and made a run for the toilet with him, trying all the way to keep his mouth covered, trying to keep the warm, melted, waxy brown slime from dribbling onto the recently shampooed Aubusson carpet.

7

DADDYCAKES

After vomiting most of the chocolate bunny, Tobias was slumped drowsy-eyed on the sofa, getting ready for an early-afternoon snoozette. I made a fast call to a local poison-control center to report his symptoms, just in case it was poison that he'd ingested. Also, with the ghastly amount of sugar Tobias had just consumed, there was the chance of an undiscovered diabetic complication. But the hospital folk assured me that it was a common syndrome around the candy-laden holidays like Valentine's Day and Easter. The best remedy was to abstain from sugar and to keep the boy's body moving. That was just what I wanted to hear, since I intended to set out immediately for Station E of the Boston Police Department and confront Detective Lieutenant Vito Branco, the burly cop whose path was once again crossing mine . . . or was mine crossing his?

I shook Tobias gently.

"Tobias, wake up. We have to go out again."

"Noo-o," he groaned. "I'm tired."

"We have to go, and I can't leave you here alone."

"Then don't go."

"It doesn't work that way." I yanked at him, and he resisted heavily with his whole little body. It turned into a kind of game, with him being as passive as possible and me trying to rouse him gently but persistently. Eventually the sheer attention of it all got him awake enough so that we could venture out. For what seemed the thousandth time that winter, I donned the layers of heavy clothing for a trip to the police station. On one arm I supported a drowsy boy, while with the other I juggled the recently arrived box of Valentine's truffles. I also wondered again about taking Branco the candy I'd lifted from Laurett's place last night. Part of me wanted to know if that stuff was poisoned, but another part of me felt like a Judas, betraying a friend I'd promised to help. So I decided to withhold that evidence a little longer. I hailed a cab and headed for Station E. Once inside the cab, Tobias dozed off again almost immediately. He'd hit the sugar slump.

Station E of the Boston Police Department is one of the crown jewels of Boston's municipal restorations. Its granite pillars and portico give the illusion of stately authority and protection and trust from days gone by, the so-called better days. It shares the same neighborhood as the recently developed Boston Center for the Arts, almost as a reminder to performers and audiences to desist from having too much fun. And, since the station building is an official historical landmark, all maintenance and renovation must be in keeping with its original design: no skylights, no smoked glass, no fluorescent lights in the public areas, no threat of conversion to condominiums.

I paid the driver and carried Tobias inside. He was sleeping heavily, but he almost looked unconscious. Now was the time to flip that on/off switch, if only I could find it. The desk sergeant asked with concern if the boy needed help. I assured him that Tobias was just sleepy, and that the urgency of my meeting with Lieutenant Branco had required me to drag the kid along with me. The sergeant responded in a friendly way, without the usual brusqueness I receive from heavy-duty straight men. Perhaps my holding a young boy in my arms imbued me with a kind of procreative aura, the kind of power that the breeding male believes is his exclusive domain. I guess having a man-child does have its advantages.

The sergeant called Branco and announced me, and surprisingly, Branco said to send me in right away. I figured he'd make up some excuse not to see me, since for someone like Branco contending with someone like me, a little goes a long way.

The sergeant offered to put Tobias in Station E's "day-care

center" while I talked with the lieutenant. The day-care center turned out to be a single windowless room—probably a converted interrogation chamber—containing a crib, a diaper-changing table, a playpen, and a plastic tricycle. So much for the City of Boston's official attempt at progressive ordinances for working parents. On the bright side, since there were no other children in the room today—or probably any other time, since the distinctive litter of young humans was missing—Tobias had the place all to his quiet little self. He was so sleepy he didn't even notice that I was leaving him alone. Such a peaceful picture.

Which in no way resembled my visit—or should I call it my confrontation?—with Branco. When I entered his office, he was seated at his desk, leaning back in the oak swivel chair and talking on the telephone. I wondered why he was always on the phone when I went to see him. Was he really so busy? Or did he just like to set the tone of the meeting—that *he* was in charge? I knew I was in for trouble when he lifted his long legs and rested his feet on the corner of his desk. The pose showed off the long lines of his muscular thighs and the dense strength of his calves all pressing against the fabric of his fine worsted slacks. The pose also showed a curious contradiction: For all his macho intent and behavior, Branco's favored shoe was not the typical cop's snub-toed blucher, but instead a sleek black loafer, polished to a chromium shine. And he chose the beefy moccasin style made in Maine, not the stylish slip-ons from Italy.

He finished his conversation with a wry smile and lively eyes, and I was a little jealous of the lucky person who was receiving such rare warmth from him. Then he slammed the receiver down, put his feet back on the floor, and stared at me coldly. "What do you want?"

"You sure know how to make a guy feel welcome, Lieutenant."

"I'm not running a charm school here. If you have something to say, go ahead."

"Fine. What are the grounds for charging Laurett Cole with manslaughter?"

"You her lawyer?"

"Obviously not."

"Then where do you get off nosing around here?"

The only place I wanted to put my nose in that room would have got me arrested.

"She's my friend, Lieutenant. Ever have one of those?"

"I got friends," he said. Then he leaned back in his chair with a self-satisfied grin. "But they don't kill people. Laurett Cole may have wanted just to scare that guy, but her plan backfired, and he's dead now."

"But it wasn't intentional."

"The poisoning was."

"You can't prove that."

Branco leaned forward, pressing his fabulous strong hands against the distressed top of the old oak desk. "Kraychik, she admitted giving him the chocolate. What the lab found in his mouth and stomach contained enough cyanide to kill five healthy adults. She's lucky the charge isn't first-degree murder."

That wasn't what Laurett had told me. Once again I wondered, Had she planned to poison her boyfriend or husband or whoever the dead guy was? The only thing that might drive her to such desperate action would be a threat to Tobias, and from what he had told me already about the dead man, sexual abuse was quite possible.

"Lieutenant, Laurett told me how it all happened last night with those chocolates. One of the special truffles had been damaged, obviously by whoever put the poison into it, so she replaced that truffle with another one. She had no intention of hurting anyone. That guy took it and ate it after she'd left the kitchen. That's how he got the dose of cyanide. But it was really supposed to go to Prentiss Kingsley. That's what I came here to tell you, among other things."

Branco leaned back in his chair again and studied me through narrowed eyes. He pursed his lips and shook his head in a slow no, as if to say, "Convince me." I could almost feel his thoughts about me. I suppose that someone with my genetic makeup would naturally rile the blood of someone like him: I was a hairdresser, he was a cop; I was resilient, he was rigid; and

I preferred men, while Branco had no visible sexual preference. He couldn't consider me a full-fledged man in his terms, but neither could he consider me part of the helpless half of the world who needed his protection, the half that included women, children, and old folks.

He took a deep breath and held it for a moment. I could see his jaw muscles clenching. "Kraychik," he said, easing the air out slowly, as though trying to release a seething internal pressure without exploding, "I want you out of my office, and I don't want to see you here again unless I call you. Is that clear?"

"Jeez, Lieutenant, I'm just trying to be a good scout, fighting for truth, justice, and the American Way."

"Out!"

"But I brung ya deez." I held out the heart-shaped box of truffles to him.

The handsome cop shook his head and muttered, "Christ!" Then his face became stern. "What's that?" he asked coldly.

"It's chocolate. I thought you'd want it."

"Is this some kind of joke?"

"No, Lieutenant. It's serious. Take it."

He sat upright in his chair and crossed his arms in front of his big chest—classic defensive body talk.

He said, "I never did anything to encourage this kind of behavior from you."

"I'm only doing what's right, Lieutenant."

He shook his head. "I don't want it."

"Then what should I do with it?"

"Give it to someone who feels the same way you do."

"But it might be evidence."

Branco's eyes opened with their glorious light. "What do you mean?" he asked.

"They were outside my door today. I don't know who sent them, but they're certainly Le Jardin merchandise. So I figured they might provide some clues for you."

Branco pondered this a moment, then chuckled nervously. "I thought maybe . . ." He smiled vaguely. "I thought with Valentine's Day . . . and you. I thought . . ." Then he actually laughed. It was the first time I'd ever heard Branco laugh, and in that new moment of hearing him and seeing him, I wanted him to laugh more, and for me to laugh with him. But he must have sensed my thoughts, because he quickly caught himself and regained his cop-ness.

"So it's not a gift?" he asked.

"Why would I give you a gift?"

He took the box stiffly. "Thanks," he said. "I'll send this down to the lab." Then he stood up abruptly and put on his overcoat. It was a full-cut job in heavy charcoal-colored melton. On someone else it might have been a mere stylish tog, but on Branco it had the aura of a sacred garment. He opened the door and gestured with his right hand for me to leave. "We're finished here."

"Late lunch?" I asked on my way out the door.

Branco scowled. "I'm gone for the day."

"So early? It's only three o'clock."

"Kraychik, if you're playing timekeeper, why don't you mark down that I've been on duty here since eight A.M. yesterday morning."

"Eight A.M. in the morning is redundant, Lieutenant."

Branco grunted.

I never intended to be sarcastic with him, but it always seemed to happen. I sometimes wished we could be friends, bonding-buddies who touch each other easily and share pitchers of beer and the stories of their petty victories and losses. But if Branco ever touched me, or I him, I'm afraid the symptoms of *my* style of male bonding would become protrudingly obvious.

He headed down a busy corridor on his way out of the station, and I tagged alongside him. With his long legs, Branco moved easily, yet his step was almost silent against the marble-tiled floor, not the typical clumping tread of authority. His overcoat, still unbuttoned, unfurled itself around and behind him like a big dark cape.

"Lieutenant, I was at the Gladys Gardner factory this morning, and I think they're hiding something."

"I don't care, Kraychik. I'm off duty now."

"But they wouldn't show me where Le Jardin makes their truffles."

"Believe it or not, they have a right to privacy, especially from people like you."

"But I think the poisoned truffle came from that factory. Someone in that place loaded that truffle with cyanide."

"It could have been done anywhere. In fact, it's a strange thing—we searched Laurett Cole's place and didn't find one piece of chocolate there. Now, for a woman who was supposed to be managing a chocolate shop, wouldn't you say that's odd?"

"Well . . ." I replied haltingly, since I was withholding that very evidence myself. "Maybe she's just so sick of the stuff that she couldn't stand the sight of it at home. I mean, I don't keep hair rollers and frosting caps around."

"But wouldn't she have some of it around for her boy?"

"No, no, Lieutenant. His nutritional health always comes first," I lied. "I think what happened, though, is that you were looking for incriminating evidence at Laurett's place and you didn't find it. So rather than believe the facts, you'd prefer to suspect foul play."

"Those are your words."

"Isn't there a chance you're on the wrong track?"

Branco stopped walking and faced me.

"*You* are on the wrong track, Kraychik. We've got a corpse, a suspect, and a motive. All you've got are some crazy ideas."

"But—"

"I told you, I'm off duty." He turned away from me angrily and walked toward a door marked MEN. What could I do but follow?

Inside, the walls had been refurbished with slabs of grey marble three-quarters of the way up, the remainder painted with high-gloss enamel in a cozy shade of robin's-egg blue. The floor was a spotless mosaic of tiny white hexagonal tiles. Everything was austere and functional. Even the cool air was heady with pine disinfectant. Branco stationed himself at one of two urinals while I washed my hands. I always wash first. You would too if you had your hands in other people's hair all day. Don't worry, though—at the shop, I wash afterwards as well.

Branco glanced at me, then fixed his gaze on the marble wall directly in front of him. I stood at the urinal next to him. Odd, but it seemed a kind of friendly thing to do together, Branco and me, as though we were re-enacting some kind of archetypal ritual: No matter what we do, or who we like, or how we feel, this is how men pee. So I'm standing there, gushing forth with my usual noisy splash, imagining all kinds of anthropological evolutions, how this act hasn't changed much through the millennia, that zillions of men have peed like this, and with any luck, zillions more will too. I mean, I wasn't thinking sex, per se. But then what happens? Branco suddenly turns away from his place and goes into one of the empty stalls. Then he closes the door and latches it as though he's afraid of catching something from me. I felt horrible. And then, just as suddenly, when I finally heard his tentative flow, I understood his behavior. Lieutenant Vito Branco, that unnerving male animal with a magnificent body and a powerful will, that epitome of Italian machismo, was pee-shy.

He emerged from the stall and washed his hands at the sink, while practicing his sullen look in the mirror. I pretended to adjust my short hair in another part of the same mirror. Branco frowned at my reflection. I stared directly back into the reflection of his eyes, my whole face one big dopey grin. His lips seemed just about to lapse into a smile too, but instead he began methodically checking his teeth in the mirror.

Outside, in the cold air, Branco's curly black hair glistened in the bright sun. The guy could have been a magazine model in his youth, but in those days the publishers were still reluctant to put such sensual men on their front covers. I followed him to his car, a vintage Alpha Romeo coupé whose once vibrant racing-green lacquer was now discolored and matte.

"Lieutenant, will you at least question the people at the chocolate factory?"

Branco looked at me wearily. "Kraychik, I told you to stop intruding. I know you want to help your friends, but you're getting in the way."

"I'm finding facts."

Branco shook his head no. "You're just repeating what other people tell you. For all you know, everyone is lying to you. Why don't you wait until tomorrow, and see what kind of cockeyed theory you come up with then?"

"Tomorrow may be too late, Lieutenant. There's a killer still out there who wants Prentiss Kingsley dead. Why should he stop just because you're tired?"

"If that's true, he won't stop." Branco got into the car. "But I don't think it's true."

He closed the door and started the engine, while I vainly polished a small spot on the hood with my fingertip. "Car needs a paint job, Lieutenant."

A small cloud of blue smoke rose from the exhaust pipe. "And a ring job," he replied, and then pulled away, gunning the Alpha's engine to make its distinctive wild, roaring sound.

I kicked at the soot-blackened snowdrift at the edge of the sidewalk, then turned up Berkeley Street and walked back to the shop. For some unknown reason, in spite of the typical argumentative exchange with Branco, I felt that a weight had been lifted from me. I walked more easily than I had since the killing last night, and I felt my legs reaching out freely with their usual long stride. At least Branco and I had long legs in common. That was something, wasn't it? The walk felt good, and I thought maybe if I did more of it, I'd finally shed the extra weight I carried around my middle. It wasn't until I got to the shop and greeted Nicole that I realized what I'd done, or forgotten to do.

"Where's Tobias?" she asked.

Without a word I made for the phone. I quickly called Station E and told them that I'd forgotten my ward there.

The desk sergeant half-chuckled and said, "It's no problem. The little tyke's been keeping us entertained." It seemed strange that the very people who'd imprisoned Laurett Cole were the same ones being entertained by her son. The officer continued, "Do you want to come and get him, or should we bring him by in the cruiser?"

"If you could drop him off, that would be fine," I said, but Nicole interrupted me.

"Don't you think the boy's been through enough today?" she asked.

Confused and feeling helpless, I shrugged.

Nicole frowned in dismay. "Tell them I'll go get the boy. It looks like this situation needs a *real* woman to set it right."

I explained to the sergeant that Nicole would pick up Tobias shortly. Then I hung up and turned to her.

"Doll, I'm stressed out. It was a simple mistake."

"Does your stress have anything to do with the lieutenant?"

How could I confess that those seemingly innocent moments in the men's room with Branco had derailed my sexual notions about myself? Tea-room trade has never been my style, yet those few minutes alone with Branco had struck a new chord within me. With horror I wondered, Was I a latent piss-pig?

"Nikki," I said blithely, "it's my day off. I don't have to explain myself."

"You never do anyway. But as for your day off, you just trot on over to your station and take this walk-in who just arrived."

"But, Nikki—"

"Stanley, I did you a favor this morning, and I'm doing one now. Is it so much to ask?"

"But there are other people who can take her."

"But I want *you* to take her, and I want you to make sure you keep her in the chair until I return with the boy."

"Why?" I asked—but when I saw the woman, the answer was clear. At Snips we take walk-in business, provided the clients pass our unofficial, unstated, undocumented requirements. Requesting a specific stylist, for example, gives an advantage. For this woman, though, one thing alone got her past Nicole at the gate: the full-length chinchilla coat she was wearing. Nicole was mesmerized by the sea of frosty grey fur that billowed around the woman as she rose from one of the spacious lounge chairs in the waiting area. She removed the fur coat with a languid flourish and handed it to Nicole.

"Keep this safe, would you, honey?" she said to Nicole with

a condescending tone, though she appeared to be only a few years younger than Nicole, who is on the other side of fifty.

Nicole smiled broadly. "I promise I won't let it out of my sight."

The woman continued, "My boyfriend would scream if I lost it, even though it *is* insured." She threw her head back and laughed, as if she'd just told us a joke. Little did she realize that she and Nicole were roughly the same size, and that the coat would be tried on—nay, *worn* to Station E to pick up Tobias— while I dealt with the woman's overprocessed hair. Her problem? She was a suicide blonde—dyed by her own hand—and in desperate need of color adjustment, along with industrial-strength moisturizing.

I handed her a robe and showed her the way to the dressing room, then returned to Nicole. "Run your fingers through that hair, doll, you'll ruin a manicure."

Nicole nodded, caressing the fur coat that was still lying in her arms. "She's an out-of-towner, but the boyfriend's local."

"How'd you find that out?"

"She told me his name and even where he works," Nicole replied, proving once again that she could extract almost any fact from anyone. "I swear she wants to share him with me."

"Nikki, I'd think twice about acquiring another fur coat. Those animal-rights folks can get pretty nasty."

"Stanley, the meat and bones are used for pet food, so the whole carcass is utilized, just like the Eskimos and Native Americans did."

"No," I exclaimed in mock disbelief.

"I swear it's true. She just told me that now. Ask her yourself. Her boyfriend is with Kouros furriers. She's staying at the corporate suite at the Ritz."

How could I expect Nicole to sympathize with the unglamorous side of the animals? To her, all the earthly critters were arranged in a simple pecking order, the topmost rung of which was occupied by the noble humans, and the best of those were manicurists. Whatever resided below was at the disposal of those above. I'd often argued that the roaches and the rats shared the

rung *above* us, and they knew enough not to destroy us, just to live easily off us.

A cab tooted its horn in the service alley, and Nikki slipped out the back way. I caught a blurred gray glimpse of her leaving, wrapped in the fluffy fur coat. She'd be warm, if politically incorrect, on her mission of mercy to rescue Tobias.

With the woman now seated in my styling chair, I began my diplomatic but stern lecture about using hair-coloring chemicals at home. She replied, "But I don't do my own hair. My previous hairdresser . . . well, he had a little problem with drugs."

Which explained her fried hair. Unfortunately, chemical abuse is not limited to the sinks and styling chairs in hair salons. The personnel are susceptible too. I was lucky that my addictive side satisfied itself mostly with food.

I began working on the woman's hair, applying artfully blended color to the roots only. The rest of the hair shaft needed loving kindness, not more ammonia or peroxide. I'd treat that part separately, later on. While I applied the color, I mulled the facts I knew so far about last night's killing. When you and your client aren't idly chattering, hairwork can actually be a kind of meditation. Fortunately this woman only purred, which helped me think quietly to myself. I was still concerned that the poisoned truffle was supposed to be on Prentiss Kingsley's plate last night. If that was true and things had gone according to plan, then Prentiss would be dead now, and the case would be completely different. So was the killer waiting for the next best chance to get him? Or was Laurett simply trying to shift the blame from herself and her intentional killing of Trek Delorean? Had I naively fallen for her deception? It always seemed to come to that—what the police believed versus the claims made by the victims and perpetrators of a crime. For my part, I didn't like the doubt that was growing inside me. I wasn't sure whether a friend of mine, namely Laurett, was involved in this killing by choice or by accident. The police thought she was guilty all the way. I didn't want to.

I finished applying color to the woman's hair, then wrapped it all in plastic and left the chemicals to oxygenate their way to

a miracle. While it all cooked quietly, I went to the back room
and poured myself a cup of coffee. Since it was technically my
day off, I added a shot of Nicole's cognac to it. Drinking on the
job is forbidden, but Nikki wasn't there to scold me. Besides, she
was playing her own pranks. So, sipping my brew, I pondered
what my next move would be. Prentiss Kingsley was the intended victim, but I'd already tried and failed to find him. Perhaps Liz Carlini or Dan Doherty might know something that
would explain why someone was trying to kill him. I chose Dan
Doherty as my next subject, since he lived in town. I'd pay him
a call as soon as Nicole returned with Tobias.

To extend the time my client would be in the chair, I suggested that I do a temporary rinse to color the abused hair shafts
without causing further damage. That way the hair would have
a chance to grow out healthy again. I did chop about three-
quarters of an inch off the fried ends too.

By some psychic miracle I timed the finishing touches on the
woman's hair to coincide exactly with Nicole's return from Station E with Tobias, again through the back door. The woman
never guessed that her coat had taken a crosstown excursion
without her. When I finished my work, her golden hair had a
sheen and glow she'd never seen in it before.

Tobias ran into the shop and tackled my legs.

"Uncle Stan, you forgot me."

"I'm sorry, Tobias. It was a mistake."

My new client eyed me in the mirror. "Your nephew?"

I nodded and almost immediately felt the familiar, intentional pressure of a forearm rubbing against my hip. Working
with people, you get touched a lot. Sometimes it's accidental,
sometimes it's friendly, sometimes it's loaded.

"I *love* what you did for my hair," she said.

"I just gave it what it needed."

She stared directly at my reflection in the mirror. The steady
gaze of her eyes into mine conjured for me all the tawdry experiences of her life so far, and she asked, "Are you so good with
other parts of the body?"

I winked and smiled. "Some think so."

She went and changed back to street clothes, then got her fur coat from Nicole. After paying my exorbitant fee at the front desk, she returned to my station and reached inside her small beaded purse, which was just big enough to hold about two thousand dollars . . . and a lipstick. Her manicured, bejeweled fingers pulled out a crisp twenty-dollar bill. "You're a genius," she said. "I'll be back next week." Then she left the shop in a swirl of plush dead animal skin.

"Beware of heavy tippers, Stanley," said Nicole.

"Don't be jealous, doll. You can always have the boyfriend."

"So can you, probably."

"I could never date an animal killer, never mind a straight man."

"Straight hasn't stopped you before."

Since it was almost closing time—earlier on Mondays—I joined Tobias in the waiting lounge. I read to him from one of the fashion magazines, figuring I might launch his sense of style early, on the right track.

Nikki asked, "Aren't you leaving?"

"I thought I'd stay around and have a drink with you."

"You must want another favor."

She was right, but I couldn't admit it.

Shortly after, with the shop closed and locked, Nicole and I were having a cocktail in the back room. Tobias remained out on the shop floor, happily playing cosmic battle scenes with the aluminum rollers and the plastic rods at my station. Nikki lit a cigarette, one of her custom-blended fags from Perretti's, rolled in pastel-tinted rice paper. Tonight's choice was the palest teal blue, which she lit and smoked with the kind of ritual reserved for Japanese tea. Meanwhile, I was facing the question of what to do with Tobias that night. This incipient child-care problem was going to require special tact and diplomacy, especially tonight, when I needed time to visit Dan Doherty and press him about the intrigues and politics between matronly Gladys Gardner Chocolates and her chic-bitch sister, Le Jardin Chocolatier. Nicole had adamantly stipulated that she wouldn't take Tobias overnight. That was last night, though.

"Uh, doll . . . ?" I began tentatively.

"No, Stanley," she replied sharply. "You may not have a cigarette. You've already tried numerous times and failed. If you want to waste cigarettes, try one of the commercial 'lite' variety, and leave mine alone." For dramatic emphasis, she downed a generous mouthful of cognac.

I swirled my bourbon-and-bitters in its environmentally responsible glass-glass. "It was something else, doll," I said, staring pensively into my drink.

Nicole eyed me cautiously. "You must want me to take the boy tonight."

I nodded, feigning a troubled brow.

Nicole continued, "Because you want to question some people about the killing."

I nodded again, ever more gloomily.

"And the lieutenant's not helping you again."

I shook my head a despairing no, but inside I was happily relieved, since she was saying all the hard parts for me.

Nicole sighed, gently rolled the accumulated ash from her cigarette, took another deep, pleasure-filled drag from it, and said, "All right, Stanley. I'll watch Tobias tonight."

"Oh, thanks—"

She raised her finger at me. "Quiet. The boy shouldn't hear this."

"I'll make it up to you, Nikki."

"There's no need, since it will be just this once. It's not to become a regular thing. Taking care of him was your idea, not mine. Though I don't approve of placing him in the court's custody, neither do I want a child in my life, especially at my age."

"Consider him a lovable grandson then."

She glared at me. "You're treading on thin ice, you ungrateful ageist."

"Sorry, Nikki. I just need the time badly. As usual, Branco's got the case just about solved and closed already, and here I am believing, hoping, that Laurett really didn't kill anyone, and I'm trying to prove it."

Nicole raised her glass to me and said, "Stanley Kraychik, the people's hero."

"Or all-time fool," I replied.

We drank, and my bourbon went down warmly, leaving its pleasant aftertaste of burn and sugar.

Nicole said, "Sounds like you still have doubts about Laurett."

"I don't know. I want to believe her, but her story is as neat and tight in its own way as Branco's, and I never accept his side of things."

Nicole said, "Laurett does have a lawyer, Stanley. Chaz fully intends to get her acquitted."

"But does he care about what really happened, about the truth?"

"He's not the villain you make him out to be."

"Nikki, I never accused him of villainy. Arrogance, chauvinism, and greed, perhaps, but not villainy."

"Chaz has been good for me, Stanley, and he agreed to represent Laurett at no charge."

"That's just until she's acquitted. Then he's probably going to sue the City of Boston for damages on her behalf."

Nicole nodded. "Along with the Commonwealth of Massachusetts. But anything you can do to help him now will be greatly appreciated by me, personally."

I gulped the rest of my bourbon. "Thanks for taking Tobias, doll. I'll call later to check up on him."

"There's no need, darling. Besides, Chaz will be with me tonight."

"Well, maybe I should talk with him then."

"Why?"

"Didn't you want me to help him?"

Nicole paused. "I don't see the need yet. Chaz is quite competent. If he wants you, he'll call you."

That was Branco's attitude too: Why was Nikki suddenly becoming cool with me? Usually she was like a protective older sister who could refuse nothing to her baby brother. For some reason, recently, there was distance. I suspected that Charles was at the root of it. Though he liked to portray a smart young professional, tolerant in his actions and progressive in his words, I sensed a latent bigot to the atom. And in my lexicon, bigot equals homophobe.

Nicole continued, "Don't forget that tomorrow is *my* day off, and I don't intend to keep Tobias with me all day."

"But I'm working here."

"I'll send him to you in a cab."

"Maybe it's better if I come by early, for coffee, and pick him up in person?"

She paused again. "I suppose that will be fine," she said with obvious reluctance.

"Around eight?" I said.

Nicole grimaced. I suspected what she wanted was an uninterrupted morning with Charles. Then she softened.

"Well, with the boy there, we'll probably all be awake anyway. And since you're coming for coffee, would you pick up something from Sally's Kitchen? Chaz adores her stuff." Sally's was an excellent bakery that used butter, sugar, cream, and chocolate—life's basic nutrients—in such imaginative combinations that the resultant clogged arteries seemed a minor consequence to the velvety oral pleasures her baked creations produced.

"Yes, ma'am," I said with a salute. "In return for one night's baby-sitting, I'll bring one cream tart with pine nuts for Mas' Chowz."

I got up, reapplied the multiple layers of winterwear and donned my mukluks—again. I felt like Nanook of the North setting out into the wintry blast. I kissed Nicole good-bye, gave Tobias a big hug, and left the shop. I'm ashamed to confess how free I felt without having Tobias with me. After this visit to Dan Doherty, I was looking forward to going home for supper and a short rest, then maybe heading out again for some fun and relaxation. It hadn't even been twenty-four hours, and already I abhorred parenthood. Then again, being a Gemini with Gemini rising, how could I possibly expect to be tied down by anything, especially a young boy?

8
KAFKA REDUX

Out on the street it had begun to snow. It wasn't the usual February sleet that stings your face like a thousand tiny needles. Instead the snow was the big, wet, heavy flakes that you could catch easily on your tongue. It was friendly snow, which I took as a good omen. I even got a cab easily, and I headed for Dan Doherty's place. I hadn't called him first, which might seem rude, but there's an advantage to showing up unannounced and catching people off guard. There's also the possibility of a wasted trip, but I took the chance.

Dan lived in a trendy new housing concept called the Nouveau Côté du Sud, which some of us remember as the South End row houses. One whole block of the tiny houses had been razed and replaced by a self-contained community of urban bungalows. A new ten-foot brick wall completely enclosed the block, providing privacy to the contented new residents while also insulating them from the terrors of the real city outside. At the main entrance a uniformed guard sat in a heated booth. I told him who I wanted to see, and he rang Dan's cottage to announce me. After some brief remarks on the phone, he turned to me and said, "You can go right on in."

I entered the complex and walked through a brick-paved maze of evergreen-lined paths. They were snow-free and dry, heated from within the pavement. These folks didn't have to suffer the inconveniences of snow, at least not while on their own sacred property. I got to Dan's unit and rang the door buzzer.

When the door opened, a tanned, blond stranger stood there in shorts and a T-shirt—not exactly New England winter togs.

"Hi," I said, oozing vacuous charm. "I'm here to see Dan Doherty."

The stranger looked me up and down, then said flatly, "Dan's not here."

"Do you expect him soon?"

"No."

"Do you know where he is?"

He looked at me suspiciously.

"It's okay," I said. "I'm his hairdresser."

"What's it about?"

"It's personal."

He started to close the door, so I blocked the attempt with my strong Slavic foot. "Look," I said, "whoever you are, you told the guard to let me in. Now why can't you tell me where Dan is?"

He squinted one eye at me. "I thought you were bringing the pizza I ordered."

If I could be mistaken for a pizza delivery man, my winter wardrobe needed serious evaluation. But more important, what ruse would this "friend" of Dan Doherty's believe? I thought quickly and said, "I owe Dan some money, and I wanted to pay him back, but if I can't find him . . ."

The mention of money caused him to reconsider. "You can give it to me. I'll make sure he gets it."

"No offense, but it's a lot of cash, and I don't know you."

"Fuck," he said. "Then go find him yourself. He's in Abigail."

"Abigail-by-the-Sea?"

"Is there another one?" he replied sarcastically. Then he pulled the door open, but I sensed he was preparing to bash it closed against my foot. I prefer my instep unbroken, thank you, so I removed my foot. The wedge gone, he slammed the door shut, but he'd given me my next lead. If Dan Doherty was in Abigail, perhaps he was with Prentiss Kingsley at his summer house. Abigail was too small a place for any other conclusion. In fact, it's so cloistered you almost need a permit just to drive through.

I left the protection of the walled complex and returned to the street where the snow was driving harder now, unpleasant and more in keeping with the hardship aspect of winter. I guessed I wouldn't be going out later, not with the snow and wind coming up like that. Maybe a hot herbal bath and an even hotter video would fill the cold, empty place where there was no love to keep me warm on a stormy winter night. Despite the weather, though, I decided to walk home, just to burn off some of the extra calories that lingered around my midriff. I got home around nine o'clock.

Outside my apartment door the building superintendent had left the regular weekly package from my mother in New Jersey. I could smell the buttery pastry through the wrapping paper. I knew she'd made them by hand during the week, then wrapped them like porcelain and sent them to me, insured. I always wondered why she insured homemade pastries. What could they be worth, since to me they were priceless?

Inside the apartment, Sugar Baby greeted me somewhat cautiously. She wanted to make sure the coast was clear of Tobias before she did an elaborate little welcoming dance for me—two figure eights, two circles, a fall-down, a long crescent stretch, and finally a roll onto her back followed by some very unladylike squirmy-wormy writhings across the carpet, belly and crotch exposed shamelessly. Sugar Baby's vocabulary comprises mostly throaty vowels expressed throughout the audible range for humans. For variety, she adds the occasional G or W or K. A visiting friend once remarked that Sugar Baby had said "Beowulf" to him one night, but I never heard it. Tonight, her little fandango meant she was happy to see me again. Perhaps she sensed that after my recent adventures I needed some extra kindness, instead of a haughty and disdainful sniff that meant, "Who needs you, human?"

While I peeled away the layers of insulating outerwear, Sugar Baby continued rolling around on the carpet, purring loudly. I picked her up while I checked my mail: Today it was bills and trash, and, in a plain brown envelope, an unsolicited copy of the operating instructions for the Spring Waters Septic Tank System. Someone's marketing demographics were slightly off-target.

I checked my answering machine. After a couple of the usual blank messages, I recognized a welcome voice saying, "Stan, it's Tony. Remember me? I'm in town tonight and wondered if you want to get together. Are you there? Pick up the phone. . . . Hello? I guess you're not in. I'll try again later. I hope I can see you tonight."

Did I remember him? Was he kidding? I once spilled so much of myself thinking and dreaming about Tony that I was declared a National Drought Area. I met him years ago, when he was still a church organist and choir director in Maine. Even back then I was convinced he was on a one-man crusade to redefine the staid image of his churchly duties. Tony is, as they say in the vernacular, hot, with the best genes from an Italian father and a Polish mother. He also has great musical talent— world-class, in fact—and it was only a matter of time before the world noticed it. These days he lived in London and conducted opera at major houses throughout Europe. Occasionally he returned "stateside" for guest appearances. And tonight he wanted to see little old me. All I had to do now was wait for his call and then keep my heart still as I said, "Come on in."

One more blank message, and then I heard Nicole's voice sounding serious and alarmed.

"Call me immediately!"

I didn't bother listening to any more, but called her right away.

"Nikki?"

"Tobias is gone. We can't find him anywhere."

"When?"

"About half an hour ago. He was in the living room. Chaz and I were in the kitchen preparing dinner. When we came out, he was gone."

"You've looked everywhere?"

"Of course! The security guards are still going through the entire building."

"What about the police?"

"Chaz has already called them."

"I'm on my way, Nikki."

"Stanley, wait. Chaz thinks you should stay home, in case Tobias tries to get to your place."

That gave me pause. "All right, I'll stay put. But call me if anything turns up."

"You do the same."

Then she hung up.

I poured myself a drink—my usual winter libation, bourbon and bitters—and had just taken a good slug when I heard someone banging loudly on my apartment door. Could it be Tony, so impatient? How had he got into the building? I peered through the peephole and saw two uniformed cops outside. I opened the door.

The bigger brute said, "Mr. Kraychik?"

"Yes," I answered.

"We'd like you to come down to the station and answer a few questions."

"Can't we talk here?"

"We got orders to bring you in."

"For what?" I asked, alarmed.

"Questioning. Just come along."

"Okay, but I have to make a phone call first." Nikki would have to know where I was.

"You can call from the station if necessary."

"But I—"

"Get ready."

What do you do when two armed cops are giving you orders? You obey them, that's what you do. Back on went the wet winter clothes. Sugar Baby made a sad little questioning sound—Gwow?—as I once again closed the door and left her alone.

There I was, back at Station E. You'd think I wouldn't mind seeing Branco again, him and his long Italian love-thighs. But I had other things on my mind, like finding Tobias, and then relaxing and getting warm for the night. For his part, Branco didn't seem pleased to see me. He was sitting at his desk, arms crossed, when I was thrust roughly into his office by the two cops who'd hauled me in. In a second, I took in the classic proportions and lines of Branco's whole body. Even without knowing exactly what lurked under the fabric of his clothing, I sensed that the musculature was worthy of a permanent record in marble.

"There are easier ways to beckon me, Lieutenant."

"Sit down, Kraychik." His eyes glittered angrily at me. "We got a problem here."

"So have I. I don't really like being hauled—"

"I don't care what you like." He got up from his desk and paced around his office with a heavy, aggressive tread unusual for him. He finally stopped when he was standing directly behind me. "We found Tobias Cole."

"Where? Is he okay?"

"He was wandering around Government Center . . . alone."

"But he's all right?"

"Aside from being scared, yes. But he doesn't let on about that. He says he's fine."

"My brave little tiger," I said, relieved that Tobias had been found and was safe, especially with the weather so harsh now. "What was he doing out there?" I asked.

Branco answered with a voice too severe for the circumstances. "He was lost, so he got a passing stranger on the street to call us. Then he told the patrol car that he wanted to see his mother. My men brought him here instead."

"Thanks for calling me, Lieutenant. I'll take him home now."

"That's where the problem comes in, Kraychik." His words bristled with anger.

"Lieutenant, what exactly is this problem you keep mentioning?"

Branco walked around to face me directly. He sat on the edge of his desk and folded his arms across his chest. The scent of pine around him softened his belligerent stance. His shirtsleeves were rolled up for work, with the cuffs of starched white cotton embracing his strong forearms—olive-toned skin veiled with shiny dark hair.

He said, "That kid said something that's bothering me."

"He says a lot of bothersome things, damn precocious four-year-old."

"But this one is a real problem for me." Branco's look was almost hateful, and I wondered what I'd done to earn it this time.

"Lieutenant, are you going to tell me, or just keep me curious? What did the little bugger say?"

"Don't push me, Kraychik." Branco stood up and leaned toward me, putting his face close to mine. "What he said was, and I quote, 'My Uncle Stan's got a nice dingdong.' " Branco said the final word with such force that a few flecks of spit flew out and landed on my jacket, which I took as a gift bestowed from an angry god. I felt my face and ears getting hot with blood.

"Lieutenant, I think I can explain—"

"I don't want your explanation. Not yet. I want to say what's on my mind first." He sat down and put his one hand to his forehead, momentarily at a loss for words. "You know, Kraychik, I try to be reasonable with people like you. I know you have the right to choose a different kind of life, even though I don't know why you do it. But I also know that the way you live can cause . . . problems . . . the kind that normal folks don't have."

The skin around my nipples tingled.

"Lieutenant, my preference for men is not a problem for me."

"It is for some of us."

"Then face it yourself."

"I do." Branco shot me a spiteful glance. "But when you start fooling around with kids, that's beyond a matter of choice. That's breaking morals. It's just plain wrong."

"I did not fool around with him."

"Then how does he know about your 'dingdong'?"

"Damn it, he stayed with me last night. He had to, since you so clumsily decided to jail his mother. When I woke up this morning, I forgot he was there, and I walked into my kitchen without a robe. Is that against your morals too?"

Branco twisted his mouth while he considered what I'd said.

"I live alone, Lieutenant. Sometimes I don't bother with clothes. Don't you ever do that?"

"Never mind about me."

"Tobias saw me and made the comment. Believe me, it made me squirm too."

"It's strange for a young kid to be so interested in sex."

"No, Lieutenant. Not strange at all. In fact, it's completely natural. At that age, sex is just part of their world, without all the religious and emotional traps that adults insist on applying to it."

"If a kid ever said that about me, I'd . . ."

"You'd what, Lieutenant? Hit him? Put the fear-of-god in him? Screw up his view of sex forever?"

No answer from the he-man.

"You ever have kids around?" I asked.

"I'm not married."

"The conditions are not mutually dependent."

"If you believe in God and family, they are."

"There's nephews and nieces. Being Italian, you ought to know."

Branco dismissed my logic with an annoyed flick of his hand. "I can't figure out why the boy would say that unless you tried to do something to him."

"Come on, Lieutenant. It's me, Stan Kraychik. I'm not a goddam child molester. I may be lonely, but I'm not desperate." He stared at me as I continued trying to appease him. "Look, Tobias's mother has a boyfriend who's naked around the boy a lot."

"You mean the dead man?"

"Well, yeah. . . . But Lieutenant, Tobias's interest in male organs is just a phase. Even Freud claimed that girls have penis envy." I shrugged and added, "Maybe boys have penis curiosity." I almost wanted to ask him, What's yours like? But I didn't.

Branco set his face into a pensive scowl. Apparently my version of pop psychology was reaching some remote gate in his logic circuits. Finally, he said, "I'd like to believe you wouldn't do anything perverse, Kraychik."

"I can't guarantee that, Lieutenant, but I can assure you that I don't want sex with children. Sheep, goats, and chickens, maybe, and the occasional plastic bag filled with Jell-O, but not children. Now, can I take Tobias home, please?"

Branco grunted, which meant he'd heard me at least. "Let's see how he feels about it," he said, then made a phone call and ordered someone to bring Tobias into his office.

When Tobias entered and saw me, he exclaimed, "Uncle Stan!" Then ran to me and hugged me. "I didn't do it. I didn't run away. I just wanted to see my ma."

I held his little body close to me and said, "It's all right now."

Of course, Branco had to intrude. "Son, do you want to stay with this man?"

"I have a name, Lieutenant."

"Quiet, you." Then he knelt down and spoke directly to Tobias. "Do you want to go home with Stan?"

Hearing my name from his lips caused my heart a little skip.

Tobias nodded energetically.

"And you'll feel safe with him?"

Tobias nodded again.

"You're not afraid?"

Tobias shook his head and said, "Uncle Stan will protect me."

I couldn't have paid him to say it better. "Can we go now, Lieutenant?"

"I guess so," he said tiredly. "Just one more thing, though. How did the boy end up staying with you in the first place?"

"His mother asked me to take care of him."

Branco nodded at my answer as though he'd happily found a loophole. "We'll have to get a signed affidavit from her if she wants to continue the arrangement. Otherwise the boy will have to be placed in court care."

"No," said Tobias. "I'll stay with Uncle Stan and Nick."

"He means Nicole," I added quickly. "Matter settled, Lieutenant?"

"Not officially. Good night, Kraychik."

I was leading Tobias out of Branco's office when I thought of something. "Lieutenant, do you know where I can find Dan Doherty?"

"Why?"

I lied, "His facial products arrived today, and I know he wants them, but I can't reach him at his place."

"So?"

"I'm sure he wouldn't leave town without telling you, and I thought maybe—"

"I can't help you," Branco interrupted.

"Is he staying in Abigail?"

"If you know, why are you asking me?"

"I don't have his address there."

"I'm sure you'll figure it out."

"Just thought I'd ask."

"You just keep yourself covered up at home."

"Are you policing my bedroom now?"

"Get outta here!"

Tobias and I got to ride back in a cruiser, and despite the slippery roads, we were back in front of my building by ten o'clock. As I was opening the outside door, Tobias asked if we could watch a video.

"Sure," I said agreeably, hoping to curb any other ideas he might have to run away again. Besides, a movie had been part of my alternate plan that night anyway, when I was going to be holed up warm and cozy and alone. No, not alone. With Tony. Tony! What if he'd called while I was out? Had I lost my chance? And now Tobias was with me. How was I going to stage this scene?

The video store was just around the corner from my apartment, and since the snow was letting up a bit, Tobias and I walked there together. Once inside I headed us directly for the animation/children's section, but Tobias had other ideas.

"Where are you going, Tobias?"

"I want *Body Talk*."

"Tobias, that's for adults."

"Trek watches it all the time. When him and Ma go in the other room, I play it slow-motion."

What, I wondered, was going on here? Just minutes ago I'd been arguing with Branco about not limiting a child's experience of sex, yet here I was myself resistant to rent a sexy movie that Tobias wanted to see. If I said no, would it adversely affect Tobias's attitude about sex? If I said yes, would I be too permissive? Perhaps Branco had a point after all. I solved it quickly by telling Tobias that if we were going to watch a video, it should be something that we both wanted to watch. And truthfully, *Body Talk* was not on my list of must-see's. We finally agreed on *Bambi II*, not a sequel to the classic but an "adult animation sensation" as it was billed on the box.

We got home, and sure enough, Tony had called again and left a sad little message.

"Well, Stan," he said with a mournful tone, "looks like you're out whoring. Too bad I missed you. Maybe we can try again next time I'm in town."

So much for romance that night.

While I fed Sugar Baby and put a frozen pizza in the oven, I called Nicole.

"Nikki, I've got him. He was at the police station trying to visit Laurett."

"That boy gets around for a four-year-old."

"He's got definite opinions about film too."

"Did you talk to Dan Doherty?"

"No."

"It's probably just as well, darling. Stay warm tonight and get some rest."

"Same to you, doll," I said with a note of envy.

Click.

Yes, I was slightly jealous of Nikki and her ardent, handsome, financially successful young lover. I was feeling old, unwanted, withering on the vine. Tobias tugged at my trousers.

"I'm hungry," he said.

Back to reality.

While the pizza baked, I threw together a quick salad. At least part of our dinner would be dietetically sound. Tobias would have nothing to do with the vegetables though. His idea of vegetables was potato chips. I told him if he wanted them, he'd have to go himself to the corner store for them. When he made for his coat, I stopped him.

"You've already painted the town tonight, buster. I'll go get the chips. You don't move. Clear?"

"Yup."

When I returned, the terrorist child from hell had already started watching *Bambi II*. It turned out to be pretty erotic and explicit, but I figured it was only consenting cartoon animals cavorting in the comfort of their own forest for the benefit of two insignificant human voyeurs. Once we'd eaten—and I'd had a double bourbon—we both fell asleep on the couch, while the animals played on.

I was awakened by the sudden sound of white noise whooshing at me when the tape had finished. I tucked Tobias in to sleep on the couch while I took the bed. This time, I laid my robe across the covers, hoping that would remind me to put it on tomorrow morning. Sugar Baby joined me shortly after I lay down. As she squashed herself up against my thigh and started purring her lullaby, I wondered, Is this what parenthood is about? It seemed like lots of concerned activity that signified nothing.

I turned my mind back to the mysterious poisoning of last night. I wondered about Dan Doherty and Prentiss Kingsley. Were they together in Abigail? Was Liz Carlini with them? And what about those other two from the Gladys Gardner factory, Mary Phinney and John Lough? What was their strange connection? Tomorrow was going to be a busy day. Perhaps I'd even find some answers.

9

CHARM-SCHOOL
DROPOUTS

Early the next morning I took Tobias to Nicole's place at Harbor Towers. Yes, I knew it was her day off and that she'd planned to spend it alone with Charles. I also knew that since I wasn't picking Tobias up as originally planned last night, I had no business there at all. But I had plans of my own that day, and they did not include dragging a young boy around with me. I had to convince Nicole to look after Tobias. I figured I'd tell her what Branco had said last night, embellishing it to make the threat of court action sound more immediate.

On the way to the waterfront I realized I was in a good mood, since I was noticing the beautiful side of a winter day in the city. Last night's storm had long passed, and all along Marlborough Street the bare, black-barked trees stood in high contrast to the blue sky and the new white snow. When we arrived at Nicole's neighborhood, even filthy Boston harbor, the featured vista of the waterfront, looked appealing in the clear early light.

It was just after eight o'clock, so I knew she and Charles would be home, probably still in bed. Invading forces know the advantage of surprising their quarry as it lies abed. The doorman recognized me with a friendly nod, and let Tobias and me enter. It wouldn't have mattered if he hadn't though. Nikki and I have keys to each other's pads.

When I knocked on the door, Nikki answered it from behind. "Who's there?"

"Me."

She opened the door and saw Tobias and me.

"You mean 'us,' " she said with a scowl.

Tobias smiled charmingly. "Hi, Uncle Nick."

"Sorry if we woke you, doll."

"What is it?" she asked coolly.

"Can we come in?"

She eyed Tobias and was already suspecting my motives, so my suffering-Stanley act had to be convincing. Fortunately, from what I could hear in the background, Charles was already in the shower, so my timing was perfect.

"Nikki, I'm in trouble. After last night's urban adventure with our little renegade . . ." I glanced at Tobias, implying that he'd caused my latest dilemma. "Lieutenant Branco put me on probation. He says if anything like that happens again, the C–O–U–R–T will take action."

"So what am I supposed to do?"

"Nikki, you know how busy it can get at the shop, especially if you're not there to direct traffic."

Nicole pondered a moment, then spoke. "Yes, Stanley, and it will be extra busy today, since Leslie just called me." With extra emphasis she added, "Which is the only reason I'm up at this hour on my day off."

"What did Leslie want?"

"She won't be at the shop today."

"Another fit of vapors?"

"Her car wouldn't start, with the snow and all."

I'd heard that excuse plenty before. Whenever it displeased Leslie to drive into town during winter, her car conveniently didn't start, even though it was one of those Swedish jobs that claims to thrive under glaciers or inside icebergs. Leslie had a kind of "let the city folk take care of it" attitude toward discomfort or inconvenience, and I often wondered why Nicole kept her on, since she was so unreliable. Perhaps it was her genius with scissors. When Leslie is cutting, there's a maelstrom of flying hair and combs and clips. You almost can't see the customer for all the Brownian motion around the chair. But the results are consistently stunning. After all, she cuts my hair.

Nicole said, "I'm afraid you're facing double-duty today, without Leslie or I to hold your hand."

"Leslie or *me*, doll." But Leslie's unexpected absence would complicate my plan to take time off to make my personal rounds that day, and I didn't want to tell Nicole that.

"That's all the more reason I need you to baby-sit, just for the morning. Please?"

"Stanley, don't start again."

"Nikki, you were going to take him last night. Just pretend you're doing me the favor now, a little later."

"Chaz and I have plans."

"Didn't you already do most of that?"

She frowned. "I'm trying to be hospitable."

"I'd say he's had his share of the open door today."

"That's uncalled for."

"Nikki, I need your help now. Charles can have it any other time."

"I'll ask him."

That stopped me. "You're going to ask Charles if you can do *me* a favor?"

Without answering, she left Tobias and me standing in the foyer and headed up the stairway to her bedroom on the upper level of the apartment. I wandered with Tobias into the vast living room with its lowered floor and stratospheric ceiling. The entire room was basically the northeast corner of the building, and it provided an unimpeded view of the city and the open harbor. I could hear Nicole's and Charles's muffled voices from the open door of a bathroom in a faraway corner of the penthouse.

Nicole returned and said lightly, "Chaz thinks it *is* a better idea for us to have Tobias this morning."

"A better idea than what, doll? Is he afraid that I'll turn Tobias gay? The police share the same horror. Then again, cops and lawyers come from the same mold."

"Stanley, do you want me to take the boy or not?"

"Yes, I do."

We agreed that she'd bring Tobias to the shop after lunch-time. She and Charles would entertain him until then. I left them quickly, without having coffee, since I was supposed to open the shop. Actually, I just didn't want to see Charles, all pink and clean and lean from his shower. I'm often uncomfortable when meeting my friends' bedmates, especially after they've been rutting like goats, and more especially if the bedmate is someone I don't care for, and most especially if he's cocksure and relent-less about it. Somehow it makes the couplings between friends and their sex-pets seem tawdry. I guess I was feeling my old protectiveness for Nicole, that she deserved better than the con-ceited young lawyer she'd taken up with for the past few months. My only consolation was that her winter affairs never lasted beyond the first thaw of springtime, and that Charles, like the others, would probably not be a permanent fixture in our lives.

On the way to Snips Salon I once again felt the great relief of having Tobias off my back. I opened the shop and called the answering service at once. What a happy surprise to hear all the out-of-towners canceling that day, all because of last night's storm. Even the winter weather seemed to be helping me, caus-ing things to fall into place so that I'd be able to get away later without too much trouble. True, I'd make less money today, but I could make that up another time.

Midmorning, when local business started picking up slightly, a male client came in to see Leslie, the absent and snowbound stylist. I explained that she wasn't in today, but since I recognized him as a former customer who used to keep regular appointments, I offered to take care of him myself. He hesitated, then asked for the next best stylist after Leslie. I told him that I was the salon's lead stylist, *before* Leslie. When I suggested that he might want to reschedule with her after all, he opted to have me do his hair. It was a good decision, since it needed color work badly.

The job was simple for a master: Apply perfectly mixed color to his longish brown and grey roots. The soft, amber blond would match the rest of the older color work, which had held up pretty well considering all the time he'd let pass since his last visit. Leslie's expert cut had held up well too, except for two "holes" on either side of the man's head. Leslie couldn't have done anything so clumsy, and I wondered how the man's hair had got that way. As I sectioned the hair to apply color, I noticed a pair of small, pink scars within the shorter hair, one diagonally forward above each ear, and another behind each ear, just back of the occipital bone. Each scar was about an inch long. Recognizing their significance, I casually asked if he'd been on vacation, since he looked so rested and, I couldn't help adding, somewhat younger. He described in surgical detail the happy time he'd spent at a tropical oceanside resort, but he didn't admit to the beautifully executed face-lift he'd recently had.

By late morning, the place was humming with enough worker bees to handle the flow of local customers into the shop. I was booked too, but they were coincidentally all clients from my B-list, the whiners and the lousy tippers. Seizing the moment, I relegated my bookings to Ramon, who was always eager to build his own clientele from the shampoo sink. The only drawback to letting Ramon work on my clients was that there'd be so much to *undo* after his work. We obviously didn't respond to the same muse.

I headed out on the first leg of my fact-finding mission that day, a visit to Liz Carlini. Again, I didn't call first, hoping to catch her off guard. Lies are more difficult to hide when a person is on the defensive. Since Liz was a client, I found her unpublished address in the private directory I keep on all my customers. She and Prentiss lived in Chestnut Hill, so I took the Riverside train, which even in winter is one of the more dependable lines of Boston's MTA, an ancient and misnamed rapid transit system that supposedly links Metropolitan Boston to its many suburbs. From the Chestnut Hill station, it was a short cab ride to their house. They lived in a small mansion—an oxymoron, I suppose—overwrought with pilasters and porticos, but in Chestnut Hill, you showed your wealth, not your taste. Nature helped today though, with ice-glazed tree limbs and soft new snow on the ground. The driveway and sidewalk had been meticulously cleared and were bone dry. Obviously, both pavements were heated. No nasty, noisy snowblowers for these folks. Just flick a switch.

I hoped someone would be home, since it was almost eleven o'clock. I stepped onto the portico and rang the bell, which caused a large dog to start barking inside. Reflexively my body tightened. Dogs and me ain't the best of friends. They tend to bite me, even after the owner claims, "She *never* bites." Then, seconds after Fido or Fidina has had a taste of my tender Slavic flesh, I hear the owner say, horrified, "She's never done *that* before." Luckily, both my skin and my nerve don't scar easily, but I still don't take naturally to dogs.

Liz answered the door herself. She was fully dressed for the day, all perky and ready to face life squarely, which probably isn't too hard when you're wealthy. The big dog standing near her wagged its tail vigorously while it sniffed and licked and nipped lightly at my hands. I instinctively pulled away. My hands are, after all, my livelihood. Liz seemed pleased to see me there.

"Vannos, what a surprise. Is everything all right?"

"Sure, Liz. Why not?"

"Well, after that trouble the other night . . ." She paused. "And . . . well, I'm just surprised to see you here in person. You've never been out here before, have you?"

"That's true, Liz, and I apologize for not calling first, but I was riding the train this morning—you know, it's so rare we get a day like this in February—and I just thought I'd come by and see how *you* were doing, especially after that trouble the other night." I purposely used her same words, a ploy to build trust. "I hope I'm not intruding."

"Not at all. Come on in. I was just about to make myself another espresso. Would you like one?"

"Sure." I love espresso.

She led the way to the kitchen, and the big dog gamboled back and forth between us. Liz noticed me keeping my distance from the beast. "I'll put him outside if he's worrying you."

"Thanks," I said. "Dogs like my blood."

"Oh, he'd *never* bite," she said as she let him out. But when puppy-dog found himself outside without me, his anticipated midmorning snack, he barked and squealed to be let back in, pawing and scratching against the sliding-glass door.

"Too bad, pooch," I said, watching him from the safe side of the door. "No warm blood today."

Liz's kitchen had been remodeled recently with expensive European appliances and cabinets, and I was happy to sense a feeling of *use* instead of just show. While Liz prepared the coffee, I gazed out over the spectacular backyard, though estate lawns might be a more correct description.

As I turned back into the kitchen, I happened to notice, squeezed up between the cookbook shelf and the bottom of the overhead cabinets, the distinctively decorated sides of a lavender-colored box. The purple irises meant it was a box of Le Jardin chocolate. After the murderous mishap the other night, I could undersand why the box was tucked away, out-of-sight-out-of-mind.

"Is Prentiss home?" I asked.

Liz clumsily dropped the coffee basket on the counter, spilling the fine dark grounds everywhere on the hand-glazed ceramic tiles.

"He's out now," she said shortly and grimaced as she swept up the spilled coffee. "He had an important errand to run. Did you want to talk to him?"

"Well, yes . . . and to you, too. As I said, I just dropped by to say hello and find out how you were doing. The other night was pretty hard on all of us there. Sometimes it's helpful to share feelings with others after suffering a calamity together." I sounded like a recovery group facilitator.

She nodded. "It's true, Vannos. I've been thinking about it a lot." Then she said with a secretive look, "And I think I know who did it."

"You do?"

"I have a theory."

It figured she would. With every other success in her life,

Liz Carlini probably imagined herself a brilliant detective too. She refilled the coffee basket and installed it into the espresso machine while she explained.

"There's a woman who is the operations manager at the Gladys Gardner factory. Her name is Phinney, Mary Phinney."

"I met her yesterday."

"Oh?"

"I took my nephew on a tour of the factory."

"Was it fun?"

"Actually, we had a little trouble, and it was with Mary Phinney."

"They really should get someone else to give the tours."

"I'd have to agree with you there. But why do you think she's involved with the killing?"

Liz ran the espresso machine. I watched the syrupy coffee flow into two small cups she'd placed under the dual spigot. I also noticed that she'd neglected to preheat the cups. After the machine stopped humming, she spoke again.

"When Danny and I asked Laurett to manage the new Le Jardin shop, Mary Phinney objected noisily. In the entire history of Gladys Gardner chocolates, there's never been a black person in the stores serving the customers. So for us at Le Jardin, choosing Laurett was a breakthrough."

Such is the political correctness of business savvy.

"But how does that relate to the killing?"

"I think Mary Phinney planted that poisoned chocolate to incriminate Laurett, since she was the one who was setting up the truffles that night."

"But then the killing would be random," I said.

"I don't think Mary intended to kill anyone—she just wanted to make them sick. But as long as Laurett Cole was suspected and accused and didn't get that job, Mary Phinney would be satisfied."

"Liz, did you tell this to the police?"

She shook her head. "It's just an idea. I have no proof."

"Tell them anyway. Let them decide what to do." I figured, if nothing else, maybe her far-fetched story would incite Branco to interrogate Mary Phinney. "Make sure you talk to Lieutenant Branco though. He's in charge."

"Should I mention your name?"

"Better not."

She set out to steam some milk, but at one point she miscalculated the steam pressure and splashed scalding milk all over the counter top. "Damn!" she said, and then banged the small pitcher against the counter, spilling even more hot milk.

Being a salon neatnik, I automatically went to the sink for a sponge to wipe up the spill. As I mopped up the milk, I asked, "Did you get burned?"

"You don't have to be so helpful. We're not at your salon now."

Her sudden bluntness stopped me. When she saw the effect her words had, she quickly changed her tone.

"I'm sorry, Vannos."

"It's only spilled milk."

She breathed deeply for a few seconds and regained her composure. "There's a lot on my mind. I didn't mean to turn on you like that."

"Sometimes I deserve it."

"No, I was wrong." Then she looked at me with needy eyes. "Actually, would you mind talking about something personal?"

"If I can help, Liz, sure. Our relationship doesn't begin and end at the sink." Devious Stanley at work.

After I'd mopped up the milk, Liz steamed what was left in the small pitcher. It was still a lousy job. The bubbles were coarse and the foam collapsed quickly. To finish it off, she'd sprinkled not chocolate but *cinnamon* on top—ugh!—and pushed one of the cups toward me. "I'm afraid it isn't very good today," she said apologetically.

"When the emotions are askew, so is everything else." But troubled mind or not, I could tell she hadn't inherited the knack for making good Italian coffee. "Now tell me," I said, folding my hands in front of me and facing Liz Carlini with kindly, concerned eyes. "What's the problem?"

She picked idly at her manicured nails for a moment. Then,

realizing it was "unprofessional" behavior, she curled her thumb and fingers into her palm, which I recognized as a classic defensive posture. "Prentiss and I are having a disagreement," she said unsurely, using a euphemism even for the simple, direct word *fight*.

"What happened?" I asked, wondering how the overly refined Prentiss Kingsley could be in conflict with anyone.

"I think it's a result of what happened the other night."

I thought, Nothing like a little death to show people's true colors.

Liz went on, "I'm sure that we're both upset by that horrible accident at the party. But he insists it's something else."

"What do you think it is?"

She sipped some of her coffee, then made a sour face, as though admitting how bad it was. She took a deep breath, looked me straight in the eyes, and said, "I *know* what it is. I just don't want to believe it. Prentiss wants me to sell my share of Le Jardin to the Gladys Gardner Corporation."

"But I thought Le Jardin was already part of the business."

"Who told you that?"

"Rafik mentioned it at the factory yesterday."

Liz let out a professionally discreet giggle. "Rafik misled you. How would he know anyway? He just drives the truck. No, Vannos, there's no fiscal connection whatsoever. Prentiss did put up part of the money, but I raised the rest myself. Le Jardin is privately owned by Prentiss and me and Danny together."

"Dan Doherty is an owner?"

Liz nodded. "He didn't contribute any money, but Prentiss and I agreed that it would be fair to give him a share of the business."

"That's very generous."

"We thought so too, even though Danny's artistic contributions to Le Jardin are almost priceless."

"How is the business split?"

Liz eyed me curiously. "That's not what's causing the problem."

"Then what is?"

"Danny and I worked hard together to make Le Jardin happen. Danny once joked that it was like having a baby together." She blushed. "Sometimes it almost seemed true. But then, as soon as the business was about to open officially, Prentiss wanted me to give it up and sell it, as though the whole thing was an academic exercise. I'm supposed to relinquish it all now and become the devoted wife again."

"And you don't want that."

"Of course not. I kept my own name for this marriage, and I'm certainly going to keep my own business alive too. Le Jardin has potential for international growth. We've already had inquiries from two European distributors to sell our products over there."

"That's big-time stuff."

"It's certainly not the kind of sophistication Gladys Gardner can handle."

"Why can't you just continue on with your plan the way the company stands now, keeping it separate?"

Liz shook her head no. "Prentiss claims that Danny is willing to sell his share of the business to Gladys Gardner, which will leave me with a minority holding in Le Jardin. Basically, I'll be powerless to direct the course of the company."

"I don't see why Le Jardin has to be part of Gladys Gardner. What's the benefit?"

"That's obvious, isn't it? If my husband's company owns my company, he regains his control over me, his chattel."

"Liz, you don't mean that. The other night I overheard Prentiss saying how much he respected you and Danny for what you've done."

"Done, yes, but not doing. He wants everything back the way it was."

"But won't Dan resist selling out—you know, for artistic integrity and all?"

Liz began a tiny cackle, then caught herself. "Danny did all that design work for Le Jardin solely for the exposure. Beyond that, the business doesn't interest him. He'll sell out in a minute. He's already planning his next project and he needs cash."

"So much for your baby."

Liz flashed a horrified look at me. "What do you mean?"

"You said the business was like you and Dan having a baby together."

"Yes, that feeling is gone now too. Our friendship has changed suddenly."

"Maybe when the trouble from the party all blows over—"

"No, Vannos. Prentiss wanted me to sell Le Jardin even before the party. As I said, once it became a reality, he wanted me to have nothing more to do with it."

"You have a contract, don't you? Lawyers?"

"Of course. But I never thought I'd be facing the classic problem of a wife having to choose between her own life or her husband's demands. I should never have let Prentiss get involved in this project."

"Why did you?"

"Because he had the means and experience. It's not public knowledge, but Le Jardin's chocolates are actually made in the Gladys Gardner factory."

I nodded. "Rafik told me that too."

Liz gave me another suspicious glance. "I know he's handsome, Vannos, but don't believe everything he says. We do have our own highly trained staff there, and they work exclusively on our products. It was just easier to start out using the existing facilities. Why reinvent the wheel, especially with the cost of tempering and molding equipment these days?"

"But aren't the intentions behind the two companies different?"

Liz's smile told me I'd asked a naive question.

"Both businesses exist to make a profit. They're aimed at different markets, obviously, but the end result is the same— money."

So simply stated, it was disturbing. Even the heavenly chocolates of Le Jardin weren't so appealing now, thanks again to my unfortunate streak of moral purity, the one that often limits and ruins a lot of life's experiences simply because of the monetary motives behind most enterprises.

"Where is your husband now?" I asked.

"I don't know," she answered quickly—too quickly, I thought.

"Maybe you can help me with something else, then, Liz. I've been trying to find Dan Doherty, but he's not in town. Do you know where he went?" I already knew, but would she tell me?

She shrugged. "If he's not at home, I don't think I can help. . . ."

I absentmindedly twirled my coffee cup on the tile counter-top. "Has Danny ever been to your place in Abigail?"

"What?"

"I'm wondering just how close he is to you and your husband."

She answered flatly. "It's a friendly business arrangement."

"You said it was like having a baby."

"Danny said that, not me."

"Liz, I have it from two sources that Dan Doherty is in Abigail as we speak. Is he staying at your summer house there?"

"Did Rafik tell you that too?" she asked with a playful toss of her head.

Liz Carlini seemed to be on the denial track, more con-cerned about the future of her carriage-trade business than about her husband or the killing the other night. The time had come to tell her the facts of life and death.

"Liz, from what I've learned recently, it's probable that the poisoned chocolate from Sunday night was intended for your husband."

Liz blanched. "What do you mean?"

"Laurett Cole told me that she switched the truffles at the last minute, and the one that killed Trek Delorean was originally supposed to go to Prentiss."

"I don't believe that." Liz shook her head angrily. "Why are you telling me this?"

"Because I think your husband is in danger. And in spite of this recent problem between the two of you, he needs your help."

Liz picked at her nails again, but this time she didn't stop. "Who would want to kill Prentiss? *Who?* Tell me."

"That's what I'm trying to find out."

"Is that what the police think too?"

"No, the police want to convict Laurett Cole and close the case. Meanwhile, someone is out there who wants to hurt your husband."

"This is absurd. You've really upset me, Vannos."

"I'm sorry—"

"Maybe you'd better go now."

"But tell your husband—"

"Just leave me, please!"

The tension in her voice was activating Jaws-n-Paws, the hungry mastiff who was barking loudly outside and scratching on the back door to be let back in. As Liz went to let him in, I headed quickly for the front door before he had the chance to taste my strong but tender thighs.

Safely outside, I walked—slid, mostly—back down the icy hill until I got to the busy intersection of Route Nine, where I got the MTA back to town. But instead of getting off there, I stayed on and continued to North Station, where I could catch an afternoon train to Abigail-by-the-Sea.

band on his left hand and the scent of cheap tobacco smoke in his wake.

I got off the train and found a local town cab at the station. "I'm going to the Kingsley house," I told the driver.

He eyed me with mistrust, then started the cab. We went through what looked like the main part of town—a pizza shop, a gas station, a hardware store, a small surf-n-turf restaurant, and a bait and tackle supplier—all the et cetera of a small coastal community, with one notable exception: I saw not one bar.

"Where do you get a drink around here?" I asked the cabbie.

"A little early for that kind of thing."

"Just asking."

"Stranger here, eh?"

"Visiting a friend."

"You know the Kingsleys?"

"I do."

"You can get a drink there."

"I don't need a drink. I just don't see any bars or liquor stores around."

"Aren't any. You want liquor, you go to Gloucester. Abigail's dry, and we like it that way."

I wouldn't last long in a town like that. I could imagine all the residents sitting around in privacy and peace, waiting for their ten-million-dollar dividend checks. Squeaky clean, sweetie-pie, neat and orderly it all was. I half-expected to see the Mary Baker Eddy Motel. Meanwhile, behind closed doors and drawn shades, these people were probably drinking, fighting, and abusing each other mercilessly. But as long as the houses were tidy, and the cars sat spotless in their heated garages, everything was okay. Even the all-white residents looked fresh and lively walking along the sidewalks in their brightly colored winter togs. These were the same folks who remark, "I'd never live in the city." They see urban life as low and dirty, steeped in sin and corruption, except when *they* come into town to suck out some money or jostle their wits. It kind of made me want to leave my working-class mark on the place, piss on a hydrant or something.

10

NOT THE HOLIDAY INN

At North Station I phoned the shop to tell Ramon I might be late getting back there. I didn't tell him where I was, nor did I say anything about Nicole's bringing Tobias to the shop later. For all I knew, she was there already, so the less Ramon knew, the better. And if Nicole was annoyed at my lateness, there wasn't much she'd be able to do, since I'd be twenty miles away, in lovely Abigail.

I just made it onto the early afternoon train, which was one of the dilapidated old coaches lingering from the golden days of the Boston and Maine Railroad. The nostalgia and romance of the rails were nowhere to be found in that old heap of metal, which smelled of diesel fumes and dried urine. After a tilty and bumpy start through the industrial wastelands of Boston's backyards, the shabby train snaked its way towards the North Shore. I lost all sense of time as I watched the varying montage pass by windows that were so filthy and scratched they were barely transparent. Still I could discern small, shacklike houses, leafless woods, frozen streams jammed with debris, rusted auto carcasses, and finally, in polar opposition to all that preceded it, a revitalizing glimpse of the ocean. Ten minutes later, a handsome young conductor, mustachioed and uniformed to almost military severity—a complete anomaly to the grimy, malodorous surroundings of the coach—marched down the aisle announcing, "Aaaab-gail! Ab-GAYLE!" Being susceptible to men in uniforms, I almost proposed to him on the spot, despite the wedding

The cab drove up a narrow winding road, and I watched the town recede below us. It didn't seem like such a bad place from high up and far away. The village and small harbor finally disappeared as we headed out onto the ocean bluff, and my attitude changed immediately as the sea came into view. Even I have trouble grouching when I'm at the shore. The tide was up and rowdy, offering an expanse of turbulent blue-green water and white foam that was a welcome relief from the claustrophobic air of the tiny village. We passed two large houses on the bluff, set far enough apart to be almost invisible to each other. The cab pulled into the tree-lined driveway of the third one. It was a huge old three-story house, covered with grey wooden shingles and topped with a clay roof, cluttered with gables and dormers and chimneys. From some of the ground-floor windows, portions of the ocean showed clear through from the back of the house.

Seeing the driveway empty, the cabbie said, "Looks like nobody's home."

"I'm early. They *are* expecting me."

I paid him and requested a business card and phone number.

"What for?" he asked.

"I'll need a ride back to the train station later, unless you'd rather share the business with your competition."

"Isn't any. I'm it. Two cars, me and my wife."

"Then I might as well meet your whole family while I'm here." I gave him a generous tip, figuring his superficial morality would compel him to show up promptly later on, since I'd just about prepaid my return trip.

I got out of the cab and walked toward the front door of the large house. The driver didn't pull away as soon as he should have. I sensed he was watching me, hoping for some extra juicy bit of scandal to spread around town. I could almost hear him recounting to his wife, "Had a stranger from the city. Wanted a drink in the afternoon. Took him to the Kingsley place. I think he was one of those male prostitutes or something." Hell, if the facts aren't interesting enough, change them.

I felt the cabbie's eyes still on me, so I turned and waved to him. Then I veered away from the front door and followed a flagstone path, which I hoped would lead me to another entrance behind the house. I finally heard the cab drive off and felt some relief. I did find a side door, so I knocked loudly on it. But as the cabbie had predicted, no one was home. Now what? I continued walking all the way round to the back of the house. A wide expanse of flat ground led to the bluff fifty yards away. The patchy ground snow was typical of the shore, since the ocean air tends to change snow into rain. But the snow that was there was clean and white and undisturbed. A grey, sun-bleached picket fence ran in a straight line the full length of the property, about ten feet from the edge of the bluff—a cautionary reminder to casual strollers that the pounding surf and craggy rocks lay almost one hundred feet below.

Still presuming that Prentiss Kingsley and Dan Doherty were staying out here together, I figured I'd hang around until they showed up. I had no place to go and nothing to do until then—Snips Salon was far away—so I sat and enjoyed the sound of the surf and the rush of the wind. The bright sun gave a sense of warmth, but the cold ocean breeze soon dispelled the illusion.

I sat for a long time with my eyes closed, letting the white noise of the surf lull me into a state of alpha consciousness. Awake in a dream, I sensed someone approaching me, and I happily assumed it was my lively subconscious, once again beckoning my incubus. However, rather than ravish me as usual, my loving other-self decided to speak to me this time.

"Did you like the chocolate?" he asked, with a French accent.

I opened my eyes and turned my head. The sun blinded me for a moment, but I could still make out Rafik, in all his tall, handsome glory. He was wearing a grey warm-up suit, without an overcoat or jacket. The wind caused the soft flannel to hug his body and reveal a slender, well-formed physique, much like a dancer's.

"Hi," I said, perhaps too enthusiastically. "I figured you had sent it."

"You did not like?" His eyelids drooped sadly.

"I took it to the police to have it checked for poison."

"Ah, *non*, I will not poison you." Then, with an inviting smile, he asked, "You are coming to see me?"

"I came to see Prentiss Kingsley. I'm curious why you're here though."

"I am here with Dunny."

"And Mr. Kingsley? Is he here too?"

With a wink Rafik shook his head no. What a charmer! It could be easy to say yes to any demand of his.

I began, "I just wanted to, uh . . ." Control your yapper, Stanislav. Don't tell this gorgeous man you came here to warn Prentiss Kingsley that someone is trying to kill him. "I wanted to plan a little surprise for Liz and Danny, so I thought Prentiss could help me with it. But don't tell Dan, okay?"

"We have secret then?"

"Yeah, that's right. A secret."

"So maybe we can have one more secret?" he asked with a sly look.

"What do you mean?"

"You like to go to bed?" He pushed his right hand up under his sweatshirt, lifting it slightly so that I could watch him caress his taut belly and finger the short, black hair there. Damn! Why was this guy so interested in me, first at the party, now out here by the ocean?

"What about Danny?" I asked.

"Dunny? He's not home."

"But aren't you two . . . ?"

Rafik shook his head no. "We are not lovers anymore."

"I thought you said you were here with him?"

"I am with him, but not together."

"Then why are you here?"

Rafik grinned self-contentedly. "Mr. Kingsley invite me."

"But you just said he's not here," I said, trying to get his story straight.

"Yes, he is not. I work at his company, driving the truck, you know?"

"Yes, I know, but does that qualify you to stay at his summer place, in the middle of winter?"

"Oh, sure." His hand pushed the jacket up further to show a well-formed pectoral. "So you want to go inside?"

"I would like to get warm."

"I have good idea," he said, and suddenly peeled off his sweatshirt. His muscular chest had a neatly trimmed, fan-shaped mat of coarse hair, clipped short and bristly. The cold air set it all on end, and the rest of his skin also went bumpy in the breeze. His nipples greeted the frigid air with a perky salute through the dark hair. "Come," he said, and undid his sweatpants as well. He jogged away from me, then stopped momentarily to pull off the sweatpants, leaving only his robin's-egg-blue jockstrap. I was right. He did look like a dancer, and he moved like one too, as though this were all a familiar sequence of steps rehearsed and performed many times before. But I'll confess, his furry limbs sure were appealing against the patchy snow. He turned toward me and beckoned. "We go to bed now." He ran toward the solarium attached to the back of the big house.

Being a lonely pile of flesh and bones, I'd be a fool to pass up a chance like that. I got up from the bench and headed toward the house, picking up Rafik's discarded clothing along the way—already the wife. As I got near the house, Dan Doherty emerged from the pathway that led around from the front of the house.

"What the hell are you doing here?" he demanded. Then he saw Rafik's near-naked body entering the solarium, while I stood there holding his clothes. Dan frowned and said, "Figures you'd get your way with him, Vannos."

"Uuuuhhhh . . ."

"Don't worry," he said, irritated but resigned. "I'm used to it. He's good for nothing." Dan watched Rafik waving energetically from inside the solarium. "I take that back. Rafik is certainly good for one thing."

"Danny, I didn't come here to have sex with him. I came to talk to Prentiss and you. I even tried to find you at your place last night. I've got some unpleasant news, I'm afraid."

"Vannos, you can cut the crap. You don't need an excuse to

have sex with Rafik. Really, it's 'anything goes' out here in the 'burbs.''

"I'm not making excuses, Danny. And you can call me Stan now. Vannos is okay in the shop, but this has nothing to do with the shop.''

His face relaxed slightly. "You mean it, don't you?" he said with less anger in his voice. "You're serious.''

"Yes, this is serious.''

"We'd better go inside then.''

We walked by the solarium. Rafik stood within, exposed and appealing in his glass cage. Cripes, I'd just about got my sludgy juices moving again, and yet again I had to interrupt the flow. I don't know why my parents didn't just name me Frustration.

Inside the house Dan removed his down-filled parka and hung it in a fastidiously organized closet. "Take your coat off, get comfortable," he said. I dropped my jacket on a chair, but Danny picked it up and hung it—arranged it—alongside his in the closet—ever the designer. Then he led me into a large, bright room with numerous bay windows, complete with window seats and chintz-covered cushions, all facing out onto the bluff and the ocean beyond. The fireplace was blazing, even though it was midafternoon. Through one of the front windows I saw Danny's car, easily identified by the vanity plates: DDDESIGN.

Danny flopped himself onto one of the sofas. I sat in a high-armed chair that enveloped me luxuriously as the down-filled cushions wheezed out their air. "Is Prentiss here?" I asked.

"No," he said, reclining and stretching himself out provocatively. I hoped it wasn't for my benefit.

"Danny, it's important that you both hear this. Will you promise to tell him?''

"Depends." His eyes seemed to be flirting, and I soon recognized a behavior pattern that I'd often seen with other couples: Love my spouse, love me.

I said, "Depends isn't good enough, Danny. I found out something about the poisoned chocolate that killed that man the other night.''

"The one Laurett Cole gave to her boyfriend?''

"That's the point. It was a mistake. The truffle that killed that guy was intended for Prentiss Kingsley."

Danny pulled himself upright and faced me with sudden alarm.

"How do you know that?" he asked.

"Laurett made a last-minute switch because the original truffle had become damaged."

"But how do you know it was meant for Prentiss?"

"Because it was almond-flavored. Laurett said that one was for him. And the almond flavoring easily covered the taste of the cyanide."

Dan began a nervous laugh that grew and grew until it verged on hysteria. He got up and poured himself a shot of whiskey from a crystal decanter. He downed it in one grand gesture, as though acting in a bad soap opera. Then he turned to me and said flatly, "The almond truffle was not for Prentiss. It was for me. Prentiss is allergic to almonds."

"Are you sure?"

Danny smirked. "I ought to know. He'd never ask for an almond truffle. The flavors obviously got mixed up."

I quickly replayed the party scene in my head. "So that's why he spit his chocolate out that night. He was afraid of an allergic reaction."

"That's right." Danny's voice started wavering. "And since I was supposed to get the almond truffle, that means someone wanted to kill me the other night."

"But who? Why?"

Without answering, Danny poured himself another drink, then realized he hadn't offered me one yet. He held the decanter toward me and asked, "Scotch?"

I replied, "Bourbon, neat."

He poured an inch of fine bourbon into a crystal tumbler and handed it to me. Then he sat in the other armchair and spoke. "Prentiss has a half brother, John Lough. He hates me."

"Why?"

"He thinks I'm corrupting Prentiss, that I've turned him gay."

"Is it true?"

Dan squirmed in his chair. "Prentiss and I have a deep friendship. He confides in me."

"Is that all?"

With an angry look Dan said, "There is no sex between us."

"Whose decision?"

"None of your goddam business."

"Isn't it a little extreme to think John Lough wants to kill you because you're close to Prentiss?"

"And because I'm gay, and therefore I'm bad."

"But why pick now to do it?"

"The opportunity was right, I guess."

"It sounds too simple, Danny. There must be something else."

He got up to refill his glass again. All along he'd been pouring himself more than an inch, yet the liquor didn't seem to be affecting him. "Well, since you're so smart, Vannos—excuse me, I mean Stan—what do you think?"

I looked into his eyes. "I think money."

Danny went back to the sofa, lay down, and put his stocking feet up on the cushions. "Money, money, money. Here's to money!" he said, and raised his glass in a toast. "You're right, of course. You're always right, aren't you?"

"Far from it."

Danny closed his eyes and spoke as though reciting from a memorized script. "Prentiss inherited his money from his mother, Helen Kingsley."

"What about his brother John?"

Danny shook his head. "Half brother. He was born after Prentiss, when their father remarried, so he got nothing. Besides, the Kingsley money always went to the women, up until the last one, Helen Kingsley. Since Prentiss was her only child—she died giving birth to him—he inherited everything, the money, the company, the property, everything that usually went to the oldest daughter."

"So that's why Prentiss retains the Kingsley name—as a kind of memorial to his mother."

Dan shook his head. "Not a memorial. Guilt. It's all guilt. Imagine killing your mother just by being born, then getting all that money."

"At least he gets to live a life of ease."

"Prentiss has plenty of problems, believe me."

I shrugged. The neuroses of the wealthy rarely aroused my sympathy.

Finally, Dan's speech was showing the slightest slur. "He tries to be generous with John. He even made up that position for him at the factory, some monkey-job in corporate administration. The salary would make you puke."

"So John should be content, not murderous."

"But he wants more. He wants bigger. He wants the whole thing. And now Liz is in the picture, and John's afraid she's gonna get some of it."

"So how do you fit into all this?"

Danny looked at me with watery, unfocused eyes. "Hey, what is this, a goddam game show with all the questions?"

"Someone tried to kill you or Prentiss the other night. I'm just trying to establish motive."

"Fine, then. Make a motive." Dan gulped the rest of his whiskey, then staggered up to pour himself another. He faltered over the decanter. "If I'm dead, John gets more. There's the motive. And he'll sleep better if he removes another of us filthy vermin from the face of the earth."

I couldn't recall John Lough having the capacity for that much passion. Meanwhile, Rafik had quietly entered the room. He looked sullen and dejected, though he'd put on a colorful new set of warm-ups.

"Quit wearing my clozhe," Dan shouted with an obvious slur.

Rafik looked at me sadly, as though I'd reneged my troth of undying love, as if to say, "See how I live without you?"

"Dan," I said, "where is Prentiss now?"

He shrugged. "Uddn' know." Dan turned suddenly to Rafik. "Hey! Why don't you go play in the snow, Rafi-baby. Maybe roll off the edge and leave me in peace."

"I do nothing to hurt you, Dunny."

"Your life gives me pain."

"I go now." He turned to me and spoke almost imploringly. "You will come to the solarium later?"

I scratched my ear. "I think you might arrange your assignations more discreetly, Rafik."

"Ah, you are *romantique*, eh? *L'assignation, alors!*"

"I'll come and say good-bye before I leave."

Rafik left us alone, then I asked Dan, "Did you tell the police any of this the other night?"

Rafik's interruption seemed to snap Dan back to sobriety, at least for a few minutes. "Can you imagine what they'd do with this piece of faggot sensationalism?"

"But you think John Lough wants to kill you."

"If I told the police that, they'll do absolutely nothing. They'll write me off as a hysterical queen."

I looked at Dan. Maybe he was right. He did tend to embody the archetypal urban American gay designer clone.

"Dan, will you promise to tell Prentiss what we talked about today? It's important that he knows that the killing the other night was not accidental, and that the intended victim may have been he or you. You said he confided in you. You owe it to him to tell him."

"Don't tell me what to do."

I wasn't going to get much further with him, and my welcome was obviously spent, at least in the main part of the house. I asked, "Can I use your phone to call a cab?"

"You can call from the solarium, when you and Rafik are done."

I got up and extended a hand to Danny.

"What's that for?" he asked.

"To show my good intentions."

"Save it for some other sap."

I left him and set off to meander through the hallways of the large house, first picking up my jacket along the way, then aiming myself in the general direction of the solarium. I found it, guided by the bright light coming from the open doorway that led out to it. Though it was early February, the glass-enclosed structure was very warm—almost too warm. Certainly it was warm enough to lie about naked on the white wickerwork furniture and feel the welcome heat of the sun penetrate your frozen winter flesh and thaw your frozen winter bones. Rafik was lying on one of the padded lounge chairs. He'd placed a towel discreetly across his crotch, but underneath it lurked a lively mound of flesh.

His eyes were closed, but he knew it was I who'd entered the heated structure. "Lie down with me," he said.

I sat on the edge of the plump cushion.

"Rafik?"

"Eh?" He opened his eyes just a slit.

"Who would want to kill Danny?"

His fiery eyes shot open. *"I* want to kill him."

"You?"

"He make us so miserable. Why he cannot say *fini* and leave me alone? We do not love each other."

"Why did you come here then?"

"I was here. He came to see me."

I knew he was lying, since the visible facts were exactly the reverse. It was Danny's clothes and Danny's car that were ensconced at the place—not to mention his confidential relationship to Prentiss Kingsley, whatever that meant. But damn, he was handsome! And the hot sun made his skin smell of mild, sweet spice. And I was hungry. The scent and the heat and the look of him made me blurt without thinking, "How did you get to look like this?"

"Is my family," he said, enjoying my admiration. "And I was dancer," he added with a complacent smile, eyes closing again.

"But now?"

"I still do *barre.*"

None of the bars I went to ever did that for my body.

"Can you help me, Rafik?"

His eyes opened again, this time with that come-onna-my-house look. "Of course I help you."

I asked, "You work at the factory, right?"

"Yes. . . ." he answered, disappointed by the kind of help I was seeking.

"I want to find out who made those chocolates, the ones for the party last Sunday night."

He weighed this all for a moment, then pulled my head down to his and kissed me on the mouth with a real affectionate smooch. "I tell you, Stani."

"You know?"

"I know everything."

"Who then?"

"You will stay with me?" His dark eyes sure knew how to tell love-laden lies.

I shook my head. "Not here. Not with Danny around."

"Then I keep my secret," he said with a grin.

In a lame imitation of Branco, I grunted. "Then *I* go."

I called for a cab and asked for the "female" driver. That done, I hung up and turned to Rafik's warm, prone body. I tweaked him lightly on his left nipple, and said, *"A tout a l'heure, diable!"* Then I stood up and walked out of the place. If Rafik hadn't been so damn appealing and hadn't stimulated my vesicles, I would have written him off as a first-class hustler and exploiter. But his body heat and his suave continental manners seemed to jam out any negative traits he possessed. When the cab arrived to take me back to the train station, my stupid crotch was still saying yes.

Some people think I'm oversexed, that sex is my focus. But in truth I'm one of those unfortunate souls who confuse sex and love. I'm just overlonesome, and the simplest way to handle it is always to be searching for the perfect bedmate. It looks to others like an insatiable libido, when it's actually an unfulfilled urge to nest and nestle. The proof? Put a porn movie on the VCR and two minutes later I'm contemplating housework. But, on the other hand, invite me away on a romantic weekend, and I'm yours forever. Well, for three days anyway. So all the rumblings that Rafik was causing within me were more related to the lack in my life of that heavenly phrase, "Honey, I'm home!" than to his sinewy muscles, his chiseled face, and his big dick.

I got back to North Station around five-thirty and went directly to Snips. I figured Nicole would be waiting there with Tobias, ready to pounce on me and scold me. I was right. She was reading to him quietly in the waiting lounge, but the minute I walked in, she got up and dragged me to the back room, where she slammed the door closed.

"Where were you?" she demanded.

"It was important. I had to go."

"So is managing this shop, Stanley. When I gave you the keys, I expected a certain level of responsibility, which is something you seem to have lost."

"Nikki—"

"Don't 'Nikki' me. I'm tired of this Nancy Drew impersonation. You lied to me this morning, Stanley. I abhor that."

"But—"

"And you're not scoring any points with Chaz either. He's thinking about dropping Laurett's case."

"But that's unethical. He can't desert her just because he doesn't approve of me."

"He's a lawyer. He knows his rights."

"And I know he's a jerk."

"Enough! It's been a difficult day."

"For me too, doll."

She pulled out a cigarette and lit it nervously. It was rare for Nicole to use a cigarette as a prop, since it usually provided pleasure for her.

"And that boy is quite a handful, Stanley. Are you sure you're up to caring for him?"

"He's not so bad once you get used to him."

"As if you should know. Well, you'll have plenty of opportunity to find out, since I won't be helping you anymore."

"Why not?"

"Chaz wants his time with me alone."

"Tarzan speaks."

"He thinks you may be a bad influence on the boy."

"Neanderthal brain."

"When Chaz came out from his shower this morning, Tobias tried to look under his towel."

"So?"

"So what's he looking for?"

"I should think that's obvious, doll."

Nicole's eyes were furious.

"Nikki, he just wants to make sure he's the same as other men."

"The difficulties don't stop there. We took him to the zoo. You know how children are supposed to like the zoo?"

I nodded and anticipated what she was about to tell me. "And the animals put on a floor show for him?"

"No, it was worse. He found some stones and was throwing them at the lions. It was pandemonium. The roaring was horrible. Finally, the guards ordered us all out."

"Poor Charles. He must have been mortified."

Nicole glared at me. "Stanley, even I was disturbed by the boy's behavior, and I'm certainly no animal lover."

"Nikki, Tobias is angry about what's happening to his mother. It's better for him to release the anger than to suppress it."

"That's bosh. He's an ill-mannered little monster."

"He's only four years old. You can't expect him to be a paragon of etiquette."

"Chaz thinks the corruption is irreversible, and he believes that you are partly responsible."

"That's absurd."

"Maybe not, Stanley."

Silence. Puff-puff. Smoke screen.

"Whose side are you on, Sis?"

Nicole faltered for just a second. "There are no sides. Chaz is a very satisfactory lover, Stanley, despite what you perceive to be flaws in his character."

"He's trying to cause a rift between us, Nikki. Homophobes tend to do that, and the educated, clever ones do it sneakily, the way Charles does."

"Stanley, I don't want to lose him. Not just yet. And at the same time I don't want to have to choose between the two of you."

"How do you think I feel? Do you think I like being pitted against an Olympic rug-muncher?"

Nicole crushed her cigarette carelessly, not with the usual delicacy. "You have a way of debasing everything."

"It clears the air."

"It's coarse."

"Everything is, at the bottom."

"You sound just like a man now."

"I am a man."

"Yes, I sometimes forget that. Well, I can no longer help out with caring for the boy. He's all yours, Stanley. And if you can't handle it, then the courts should take him."

Cripes, even if Tobias *was* somewhat disturbing to our pretty little lives, a foster home certainly wasn't the answer, not when Nikki and I could offer him friendly, familiar places to stay. Besides, I'd promised Laurett that I'd take care of him. Of course, that had been under the assumption that it would be for only one night.

"Nikki, I'm not going to give the kid up until the police come and take him from me."

"Suit yourself." She latched her purse forcefully and yanked it up over her shoulder. "And as for your shirking your duties today—I'm not asking for your keys, but consider yourself on probation for a month."

"But—"

Nicole raised her hand to silence me, much the way Branco had at the party the other night. It made me wonder if my lying to her earlier about being on probation with Branco had caused it to become a reality now with her. He-said-she-said. Were they in cahoots against me too?

Nicole spoke as if announcing a corporate policy change.

"Ramon has proven that he's perfectly capable of managing the shop. If you don't want the responsibility, he'll gladly step in."

It was happening again. Ramon was displacing me. Damn conniving little liar. I never trusted him or his story. He was supposedly from Paris, and he'd wormed his way into Snips by dropping some names that Nicole recognized from her modeling days back there. But I reasoned that if a young man knew people from her generation so well, he was probably a clever opportunist who traded on his youth and looks. Nicole insisted that he was simply cultured. Ramon also claimed to be bisexual, which was a kind of fashion statement for him, and which also seemed to increase his tips. But what I really mistrusted him for was his interest in my client list and my expert technique. He had few clients of his own and he envied my position as Snips's lead stylist. Besides, Ramon was hatefully good-looking and suave, which really grated on and exposed my blue-collar background.

"No," I said sharply in my best all-male imitation.

"Then grow up, Stanley, and do your job."

She left the back room abruptly and continued on right out of the shop, even before putting on her coat.

Nikki and I had fought before. During our worst one, I'd actually quit and gone to work in another salon. Those six weeks were hell for both of us. I even considered returning to my first profession as a psychologist. But fortunately Nikki and I made up, and we promised that we'd never get that angry again. Yet here I was being punished like a naughty boy. What had I done that was so wrong?

When I came out from the back room a few minutes later, Tobias was standing outside. "Uncle Stan, should I go away?"

He'd obviously overheard everything.

"No, Tobias. I'm just not used to having a boy around. Give me a little time, okay?" How could I explain to him that the best way he could help me would be to show me where his ON/OFF switch was? That way I could put him on a shelf, then take him down again whenever it suited me. Parenthood and I were obviously incompatible.

Back to work it was. The one remaining name on my book was a new customer. He was a good-looking man, rugged and muscular, probably in his late twenties. He told me he was an actor and was in town for the tryouts of a new show. While I was cutting his hair, he asked me if I'd like to go to the theater with him that night, since he had tickets. I figured Rafik must have activated my pheromones, because I don't usually get such easy invitations from such hunky men. Regretfully, I had to say no, since I'd be playing my own role of Daddy again that night.

With the work day over, Tobias and I headed back to my place. I asked him, "Are you ready for supper?"

He nodded vigorously.

"How about soup and sandwiches?"

Negative.

"Pizza again?"

Equally strong negative.

"Then what, Tobias?"

"Burgers."

So much for the diet. We headed for the downtown branch of Acme Burgers. Yes, there is such a place, and it's hamburger heaven. I knew they had deluxe salad plates for the chic, slender crowd, of which I seemed destined to be a nonmember. And once inside, the smell of grilled burgers and onions and fries convinced me that fifteen, make that twenty, extra pounds on a five-foot-ten-inch, long-limbed Slavic frame wasn't really a serious problem. I had more important matters to contend with. Like attempted murder.

11

A DAMSEL IN DISTRESS

The next morning I arrived at Snips with Tobias in tow. The shop was open and I assumed that Ramon was already exercising his new-found keys and privileges as salon manager, however long they lasted. I greeted Nikki nonchalantly, as though my recent deposition didn't faze me.

"Morning, doll. Am I forgiven for yesterday?"

"Forgiven, yes, Stanley, but not reinstated. You have a nine o'clock appointment, and after that you're booked solid."

"Sounds like all work and no play today."

"Unlikely for you."

I looked around the shop and didn't see my rival.

"Where's swivel-hips?" I asked.

"Who?"

"Ramon."

"Poor thing called in sick, so you'll have to shampoo for yourself too."

"The heir apparent crumbles under the yoke—"

"Just get to work, Stanley."

Nicole then presented Tobias with a large gift box wrapped with expensive paper. His little fingers tore into it like a puppy's paws on a chow bag. Nestled inside was a big, plush teddy bear imported from Germany. For all Nikki's complaining about the boy, her actions proved that she cared about him. "Nonsense," she remarked when I commented on her generosity. "I just want to keep him out of our way."

My first customer of the day was my friend Kris, a freelance production assistant in Boston's theater world. He said he needed a big change—what we call a new look—something to lift his spirits out of the winter doldrums. I suggested color work, specifically, a halo highlighting, where two or more separate colors are skillfully interwoven with plain, bleached hair to achieve a glowing "crown" effect. The complexity of the idea appealed to him, and I launched into the challenging project. The first step was to separate the hair into sections along its natural growth patterns.

Since theater was Kris's world, I asked him if he'd heard about the play I missed last night, the date with the hunky actor I'd had to turn down because of my recent parental charge. Kris laughed.

"Phone sex," he replied.

"A play about phone sex?"

"It should have been more than that, but our local dramaticos ruined it by focusing on porn instead of the characters and their conflict. And the cast—well, I would have *loved* to run the auditions. Forget acting, boys, just show me your stuff. Ergo, it became a play about phone sex. Too bad."

Perhaps I hadn't missed much with the hunk after all.

On Kris's sectioned hair, I wove out selected strands and painted them with one of the two colors, or with the bleach. Then I wrapped each treated tuft in a separate, color-coded piece of foil. By the time I finished applying all the color, Kris's head resembled an Aztec pyramid of fluttery, multicolored foil. When he saw his reflection in the mirror, he exclaimed, "I look like a Vegas show girl."

While the colors cooked in Kris's hair, I had just enough time to perform the weekly trim on the virile head of a popular television newscaster—a regular appointment that kept him looking perfectly groomed without looking recently cut. Thirty minutes later, Kris's color work was ready for finishing, which I did with him facing away from the mirror, to intensify the dramatic effect when it was completed. After my last masterful touch, I turned his chair around to face the mirror. He seemed awestruck by the effect: The two shades of blond along with the bleached hair blended into his former mousey brown head made it seem to glow from within itself, really like a halo. He didn't say a word, so I supplied my own compliment.

"I like it," I said. "That's all that matters."

By late morning, Tobias had become restless from being in the shop, so I took a short break with him and went for a walk in the Public Garden, which is only half a block away. Once in the garden, Tobias ran full speed toward the snow-covered banks of the Swan Pond. He tumbled down into the snow and rolled himself like a big snowball toward the empty lagoon. When his small body came to rest, he played dead in the snow, facedown. I knelt down over him and gently tickled him. I could see him tensing up and refusing to laugh, but I persisted until I overcame his resistance. He rolled onto his back and faced me, now laughing loudly and flailing about in the snow, tossing some of it up onto me until I had to pin his arms down to stop him. But the physical restraint only caused him to laugh louder.

"Want to make snow angels?" I asked, crouched over him.

"Is that like making love?"

"Tobias, don't talk like that." I feared that passersby might overhear and get the wrong idea. Why was this kid so insistent on proving me a pederast? "No," I said. "It's like doing this." I rolled off him and lay down in a clean patch of snow and made the requisite motions with my arms and legs. Then I stood up and showed him the splendid angelic form I'd created in the snow, a kind of reverse bas-relief.

Tobias studied the neatly depressed snow, then remarked, "Why is it wearing a dress?"

"That's a holy robe."

"I'm going to make a bum-angel," he said and started to unfasten his pants. I realized instantly what he was about to do, so I snagged his little arms.

"No you don't, young man. Not with me." I quickly halted his imminent exhibitionism, but it was too late. People had already seen and heard enough to wonder what a red-haired man in his early thirties was doing diddling with the trousers of a blond-haired brown boy of four. "It's all right," I heard myself begin to explain aloud, but I realized that explanations only sounded defensive. I dragged Tobias out of the garden and headed back to the shop. Once inside, he grabbed his new teddy bear and fell asleep on one of the big cushioned chairs in the waiting lounge. I wondered how the little monster could appear so peaceful and harmless in sleep, while awake he challenged mind, body, and soul.

I was checking the book to see who my next customer was, when the phone rang. The receptionist answered it and told me, "It's for you. Personal. She sounds pretty upset."

I took the phone, prepared to hear some customer complaining that her hair didn't look the same as it had after my recent ministerings. But it was Liz Carlini, and she was frantic.

"Vannos, thank god you're there. I don't know who to turn to."

"What's wrong?"

"Something horrible has happened."

"Are *you* okay, Liz?"

"I'm not injured, if that's what you mean."

"Then what happened?"

She paused, then spoke as though she was telling a group of stockholders that there'd be no dividends this quarter. "Someone tried to shoot me."

"Did you call the police?"

"Of course. They're on their way."

I wondered why she'd called me then. I got my answer fast. "Vannos, can you come here now? I'm at home."

"I'm working, Liz. It's—"

"Oh, please. I need someone I can trust here with me."

I didn't answer her. I couldn't.

She continued with a slightly calmer voice. "I hope you've forgiven me about yesterday. I was a perfect fool."

"Those things happen," I replied, but I wondered why she wanted me there with her instead of her husband.

"Vannos, please come. Take a cab, I'll pay for it. Just hurry."

She seemed awfully eager to see me. Then, too, maybe I'd find out something by going.

"All right, Liz. I'm on my way."

I hung up and went to Nicole's table. She was trimming thick cuticles from the clawlike nails of a Beacon Hill dowager. "Doll . . . ?" I asked tentatively.

"No, Stanley," she replied, her attention still focused on her surgery.

"But Liz is in trouble."

"So are you, Stanley. You've already taken an unscheduled break, and your next client is waiting."

What could I do but get back to work? Fortunately, it was a no-frills wash-and-set. I'd have her in and out of my chair in fifty minutes, just like a real shrink. Ordinarily I would have lingered and fussed with her hair, cultivating a stronger bond between client and stylist. But I had more pressing concerns than nurturing my clients now.

When I finished, I announced to Nicole, "I've got to go. It's an emergency."

"Fine, Stanley. Leave. I suppose you expect me to baby-sit Tobias while you're gone?"

"Would you?"

Without a word, Nicole wrote something down in a small leather-bound ledger.

"What's that?" I asked.

"I'm keeping an account of all the favors I do for you."

"Since when?"

"It's a little survey Chaz suggested. And now I'm curious myself to find out just how much time and energy I spend on you. There's a column here for the favors you do for me as well."

"Why keep track, Nikki? With friends it all comes out in the wash."

"We'll see, darling. Now just toddle off on your white knight's mission. Leslie's here today, so she can cover for you— admirably, I might add."

Vaguely annoyed, I hurried outside and got a cab to the Prentiss-Carlini mansion in Chestnut Hill. I told the driver,

"Pedal to the metal," and she got me out there in fifteen blurry minutes. On arrival I saw two police cruisers still parked on the street, so I wasn't too late, despite my delayed start. Then I noticed the curious presence of Lieutenant Branco's green Alpha Romeo parked in the driveway. Perhaps police protection in the wealthy suburbs had an element of overkill.

I trotted up the dry asphalt, then tried to convince the cop guarding the door to let me in. After checking with the others, he allowed me to enter. I followed the sound of voices coming from the living room, which was decorated to resemble the main reception room of a London town house.

Liz Carlini was sitting on the edge of a creamy mohair-covered sofa. Branco sat in a matching chair, facing her directly and asking her questions. Two other uniformed officers were also in the room. Both were good-looking men, probably expressly chosen for this particular Chestnut Hill beat. One stood taking notes behind Liz where she sat on the sofa, the other one stood next to Branco.

When I walked into the room, Branco said, "What are you doing here?"

Liz answered him quickly. "I asked him to come."

I waved to Branco in a friendly manner, and noticed that he actually looked tired. I felt kind of sorry for him. Maybe he really did work hard. Branco turned back to questioning Liz.

"Think again, Miss Carlini. Are you sure there's no one who might want to hurt you?"

Long pause.

"No. . . ."

"What about your husband?"

Liz shot an accusing glance at me, as though I'd told the police that she and Prentiss were temporarily separated. "We had a small disagreement, but that wouldn't drive Prentiss to such extremes." Then she added with a little snicker, "Nothing would."

"He might be more angry than you realize."

"It's not his style, Lieutenant."

"Miss, someone tried to hurt you." Then Branco's eyes

dropped, and I realized he was focusing on Liz Carlini's shapely legs. She was an appealing woman—not like a model or a goddess—but attractive and healthy, and in very good shape. Liz cared for her body as seriously as she did her career. Perhaps Branco was seeing the strong-willed Italian girl who had finally broken from a repressive family to succeed as a glamorous businesswoman. That was probably the kind of woman he'd pursue, someone independent, who would be a challenge to win. Not like me, who would submit to his merest whim in gratitude. But didn't Branco see that an aggressive person might also want to dominate his angry-stallion side, perhaps even render him a gelding?

Liz caught his appraisal of her limbs and coyly changed her position to show them off even more. No wonder this police report was taking so long.

"Lieutenant," she said, "maybe I'm making too much of it. Perhaps it was just some young boys, high on drugs or something." I noticed a slight change in her voice, a softening of the edge, an inviting inflection. "I really should have thought twice before calling you here. I'm almost ashamed to be making such a fuss."

But her body language was saying, Here, kitty-kitty.

"Miss Carlini," Branco said boldly, "gunfire is not something we take lightly." Big man protects helpless maiden. "Did you get a make on the car?"

Liz shook her head. "It all happened so fast. All I remember is a big maroon sedan."

"Do you know anyone who owns a car like that?"

Liz thought a moment. "Not offhand," came the breathy reply.

It was time for this little minuet to get some jazz, so I chimed in.

"What kind of car does John Lough drive?"

Branco scowled at me. "Kraychik, don't you have something else to do, maybe change the diapers on that kid of yours?"

"He's potty-trained, Lieutenant."

Liz thought a moment, then gave a troubled answer. "Lieutenant, Vannos is right. My brother-in-law, John Lough, drives a large maroon sedan."

Branco spoke into a small two-way radio clipped onto his belt. I knew the signal would be relayed through the transmitter in his car and back to the station. I heard him order an APB for John Lough's car, which I knew was cop-talk for "all points bulletin." Meanwhile, I asked Liz what had happened. She explained that someone had driven by her house earlier and fired numerous shots through the front windows of a seldom-used study on the side of the house. Another cop was in there now, investigating the broken window and the bullet holes in the wall.

"Liz," I said, "how can you think it was kids on drugs?"

"I don't know what to think anymore. Would John really do such a thing? He might have killed me."

"Or your husband. This could have been another attempt on his life."

When Branco's attention was back on us, I said, "Well, Lieutenant, at least you can't blame these gunshots on Laurett Cole."

Except for an annoyed scowl, Branco ignored the comment.

Liz said, "Lieutenant, there is something else, though I'm not sure it's relevant. My husband has been having some trouble with John Lough about the company too."

"The company?" asked Branco.

Liz smiled politely—or was it coquettishly?—before she said, "My husband owns Gladys Gardner chocolates."

"The whole company?"

Liz nodded.

Branco whistled quietly through pursed lips.

Without thinking, I blurted, "Tidy little parcel, eh?"

Branco whirled at me. "Kraychik, I want you out of here!"

"Lieutenant—"

"Now, before I have you hauled out."

I got up and shuffled through the deep carpet and left the room. I loitered in the foyer, hoping to eavesdrop, but one of the uniformed officers shoved me toward the door. So much for that idea. I wanted to talk some more with Liz, so I decided to wait around outside until the cops left. I wandered over to Branco's car and leaned on the front fender. The sun had warmed the metal up, and the heat penetrated my chinos pleasantly. With my fingertip I rubbed at the dull paint on the hood. A few moments of that uncovered the glossy paint hiding under the oxidized surface. So, there on the hood of Lieutenant Vito Branco's car I rubbed and rubbed and rubbed until I'd drawn the outline of a Valentine's heart. I retraced the design until the shape gleamed through the dull paint. I even made an arrow, and then his initials—V.B. As I was about to add the remaining initials to the valentine, Branco came out of the house.

"You still here?" he asked gruffly.

"I came to see Liz, not to bother you, Lieutenant."

"How do you know her?"

"I do her hair."

He grunted. "Looks like you do good work."

I nodded and said, "Thanks." So he *had* been admiring her. "I'm sorry if I got in the way though."

"Since when do you apologize?"

"Whenever I accidentally step on someone's toes."

"Skip it. Sometimes an extra voice doesn't hurt."

That was Branco's version of absolution. He got in the car and started it up. Through the windshield, I could see him studying my artwork on the hood of his car. The corners of his sensuous mouth curled in the tiniest smile, then he put the car in gear and backed down the driveway. Liz Carlini's legs had put him in a good mood.

I returned to the house just as the crew of uniformed cops was leaving. Liz saw me and said, "Thanks for coming, Vannos. I was hoping you'd stay around. I could use some company."

"After yesterday, I wasn't sure."

"I'm sorry about that. I'm truly sorry."

"I was probably a little pushy myself."

"I've been under so much pressure, between the business and my marriage, I seem to lash out at anything, even people who care about me and who want to help. I'm afraid I attacked the messenger along with the message. Will you forgive me, Vannos?"

"Consider it done."

"Thank you," she said. And with that bit of social interaction promptly and successfully executed, she went and put on her winter coat. "I'm going out to Abigail now, to tell Prentiss what's happened here, to warn him. I'm sure he's in danger now. I know it was John who fired those shots, but I didn't want to tell the police that."

"Why not?"

"Our family problems are none of their business."

"But you could have been killed."

"My only concern now is to warn Prentiss."

"Why don't you call him?"

"He won't talk to me. He hangs up."

"Try again. You can't stand on ceremony if someone is trying to hurt him."

She considered my words. "Maybe you're right," she said, then went to make the call. After she dialed the number I heard her talking to someone, but it was without pause, and I guessed that she was leaving a message on an answering machine. When she was finished, she returned to me and said, "He wasn't there so I left a message. At least he knows now. I just hope I'm not too late." Her desperation was building, as though she was about to lose the bid on an important contract. "Vannos, do you think you can come out there with me?"

I considered her question a moment, then shook my head no. "I have work to do at the shop, Liz."

"But if you come with me, you can back up my story. Maybe Prentiss will finally believe that I care about him."

"Liz," I said, hoping to back out of this entanglement gracefully, "I think this is really a family matter, something for the two of you to work out. If you need an objective listener, there are professionals who can help."

"I'm not going to pay some stranger to act like a friend. I thought you cared."

Great, Stanley. Nice, heartless, insensitive work. It did

occur to me that the real cause of Liz Carlini's emotional state may have been the recent visit by Lieutenant Branco. I could understand that. More than once I'd been close to hysteria after I'd spent time with him. But I usually channeled it to more positive actions, like eating half a pound of chocolate pecan fudge.

I surrendered to her apparent need. "Okay, Liz," I said. "I'll call the shop and explain that I'll be delayed. Then we can head out for Abigail together."

She nodded approvingly. "Thank you."

There was something a little too smooth about the whole thing. I felt that I was playing a part that had been set up for me, and it bothered me. Still, I went along with it.

When I called Nicole, she took the news coolly. I could hear her making a notation in her ledger of unreturned favors. I asked facetiously, "Are you keeping track of the favors I do for others too?"

"Of course. Those count as two marks against you."

So Liz Carlini and I set out on our trip to Abigail to warn her husband of imminent danger. There's nothing like the honest concern of a loving spouse to patch up a conjugal squabble. Then again, if Dan Doherty or Rafik answered the door instead of her husband, would she still feel so caring?

12

WHAT GOES AROUND
COMES AROUND

Driving out to Abigail-by-the-Sea with Liz Carlini in her big British saloon certainly beat taking the train, both in time and in comfort. Riding in the speedy car was like being inside a soundproof bank vault. The thing probably cost the contents of one too. But it seemed the perfect vehicle for Liz Carlini to rush off dramatically and save her estranged husband from impending doom.

Once we were under way, I asked her, "How long has Prentiss been staying out at your summer place?"

Her eyes flashed toward me, then shifted back onto the road, which was good, since she was doing over seventy.

"Vannos, you might as well know the facts. Prentiss and I are having a trial separation."

I'd already guessed as much. "So there's more to it than just the business problems, right?"

Liz squirmed, but didn't answer.

I pressed her. "Is it Danny?"

Liz's face twisted in anguish, but no sound came from her. The snowy scenery whizzed by, and the only road noise was a muffled rush of air outside and a politely tempered hum from under the hood. A few minutes and many miles later, Liz regained composure from her tasteful breakdown and said, "I don't know who to turn to."

I gave her my best empathetic look to encourage her trust, but I couldn't stifle that damned internal voice that went, *whom*, not who.

She went on. "I hate myself for suspecting anything. I know that they've become good friends from spending so much time together this past year, getting Le Jardin launched and all."

"But you're afraid it might be deeper than just friendship?"

"No, not anymore. I was wrong. I was foolish—a simpleminded, jealous fool. It was other people who made me suspicious. They seem to think that any close friendship between two men is suspect. But I know Prentiss and I know Danny. Prentiss loves me, despite our recent problems. And I'm sure his interest in Danny is more fatherly than anything else."

I didn't want to remind Liz that that kind of arrangement didn't exclude hanky-panky, or even spanky.

"And Prentiss really wants children," she added, as though to exonerate her husband from any involvement beyond the platonic. "I'm sure he sees Danny as a son." Liz shook her head and sighed heavily, while her grip on the leather-bound steering wheel tightened and the car accelerated. "Perhaps this is all a mistake, coming out here like this. Maybe we should turn back. I'm sure Prentiss and Danny are fine. They're probably sitting peacefully by the fire, and here I am barging in on them, looking like one of those possessive, neurotic wives who intrudes on her husband's privacy. Oh, God, I'm a fool!"

"Liz," I replied calmly, "it's okay." But I was thinking, Just slow down, girl. This buggy's going too fast. I continued, "I know that Danny is still involved with Rafik. And I'm sure you're right—he's probably looking to Prentiss for stability, which is exactly what Prentiss can offer him. From what I know of Danny, he doesn't go after straight men. I'm sure there's nothing sexual between him and your husband."

But the more I said, the faster the car seemed to go. Its twelve cylinders were on the verge of an impolite growl.

"Actually, Vannos, what does it matter, especially if someone is trying to hurt Prentiss? So what if he has a fling with a boy? So what if he wants to make him an heir?"

"An heir?"

Liz nodded. "Danny's in his will now. I protested, but Prentiss wouldn't listen. I think it's his guilt over inheriting his mother's fortune. Without a natural heir himself, Prentiss feels he has to give his money away."

"It *is* his to do with as he pleases, Liz."

"But it's time for a change, not recklessness."

Hold that thought, Liz, and ease up on your right foot. But she sped up even more as she spoke. "Sometimes I think the Kingsley pedigree is nothing more than sludge. I wanted Le Jardin to show Prentiss that everything eventually changes, even the Kingsley tradition."

"What if you and Prentiss have a child? Wouldn't that continue the Kingsley line?"

Liz smiled as though she knew a lovely secret. "That would certainly change things," she said. I wondered what the secret was. Perhaps she was pregnant? It would fit in with the image of the modern woman who has everything. But from what I could see, the love between Liz and her husband was based on balance sheets, financial projections, and marketing demographics, rather than percale sheets, throbbing projections, or pornographics. Then again, some people experience their most ecstatic moments with money in mind. I had to hand it to Liz Carlini. She was a woman who worked hard to put her life in order, to control her destiny. But any fool knows that even the tiniest murder can ruin the best-laid schemes.

Suddenly we heard a quiet beeping from under the dashboard. She immediately let up on the gas, and we re-entered the sound barrier. I looked her way with alarm, and she smiled back. "A call," she said as she picked up the car phone from the padded leather console between our seats. She obviously loved the glamor of receiving phone calls in her British touring sedan. But within seconds she slammed the phone back into its cradle. "Wrong number," she said.

"So?"

"I still get charged for them."

"You're kidding."

"They eventually credit my bill, but it's months before it happens."

At least the phone call had slowed us down. I asked Liz if the plans for opening Le Jardin were still on, especially since a killing during the gala celebration might be interpreted as a bad omen.

"That's medieval thinking. You've got to turn adversity into advantage. I'm going to use all the publicity to help promote the business. You can't let a little trouble with the police affect your plans."

As we approached our destination, Liz turned off the highway and headed into the town center of Abigail. As though announcing our arrival, a delicate chime sounded from the dashboard and an amber light flashed discreetly from the instrument panel: CHECK PETROL.

Liz said, "I need gas."

She pulled the car into the only filling station in Abigail. An old salt came up to the window and greeted her.

"Halloo, Mrs. Kingsley. Back again?"

She answered curtly, "Just fill it, Ben."

"How's she runnin' now?"

"The car is fine, Ben."

"Right," he said and went about his work.

Liz muttered to herself, "He insists on calling me Kingsley."

Meanwhile, I was happy to see that old-fashioned, friendly, English-speaking service was still alive in some places, especially if you were rich enough to live there.

I asked Liz casually what had been wrong with the car, wondering how a vehicle costing as much as some houses could even so much as sputter. She explained somewhat defensively that it was just a minor adjustment and added, "These are still the most prestigious sports sedans on the road." I guess even a high-strung thoroughbred needs a little down-home love and attention.

After filling the tank, Ben said, "Something going on at the house today, eh?"

"Why?" answered Liz.

"Ohhhh, I saw Mr. Lough was here earlier too."

Liz suddenly looked worried. "Thanks, Ben," she said, and quickly started the car and pulled away from the pump. Then she put the big cat through its paces, swerving up the winding road like a slalom race—a little too sportive for my sensitive tummy—to the Kingsley summer house. Finally we reached the top of the bluff, and for the second time in two days I got to admire the view of the town and the marina from high up on the hill. It *was* a swell place for an ocean house. But when we arrived at the homestead, we had an unpleasant surprise. The roadway in front was lined with police cruisers, flashers going, squawk boxes yapping.

"Oh, no!" Liz exclaimed. "Prentiss!"

We had a hard time getting by the two cops blocking the door. They didn't seem to recognize Liz Carlini as Prentiss Kingsley's wife. I'm sure that I, her fey, red-headed companion didn't much help her credibility either. But Prentiss himself appeared at the door and solved the problem. Liz clutched him in a desperate embrace. "Oh, Prentiss, thank God you're all right. What happened? Was it John? Did he come here too?"

Prentiss held his wife close to him and advised her quietly but firmly, "Elizabeth, don't say anything until our attorney arrives."

"But what happened?"

"It's Daniel," he said icily. "He's dead."

That stunned us both.

I started to say that I'd just seen him in that very house yesterday afternoon, but I stopped myself. No one needed to know that, especially the police. Once Prentiss had identified us, the police allowed us in, but they also quickly informed us that we'd be detained for questioning. Then they took the three of us into the solarium. It may sound ghoulish, but my morbid curiosity wanted to know what had happened. I casually asked the officer who accompanied us, "Where's the body?"

He didn't answer.

I pressed him. "Was it an accident?"

"Look, you," he said shortly, "you be quiet. You'll get your turn to talk."

They left Liz and Prentiss and me together in the solarium. Though it was freezing outside, the winter sun was toasty warm under the sparkling glass panels. I remembered the brief sexy moments I'd spent with Rafik in that place, just twenty-four hours ago. As I sat awaiting interrogation, I wondered where he was now.

Liz spoke sotto voce to Prentiss, "John fired some shots at me this morning."

"That's ridiculous," whispered Prentiss.

"I thought he might have come to hurt you too."

Prentiss gave his wife a hard, cold look. "Elizabeth," he said, "John is my brother, my half brother, a fact you still refuse to accept. He would not hurt you or me."

Liz looked at me in exasperation. "Vannos, please tell my husband what happened at our house this morning."

I complied politely, saying, "I wasn't there when it happened, but I can vouch for the broken windows and the bullet holes in the wall. They were real. So were the investigating cops."

Liz insisted, "I'm sure it was John who fired those shots." She faced her husband squarely. "Who else would want me dead, since he stands to inherit my share?"

Prentiss answered her sharply, as if instructing a stubborn child. "No one will inherit anything until I die. You are accusing someone without proper evidence."

"John resents me."

"You imagine that. You always have. I've known John all my life, and he is not trying to hurt either of us."

"He's a hateful leech."

"He is my brother."

"Half brother," retorted Liz, as if to prove she'd learned the correct word. Then she turned away from her husband and sulked.

A police officer arrived and asked her to go with him. As she left the solarium, Prentiss said to her, "Elizabeth, remember, don't answer anything until our attorney arrives."

"I can think for myself, Prentiss," she said, and she set her jaw forward and walked away with the officer.

Prentiss Kingsley shook his distinguished head in dismay, then he dropped his forehead into his upturned palms.

I asked quietly, "Who found Danny's body?"

He kept his head down as he spoke. "I'd just come back from my morning run. He was on his bed. . . ." Then Prentiss Kingsley, heir to a mega-million-dollar chocolate fortune, began to sob quietly. He raised his head and looked at me with wet red eyes. "Do you know what they did to him?" he moaned. His chin was quivering and his cheeks were streaked with tears. "Did you see?"

I felt bad for him. He'd obviously been trying to keep his composure for his wife and the police, but now, seated alone with me, he'd lost control. It's an effect I sometimes have on people.

"I'm sorry," I said. "Do you want to tell me?" My Slavic curiosity was hoping for excruciating detail.

He bit his lip, then spoke. "They took a gun . . ."

"Yes?"

"And they put it . . ." He paused and suppressed another wave of sobbing that was building in his body.

"Go on," I encouraged him. "It's best to say it."

"They put it in him. . . ." Then the sobbing won out, and he couldn't continue. I moved near to him and put my arm around his shoulder—and quickly discovered that Prentiss Kingsley's retiring personality, now stirred to agony over the death of a young friend, couldn't hide his powerful body. It's strange how some men give the impression of softness and refinement, while possessing strong, virile physiques beneath their clothes. At my touch, however, he jerked himself away. He heaved and cried and gasped for another few minutes, then stopped abruptly.

"Now my wife won't even listen to me."

I sat and stared with a blank expression, one step removed from the shrink who typically asks, "Why do you feel that way?"

Eventually people will talk themselves out, into either resolution or impasse. Sure enough, Prentiss Kingsley continued on his own, without further prompting.

"My brother John—there's such a strain between him and my wife. He was always so easygoing and friendly, but when I married, and then when my wife hired Daniel to help with the new store, well, John became aloof. Little by little it's become open hostility, so much so that it's easy for my wife to blame him for any trouble we have now."

As he talked, I stared at him with intense dispassion, the kind of look that costs over a hundred bucks an hour in a therapist's office. It seemed to work, and he went on.

"Perhaps it comes from Elizabeth working so hard to get where she is. I've tried to tell her it doesn't matter anymore, that she doesn't have to strive so much."

I remained silent. Why spoil a potential gush of information? When people have just experienced a major trauma, they often tell the most intimate things to a convenient stranger. How else do you think those funeral directors find out about the bank accounts and the trust funds and the investment portfolios?

Prentiss rambled on, as if talking to himself. "Where is my attorney? There's so much to be done now."

I sensed his free flow of facts slowing down, so I tried a direct question. "What about an heir?"

Prentiss's eyes flickered angrily. "Really, I think that is none of your business."

I'd gone too far, stepped over the boundary of propriety. Perish the notion that Prentiss Kingsley and his vibrant young wife didn't "do the job" together.

We sat together in silence until Liz returned to the solarium, this time with an officer of the local police, who was apologizing for the inconvenience all the nasty questions were causing her and her esteemed husband. Never mind the inconvenience to Dan Doherty, wherever he was now.

The same officer asked me to follow him to answer a few questions. I told him I had to use the bathroom first, which was a deceit to let me look around. He said okay, then led the way.

As we passed by the bedroom where Danny's body was, I paused at the open doorway and gazed inside, taking it all in quickly before the cop realized I wasn't directly behind him. The most obvious thing was the blood. Red was everywhere, in splatters and gobs and puddles. It was hard to imagine that a body held so much blood inside. Dan Doherty was lying naked, face down on the bed. It took my mind a few seconds to realize what the fleshy gunk on the sheets meant: The gun had been shoved into him from behind and fired. My stomach heaved, and my ploy to use the bathroom became an urgent reality. I ran past the cop and got my head over the hopper just in time.

The questioning that followed was routine and simple, at least for the moment. The local cops just wanted to know whether I'd known Danny, and why I was there. I explained that both Dan Doherty and Liz Carlini had been customers of mine, and that Liz had invited me out with her today. I purposely didn't tell them about her suspicions concerning John Lough. That was only her side of things anyway. The police seemed friendly and cooperative enough, which further confirmed my theory that if you live in a wealthy community, even the police are nice.

On my way back to the solarium, I paused once again at the bedroom door. Danny's body was now covered, which gave me a chance to notice something I hadn't seen earlier. On the nightstand near the bed was a heart-shaped box of Le Jardin truffles, spattered with Danny's blood. The box was open, but from what I could see, none of the candy had been eaten. Again I wondered where Rafik was.

Minutes later the police told me I could go, so I went to say good-bye to Liz and Prentiss, who were finally in conference with their attorney. Liz seemed brighter now. Perhaps the all-knowing presence of their attorney had renewed her confidence. She even insisted on paying for a cab for my return trip to Boston. I protested the extravagance, but she convinced me, explaining that she'd asked me to accompany her out there in the first place. Then I reasoned, she could afford it.

Even with the cab ride back to town, I got there too late to pick up Tobias at the shop. I called Nicole at home and apologized for not returning sooner, yet another of my broken promises. She seemed to accept it all in good spirits. I wondered, Was Charles there, tallying the chits on my personal Judgment Day Account? And with Nicole being so pleasant, why did I still feel the floor dissolving from under me?

"Nikki," I said hesitantly, not sure how to begin what I had to tell her next. "This whole shuffle-and-deal with Tobias will be over soon anyway."

"It will?" she asked with little interest.

"Yes. Laurett Cole will be released soon, I promise."

"Stanley, what are you talking about?"

"There's been another killing. Dan Doherty was murdered in Abigail today. There's no way Branco can hold Laurett for that one."

"So that's what delayed you!"

"Yes, Nikki. It was real life today."

I recounted everything to her, from my visit to Liz Carlini's house in Chestnut Hill to my leaving Abigail by taxi. If I slyly censored some gruesome detail, she would instinctively sense the gap and pounce on me immediately and command me, "Tell me everything." Never skip details when dealing with a gossip-monger, even if you have to contrive them.

At the end of it all Nicole said, "Darling, forgive me for doubting you. I had no idea what had happened. Would you like some time off tomorrow, well-deserved if not earned?"

"Thanks, Nikki, but I'm fine, I think. Numb, anyway. It hasn't sunk in yet."

"Call me if you have to."

"Sure, doll."

She hung up, and I knew we were friends again.

Alone, finally, and psychologically exhausted, I took a double shot of bourbon, scrubbed myself almost raw under a hot shower, then went to bed. I was asleep in seconds.

13

HOUSE CALL

The clock dial says 2:40 A.M. when the noise awakens me—the sound of a heavy leather jacket falling onto the floor. Sugar Baby is sitting high up on her haunches, purring loudly from her place on the down pillow next to my head. She seems excited but not frightened. I realize that the fallen jacket isn't mine, that someone is in my bedroom. I freeze, trying to discern the uninvited form that lurks in the darkest corner of the room. The air is still, and for a moment I hope it is all imaginary. But I hear him take a breath, and I am terrified. I am helpless, lying naked in my bed. The telephone is nearby, but what good is it? How can I call the police when whoever is in my room can see me in the dim light coming in from the street window?

His voice breaks the silence.

"Do not have fear."

I recognize the French accent at once. It's Rafik.

"What do you want?" I ask, as I reach for the lamp on the night table.

"No light."

"Why not?"

"*Non!*"

"Are you afraid I'll see the blood on your clothes?"

"I did not do it." He moves closer to the bed. "I did not kill Dunny. I do not have to. He will give me anything I ask for."

"Except sex."

Rafik replies almost sadly, "Except love."

I sense him removing his clothes with all the familiar sounds of a lover undressing in the dark: the putt-putt of shirt buttons released, the rustle of cotton sliding off shoulders and down arms, the creaking of heavy leather boots pried off, then dropped—clunk—to the floor, the loose jangle of a brass belt buckle, the secret whisper of a fly zipper lowered, the soft crunch of blue jeans pulled down and off muscled limbs, the snap of elastic. Has he purposely left his white socks on, knowing that's a peculiar weakness of mine?

He kneels down and pulls something from his jacket pocket. Then he approaches the bed, rests one knee on the edge. He places the thing from his jacket on the nightstand. In the darkness I can make out the form of a gun. The air between us pulses with my fear and his desire—and probably my desire, too.

He says, "I want to be with you."

"I can't. Not after what you did."

"What did I do? I just want to love him, but he says no. Don't say no, Stani."

He has the advantage on me. If he is a killer, I don't want to press the wrong buttons and get myself destroyed. He lifts the duvet and slides into the bed beside me. Sugar Baby remains in her spot on the pillow. That's a comfort at least. My pet remains constant, even though I might become the victim of a sexual murder.

"Relax, *mon cher*," he murmurs. "I will not hurt you."

He touches my shoulder. His hand is warm and strong, not the way I imagine a killer's hand to be. I'm certain he'll be an expert lover too, marred only by the tendency to kill his partners afterwards. Then a strange thing happens within me, occurs simultaneously as I realize that this naked man in my bed could end my life. It's an irony: I have no lover, and now a killer wants me. And instead of finding a means of escape and self-preservation, I feel myself surrender to him. With total awareness and calm I think, If my faltering, meaningless, stupid, petty life is to come to an ignoble end at the hands of a sexy killer, so be it. Rafik could have whatever he wanted.

He raises himself up on one elbow and faces me. He leans toward me and puts his lips lightly on mine. I feel their chiseled shape against my own mouth. Only a mouth, and what wondrous textures! But I lie rigid, wondering what he'll do next. I feel his lips tighten into a smile.

"I surprise you, eh?"

I take a deep breath, then let it slide out in a long, noisy gasp.

"Good," he says. "Now I have you."

I pray that I survive whatever is to follow.

Under the down comforter, Rafik rolls up onto his knees and crouches over me, straddles my body. His warm thighs press fast around my waist. The hair on his legs scratches my smooth skin. He bends closer and flicks at my nipples with his tongue, then grazes them lightly with his day's growth of stubble, causing kilowatts of pleasure to jolt through my body. He lowers his haunches down gently onto my crotch, then nestles around, squeezing and pulling on me with the furry warmth of his loins. Strong hands, hot hands knead my shoulders and upper arms. He drags his heavy pouch back and forth across my belly. A nip, and then another at my nipples. A moist member insinuates itself between my thighs, thighs pressed together, sealed with the pressure of his own strong legs around them. A hand finds a hand, a lip finds a lip, a sigh a sigh.

He sits up again and presses his hips harder onto my crotch. He presses, squeezes, twists, and milks my flesh with his butt. Even as he prepares to impale himself, he holds me captive in his strong limbs.

"I have no protection," I say. There's a killer in my bed, and I'm worried about safe sex.

"Voilà!" he replies, and takes a small foil packet from the nightstand, near the gun.

Hot, hopeful hands find their way down my chest and past my belly. He coils himself up and bends over to kiss me down where I am drooling clear syrup. He nuzzles in the bush, then kisses the shaft around its tip. He works his way toward the base, nibbling along the full length and following the course of his lips directly with the latex membrane that will protect us.

Now he sits up and begins the fast ride home. He grasps my

shoulders for leverage and pushes himself down onto me. He winces sharply at the first penetration, just the tip. He holds me tightly in a spasm of pain. I blow cool air on his face. We breathe together. I murmur, "It's just another sensation." He lowers his torso and presses himself against me. His clipped chest hair scratches my skin, scraping me as he squirms and burrows himself further onto me, over me, ever compressing us into one. I feel his warmth surround my cock, and from skin to muscle to bone to soul, all resistance is freed and gone, all pores and portals open. We cantor, we gallop, we race too fast, we leap through a dark dream, explode into fire and stars, shatter into sparkling dust, fall and die.

14

AIN'T NOBODY'S

BUSINESS

It was Sugar Baby's cool wet nose nudging my chin that awoke me the next morning. That and her noisy purr.

Rafik was gone. Even his scent had vanished. Had he really been there? Or had I imagined it all, like a movie in my mind, albeit a movie with Sensurround? The only evidence of our nocturnal adventure was a sadly wrinkled rubber on the carpet, and my humming haunches.

I got up and put coffee on. The telephone rang just as I was feeding and watering Sugar Baby. Sometimes I wonder if I've inadvertently created a conditioned response in my cat, that phone conversations mean food for her, since I so often do the two things together.

I answered the phone and Nikki asked, "Are you all right?"

"Sure, doll. Why?"

"Your voice sounds strange today, almost hoarse."

"I was, uh, doing a little primal scream therapy last night."

"Alone?"

"There was a facilitator. . . ."

"We'll discuss that later," she said. "Can you open the shop today? We're all going to be a little late here."

"Who's we?"

"Can you do it, Stanley?"

"Does this mean I'm manager again?"

"I suppose so."

I paused. "Then I'll open."

"Thank you," she said, and hung up.

I didn't have a chance to tell her that I'd planned to see Lieutenant Branco first thing that morning, before going to the shop. I wanted to find out what he knew about the killing of Dan Doherty yesterday. Now that would have to wait until later, after I opened Snips.

My stomach grumbled for food as it usually does first thing in the morning, especially after a rigorous "night before." I fixed myself a quick breakfast of organic fat-free whole wheat muffins slathered with extra butter, and fresh-ground coffee without sugar, but with a dollop of heavy cream. The breakfast was half-healthful, at least. Then I showered and dressed and headed for the shop.

It was biting cold outside and the sky was gray. Another snowstorm seemed inevitable. Cold, warm, cloudy, sunny, wet, dry—all in a day's work for typical New England weather. As it turned out, I was booked solid that morning, so I wouldn't have a chance to slip out to see Branco as I'd planned. Nicole and Tobias arrived shortly after noontime. She seemed a mite grumpy, though I was extra bright and cheery. While Tobias was using the bathroom, I asked Nicole if Charles had spent the night. I wanted to know if her lovemate had stayed until morning, unlike my succubus, who'd vanished as mysteriously as he'd arrived.

"No, he didn't," she replied. Nicole then grabbed my arm and hauled me off towards the back room. She told the receptionist to keep an eye on Tobias until we returned. Once we were alone, she poured us both a cup of coffee, then sat down. She pulled the solid gold cigarette case from her small leather clutch bag, and chose a pale turquoise cigarette from the pastel assortment perfectly lined up in the case. A single flick of her red-lacquered lighter ignited the cigarette and put Nicole into her happily altered state. She spoke through the cloud of aromatic smoke she'd just created. "Now, I want to hear everything." She took a second deep inhalation and added, "Down to the minute, if necessary."

"About what, doll?"

"About *your* gentleman caller, Stanley." One eyebrow went up. "I assume it was Rafik."

"It was."

"Well?"

"He's sexy, adept, and frightfully imaginative."

"Safe?"

"That too." Then I had a sudden insight. "Nikki, that's it! That condom proves I was right. Rafik can't be the killer if he respects life that much."

"Stanley, neurosurgeons have murdered people. Besides, he may have been thinking only of himself."

"No, doll. This was different."

Nicole smirked. "Of course, darling. *Yours* is love."

"Not quite. As the saying goes, I got laid but not kissed."

"He didn't stay, then?"

"No. But through it all I was afraid he was the one who'd killed Dan Doherty yesterday. That's why I had to submit to him."

"Stanley, you make it sound like rape."

"Well, no. . . ." How could I explain? "But I didn't want to do anything that might antagonize a potential killer."

"So you had sex with him."

"What else could I do?"

"Stanley, I'm sure there was at least one other choice."

"He had a gun, doll."

"You don't look pistol-whipped."

I happily recalled our brief coupling. "Pussy-whipped is more like it."

Without further comment Nicole extinguished her cigarette with an artful roll that separated the burning ember from the end, preventing any lingering smoke in the ashtray.

"Sorry, doll," I said, realizing I'd offended her.

"You can't seem to keep male and female anatomy straight."

"That's because straight has nothing to do with it." Then, for the second time that morning, I asked about her time with Charles last night.

Her forehead creased with annoyance. "I think Tobias may have scared him away. I never realized Chaz disliked children so much."

"More than you?"

"I don't mind them, Stanley, as long as I don't own them."

"What happened?"

"Chaz and I did have words about the boy being around so much. Tobias overheard us and started crying."

At that moment I realized that in all the time we'd spent together, Tobias hadn't once dropped his brave-little-soldier facade. He never cried or told me that he missed his mom. I hoped he wasn't already concerned about keeping up a macho image, especially with me.

Nicole said, "That young man misses his mother more than he lets on."

"He never said anything to me."

"He wouldn't tell you because you're a man. It takes a woman to make a man whole, Stanley."

"Cut the platitudes, doll."

Nicole sipped her coffee and said, "I think it's time to consider Tobias's safety."

"You think he's in danger?"

"I think *you* may be in danger, and it might not be wise to keep the boy with you, in case anything happens."

"Oh, swell. It's all right if I'm garroted though."

"Stanley, I agreed earlier that the boy should not be in court custody. But considering what happened to you last night, I'm not sure he should be staying with you. You may have enough on your hands just taking care of yourself."

"What happened that's so dangerous?"

"What if Rafik is the killer? What if he returns and isn't so amorous the next time?"

"Doll, he's not. I'm sure."

"Then what if the real killer tries to hurt you? No, Stanley, I think it's time for Tobias to be under safer care until his mother is released from jail."

"Are you sure your concern is for Tobias and not for Charles?"

Nicole replied flatly, "I'm sure, Stanley."

"Well, none of this matters anyway, since Laurett will be released soon. The police can't hold her for Danny's death."

"They're holding her for the other one."

"Nikki, Laurett didn't kill that man. It was supposed to be Danny all along. That's why Lieutenant Branco has to release Laurett today. In fact, I was just heading out to see him when you arrived with Tobias."

"Have you checked the book?"

"I'm clear for the next hour."

"What about walk-ins?"

"Isn't that why Ramon is around?"

"No one is indispensable, Stanley."

"Including Ramon."

Nicole stood up, preparing to return to the shop floor. She gathered the empty coffee cups and said, "Perhaps you should take Tobias along to see his mother while you charm Lieutenant Branco with your fantastic new theory."

"I thought you were worried about his safety."

"I meant at home, not here or at the police station."

"Do you think the WDU will allow him in?"

"Darling, one look at that boy, and they'll allow him anything. Just look at what he's done to me."

"I thought I detected an Old Mother Hubbard patina recently."

Nicole grimaced. "I was thinking more of Auntie Mame."

We re-entered the shop, where Tobias was entertaining the receptionist with a story of how he'd extorted a free tin of imported cocoa from the manager of the chic cafe next door to Snips.

I called to him, "Come on, Tobias. We're going to see your mom."

He cheered loudly and leaped off the desk and ran toward the door. Nicole chased after him with his hat and coat and mittens. "Put these on right now, young man."

He obeyed her, and in minutes we were both in a taxi headed south toward the Women's Detention Unit, which was in the neighborhood of Station E, where Lieutenant Branco would soon hear my latest scoop.

I took Tobias inside the WDU to leave him with Laurett. As Nicole had predicted, Tobias's elfin charm worked its magic on the female desk sergeant there. She was showing Tobias the wallet photos of her young daughter and was just about ready to draw up a marriage contract between them when a guard appeared to take us inside to see Laurett. Then, once mother and child were reunited, I was simply in the way. I told Laurett I'd be back in an hour to pick up Tobias, then I left them to go see Lieutenant Branco.

Getting into his office at Station E wasn't so easy today. I might have blamed the difficulties on my *chakras,* but after last night's session with Rafik, every nerve, muscle, and bone in my back had been realigned perfectly. No, in truth, the problem was that today's desk sergeant simply didn't like me or my delivery style. I tried to tuck in my gossamer wings to ease his nervousness, but it didn't work. The more he ignored me, the more fluttery I became to get his attention and his permission to enter Branco's sanctum sanctorum. I stopped short of performing an abridged version of the Lilac Fairy's dance from *The Sleeping Beauty*. Finally, he called another brute to take me inside to the hall of offices. We arrived at Branco's door, and without even knocking, the cop opened it and shoved me inside.

Show time!

"What do you want?" growled the handsome Italian.

Welcome home.

"Dan Doherty's been killed," I said.

Branco grunted.

"So you knew?" I asked.

"Sure, but it's not our case."

"It's obviously related to the other killing. I thought you'd be checking up on everybody connected with that first one."

"We've already done that."

"So what did you find?"

"Nothing we didn't already know or guess, except in your case."

So he did think of me. . . .

"Lieutenant, Prentiss Kingsley's brother, John Lough, never liked Dan Doherty. Isn't he a suspect?"

"The one we're looking for is that fellow Rafik. Have you seen *him*?"

I blushed. "He had nothing to do with it."

"How do you know? Or are you his alibi?"

"He couldn't have done it." I didn't want the killer to be Rafik, not after last night.

"What do you know about him, Kraychik? Or is *that* too personal?"

"You make it sound dirty, Lieutenant."

"You said it, not me."

Branco stared at me. What was he thinking? I'd come in to discuss Dan Doherty's death, and suddenly my sexuality was on the line. Did he hate me for liking men? What did it matter to him? Logically, he should have been relieved that some men were like me, since it reduced the competition in his arena, the quest for mother or saint or whore. Then again, maybe he enjoyed as much competition as possible. Then again, maybe he was curious about himself. Closet cases often conceal their guilt under the protective guise of queer-hating.

Branco said, "I don't know why your kind is always trying to sanctify anonymous sex."

With a word like that, Branco must have been to church recently. "Lieutenant, it's not exactly anonymous when you know the person."

Branco laughed derisively. "Isn't that how you guys get your kicks, with strangers?"

"That's naive, Lieutenant." Would he believe the truth if I explained myself, that it was an emotional connection that was the most satisfying to me? At the bottom of it all, no pun intended, was my need for romantic fantasy. The sex part of that kind of scene was easy, since *anything* you did or had done to you was perfect. It had to be, since it was all in the mind. Would a practical, physical beast like Branco ever understand that kind of experience?

"When did you see him last?" he demanded.

I looked directly into Branco's eyes and said, "It was after four o'clock this morning when I fell asleep. When I woke up at seven, he was gone."

"You'll do anything, won't you?"

"I didn't plan it. It just happened."

"We'll find him," he said.

"But it's not Rafik. You should question John Lough."

"Kraychik, you talk too much."

"What about Laurett Cole? Will you be releasing her now?"

"Why?"

"She couldn't have killed Dan Doherty if she's in jail."

"We're not holding her for that killing."

"But isn't it obvious that the two killings are related, along with the potshots at Liz Carlini yesterday? There's no reason to hold Laurett now. Besides, she won't skip town, and she could be home with her son. You *are* for family, aren't you?"

Branco paused, considered what I'd said, compressed his lips tightly, then asked me, "Where were you yesterday morning?"

"I saw you, remember?"

"I mean before you saw me."

"I was with Tobias Cole."

No response.

"You can ask him, Lieutenant."

"I've got to know where you were early yesterday morning, before you saw me."

"Why?"

"That's pretty obvious, isn't it?"

It took my brain longer than it should have to figure out what he was getting at. Then it clicked. "You think I had something to do with Dan Doherty's death?"

Branco replied coldly, "It was a sexually motivated act, and since you're involved with Doherty's lover, I'd say your chances of involvement in the killing are equally good."

"Lieutenant, that theory is so limp, all the hairspray in Boston couldn't hold it up."

"You still haven't told me where you were."

"I've told you the truth. If you don't believe me, you can cuff me now."

"Is that what you want?"

"Sure. Do a strip-search while you're at it."

"You might enjoy it too much."

I stood up and stared directly into his beautiful, bright eyes. "So might you," I said, and walked out of his office, slamming the door behind me. Cooperating with the police, and especially with Branco, was not easy. I wanted to like him, but it was no-go for now, not while he was acting like a tight-ass cop who played by some stupid rule book, working strictly from the crime side of his brain.

I went back to the WDU to pick up Tobias and visit with Laurett a little while, fill her in on my so-called progress. The guards had let her take Tobias into a large, open visiting room. The female guards stood nearby, within earshot, but at least the bright, airy room wasn't a prison chamber. Laurett was holding Tobias in her arms and had rocked him to sleep. He looked peaceful, and I hoped he was having a nice, secure dream in his mother's arms.

Laurett asked me quietly, almost in a whisper, "Did you take that chocolate from my place?"

I nodded, not wanting to disturb the boy's sound sleep.

She pressed me further. "Did you throw them out?"

"Not yet."

"Why not?"

"Because someone messed around with them."

Laurett's face showed that she sensed my suspicion of her. "Vannos, I didn't do it. I hated my man, but I loved him too much to kill him."

A familiar kind of pain, I thought. These days it had a new name—codependency—but it was really just plain old-fashioned chemical attraction to a certain kind of person, the kind of attraction that's genetically immutable, like with me and Rafik. Or Branco.

"Those chocolates are seconds," she said, interrupting my mental meanderings. "They are damaged, that's all."

"Then why were you so worried about the police finding them?"

"They look for anything once they get the idea that you be guilty."

I knew that all too well. The phrase "innocent until proven guilty" didn't mean much if the cops suspected you.

"Laurett, you remember those special truffles, the ones with the extra decorations at the party?"

"Sure. . . ." she replied cautiously.

"Is it possible you mixed them up that night?"

"I never did. I told you, Mr. Kingsley was getting the almond one, and—"

"I know, but maybe that argument with Mary Phinney got you confused."

"No!" she said emphatically, causing Tobias to stir in her arms.

"Laurett, I found out that Prentiss Kingsley is allergic to

almonds. He'd never take that flavor. The almond one was for
Dan Doherty."

She stared at me in silence. After a few minutes of contem-
plation, she asked quietly, "You mean I made a mistake?"

I nodded. "I'm afraid so, but it almost doesn't matter now.
You should be out of here soon."

"How?"

"Yesterday someone fired some shots at Liz Carlini."

"At Miss Lisa?"

I nodded.

"They get her?"

"No, but later on someone got Dan Doherty."

"Young Danny is dead?"

I nodded.

This news hit her hard. I'd carelessly forgotten that, being
in jail, Laurett wouldn't have heard about the killing. As for me,
coming directly from Branco's office, I had all the delivery finesse
of a ten-ton dumpster. As it turned out, Laurett had always had
a soft spot in her heart for Danny, and had felt protective toward
him. After hearing about his death, she broke down and cried
quietly. For the briefest instant I wondered how far her protective feeling might have gone. True, Laurett *had* made the last-
minute substitution of truffles. And true, she *had* confused the
flavors. And true, she *had* accidentally killed Trek by leaving him
that poisoned truffle. Was it remotely true that she'd also intended the cyanide-laced chocolate for someone else that night?
But then that pointed the way to Liz Carlini or Prentiss Kingsley.
Had Laurett intended to kill one of them? That was nonsense,
wasn't it? Yesterday's threat to Liz Carlini and the killing of Dan
Doherty had occurred with Laurett still in detention. Zounds! I
was so desperate for answers, I was even losing my focus on who
were suspects and who were victims and who were friends.

When Laurett stopped crying, I asked her what she knew
about John Lough. Since Liz Carlini had planted some bad seeds
about him in my mind, I wanted to get another opinion.

Laurett replied, "All I know is he's very religious."

And I thought, It's a short step from killing the soul to killing the body.

"But, honey, you're just chasing after smoke if you go after John Lowe." She smiled at the misnomer. "You go after the fire, and that is Mary Phinney."

"I know you don't like her, Laurett, but that's not enough."

Laurett held Tobias close to her and smiled even broader. "She's the one," she said simply, like a prophet. "She's the one who wants everything the way it was for the last five hundred years. She wants everything to stay the same. And she hates me because I know better. I got that job."

"You need proof," I said, sounding like Branco.

"Proof? You want proof? Why you think she got connected up with John Lowe in the first place? You think they're Romeo and Juliet?" She guffawed at her own joke.

"More like Mr. and Mrs. Macbeth, I'd say."

"Who?"

"Shakespeare traversed all kinds of couplings."

Laurett looked puzzled. "It's money, Vannos. And if you want to find the one who is controlling things, you go after Mary Phinney. You always go after the woman."

Laurett had ranted about her before. But then, sometimes even the most biased opinions are founded on incontrovertible truths. Maybe Laurett sensed something that I was unaware of. Or maybe she was just trying to mislead me. Maybe it was time to pay another visit to Gladys Gardner myself. This time I'd assert myself with more focus, maybe even get my hands into the old dame's chocolate recipes.

Maybe, maybe, maybe.

I left Laurett with some more comforting lies about her imminent release. Then she woke Tobias up and I took him back with me to the shop.

15

CHERCHEZ LA FEMME

Back at Snips, Nicole had bought Tobias another new toy, an exotic "spatial creativity" construction set from Sweden. It bore no resemblance to the toys of my youth, where construction sets were limited to piles of tiny plastic bricks, or miniature wooden logs, or dowels and multiholed spools, though the butch boys and the tomboys did get to tinker with perforated metal strips and screws and gears. But what Nicole had found for Tobias was a container full of small plastic beads of infinite colors and of three basic styles: male, female, and hermaphroditic—kind of an updated version of the old Pop-It beads. The point, apparently, was to interconnect the beads and create meshlike three-dimensional forms of any shape or size. Tobias's creation that day? A large solid rod that fit snugly into a matching cylinder. When he'd completed his masterpiece, he pumped the rod in and out so that its beaded surface rubbed noisily against the bumpy lining of the cylinder. The little monster was taking great pleasure in annoying and embarrassing both patrons and workers in the salon. And I finally understood one of the so-called dangers of sex education: The playful and innocent fantasies of a young mind might be too disturbing to the calcified experiences of the cynical adult. To me, naive soul that I am, it was simply nature in action. How else was a multicelled organism going to survive unless its genetic programming persisted with the tried-and-true rod-in-tunnel algorithm?

Seeing his progressive aptitude with toys, I remarked to Nicole, "Perhaps it's time to teach him how to read."

"Too late," was her quick reply. "He's already wormed his way through a few of my volumes."

"Picture books?"

"Some."

"Can he actually read?"

"He follows with his finger, but he doesn't move his lips."

"Maybe he's faking. Some people are pretty good pretenders."

"He struggles, darling, but he makes almost perfect sense when he reads aloud."

I wondered if Tobias's intelligence should be guided and nurtured more carefully. "Maybe there's a place for gifted children we can send him?"

"Stanley, do you know what those places charge?"

"Couldn't he get a scholarship from the Snips Charitable Trust?"

"Charity begins at home, Stanley, which for the time being is *chez vous.*"

"Doll, can't you at least use the familiar form, *toi?*"

"*Toi vous,* then," she said. "You have a customer."

I went to work on a familiar head of curly, dark brown hair. The young woman who owned it had spent years trying to chemically relax the natural curl. When that proved futile, she opted to keep it short, below the curl line. When she finally came to me, I offered another solution. Why fight nature? I suggested that she abstain from chemicals and let the hair grow out. A masterful, layered cut would use the hair's own weight to help keep a style in the desired shape. An added bonus was the liveliness and springiness exuded by happy hair—hair that is pampered instead of chemically disciplined.

During a free moment I checked the appointment book, which showed another short break in my schedule that afternoon, just what I wanted to see. I planned to slip out unseen by Nicole. In my absence, Ramon could handle any walk-ins. It would be good for him to learn to handle all contingencies, especially if he intended to usurp my position. So when Nicole took Tobias out for a late lunch, I followed them shortly after.

My destination? Charlestown and the Gladys Gardner world chocolate headquarters.

Alas, my field trip was interrupted at the outset. Waiting outside the shop on Newbury Street, straddling a big red motorcycle, was Rafik. He was dressed in high leather—boots, jeans, jacket, gauntlets, and cap—all shiny black in the silvery afternoon light of an overcast winter sky. He waved to me and beckoned me with a leather-gloved hand. Naturally, I went.

He was grinning. "When I will see you again?"

"You see me now."

"I mean together, like last night."

"You were so eager to leave—"

"Is not true. See how I feel?" He laid his big black-gloved hand on the inside of his thigh, where the leather was indiscreetly being stretched from underneath.

"Not here, Rafik," I said, but I was pleased that his love barometer indicated fair weather ahead. Still, I wasn't ready for a round of boy-toy jousting in front of the shop in the midday light.

"Rafik, what happened with Danny?"

He started the motorcycle. "Get on."

"Tell me."

He shook his head. "Get on."

What's a fella to do? I got on.

"Where you are going now?" he asked.

"Charlestown, the chocolate factory."

"I take you," he said. "Hold here." He placed my arms around his waist and pressed them firmly into his belly. He turned his head back to me, winked, and added, *"Comme ça."* Then without another word he pulled the big red machine out into traffic and hauled us off toward Charlestown. Just before we turned onto Storrow Drive, at the stoplight, he moved my arms lower down, so that I was holding onto him below the belt line. The whole experience—the powerful engine roaring beneath us, the breathtaking speed at which he drove, the firm strength of his body in my arms, the scent of his leather garments, the memory of him in bed—it was all, simply, sex.

At the factory, he let me off outside the parking lot, on the street. "Why don't you drive in?" I asked.

He shook his head. "Maybe they tell the police. Maybe they say I kill Dunny."

"Did you?"

"No."

"Then what happened?"

"If I tell you, you will hate me."

"What I hate are lies, Rafik."

He stared at me. He looked down. He looked back at me. He looked away. Back to me. Opened his lips. Smiled.

"I tell you, Stani. I trust you."

Ah, the dark-eyed charmer!

He hesitated another moment, then got off the bike. He stood before me, faced me directly and said, "I make love with Dunny before they kill him."

Did I have the right to ask why? Does anyone?

"I want to show him I still care, even if he hate me."

The original kiss-of-death.

"Then you must know who killed him, Rafik."

"No. We were alone. Mr. Kingsley was running."

"You didn't see anyone?"

"No. I leave him after we make love."

"Like with me."

He paused, weighing how much he should say. "No," he said. "Not like you." Then he almost snarled. "Dunny say I rape him."

"Did you?" I was sounding like Nicole now.

"I don't rape him. *C'est fini!*"

"*C'est* dead, Rafik."

He pulled me close to him and thrust his hips hard against mine, right there, out on the street in Charlestown, where the daylight and the sounds around us were eclipsed by our closeness, our warmth, our breath, our mouths, and the scent and texture of black leather. All that remained from the other world was the wind in our ears.

When he pulled away and broke the spell, he said, "I am sorry for him."

"So am I."

As I let go of him, I felt a hard, heavy object under his jacket just below his shoulder. With a shudder I realized it was a gun.

"Why do you have that?" I asked.

"To protect us."

"From what?"

"If they kill Dunny, mebbee they kill me, or you."

"Are you sure you didn't use it yourself recently?" I asked, as if he would tell me the truth.

"Ah, *non*," he said with that trademark smile of his. "I protect you, Stani."

Then he zoomed away on his red metal steed.

I zigzagged unsteadily through the parking lot toward the factory, swooning slightly from all that had just happened. On the way I spotted John Lough getting into his car. I snapped myself back to alertness and ran towards him, calling out. He turned, looked my way, squinted, frowned, then got into his car. Maybe he didn't remember me, but that wasn't about to stop me from talking to him. I got to his car just as he'd settled in and had fastened his seat belt. I knocked on the window. He looked back through the tinted glass with frightened eyes.

"It's important," I said.

He stared at me for a moment. Then, reluctantly, he lowered the window. Only then did his face soften. "I'm sorry," he said. "I didn't recognize you. One can't be too careful in this neighborhood. You never know who might accost you."

"I'd like to talk to you."

He seemed to be in a hurry. "I hope it's not about that incident the other day."

"It depends on which incident you're referring to."

"You and your nephew. I apologized to both of you, and as far as I'm concerned, the matter is settled."

"That's not why I'm here, Mr. Lough."

"Then what do you want? I don't have much time."

"Do you have time for murder?"

"What do you mean by that?"

"Dan Doherty was killed out at your brother's place in Abigail yesterday. I thought you might know something about it."

"I most certainly do not. Young man, I don't even believe you. If such a thing did happen, Prentiss would have notified me."

"It did happen, Mr. Lough, and the mechanic in Abigail said he saw you in town yesterday."

He started the car and raced the engine. Then he put it in gear too soon, causing the big car to jolt sharply against the parking brake. It stalled.

I said, "You didn't care much for Danny, did you?"

"I don't have time for this," he muttered, and started the car again.

As he backed the car out of its stall, I followed along, still trying to provoke some facts out of him.

"Why did you hate Danny? Were you jealous of Prentiss?"

He jammed the brake on. "What did you say?"

"Maybe you were jealous of your brother's friendship with Dan Doherty."

John Lough set the parking brake again, then got out of the car and came toward me. "If you insist on insulting me, you'll pay the consequences."

"Are you going to kill me too?"

"Stop saying that. I didn't kill anybody."

"Then why are you acting so guilty?"

"I am not acting guilty. That young devil was creating a problem."

"What kind of problem?"

"You know what I'm talking about."

"Refresh my memory."

"He was trying to destroy Prentiss. He was going about it methodically and persistently. It's no wonder that Prentiss was losing his senses."

"Dan Doherty and your brother were friends, that's all."

"Don't try to protect him. I know what kinds of things he

made Prentiss do out there at the summer house. It's an abomination."

"Did you see them?"

"Yes, I saw them."

"Where?"

"Everywhere. The way they'd hold onto each other, the way that young man would . . . would play up to Prentiss. It was . . . he actually *flirted* with him . . . like a woman! It was disgusting. He knew Prentiss was a confused man, and he preyed on him. It's no wonder Prentiss finally gave in to the pressure. If the young man is dead now, at least that problem is solved. Things can return to normal."

Whatever that means, I thought. "One thing isn't solved though. Dan Doherty is dead, and the killer is free. Sounds to me like you've got a good motive."

"And you have a big mouth." He opened the car door to get back inside, but I grabbed his arm and stopped him.

"Mr. Lough, I talked with the police this morning."

He turned and faced me. "So?"

"They think Dan Doherty's death was psychologically motivated, that it was a crime of passion. So maybe you did it because you secretly wanted Danny for yourself."

"If you don't keep quiet, I'll . . ." But he didn't finish his threat. Instead, he braced himself and pulled his arm back, ready to slug me.

I backed away, just out of his reach.

"You really should confess, Mr. Lough. They give you extra points if you do. And the way I figure it, by killing Danny the way you did, you can probably claim insanity. Then you can serve your sentence in a mental institution instead of a nasty prison, and you wouldn't like prison. You know what can happen there, don't you? You could end up as somebody's love blossom."

"Young man, you'll be hearing from my lawyer shortly. You're the one who should be put away, talking like that." He got into his car and drove away.

Meanwhile, I was feeling pretty smug, believing I was already in the homestretch toward nabbing Danny's killer and freeing Laurett. Why, then, hadn't I felt any danger? Logically, if John Lough had killed Danny, I should have felt some kind of dreadful energy around him. But there was none. Are killers that deceptive? I headed toward the factory feeling confused. Had I just let Danny's killer go? Or was he just some bystander who was implicated because of his family connections?

Once inside the factory, I told the security guard I wanted to see Mary Phinney. "Mary Phinney?" he asked incredulously. I nodded. He seemed surprised that anyone would call on her personally. Having already met her, I'd have to agree with him. Mary Phinney wouldn't win any popularity contests among grandmothers or candymakers.

She appeared promptly at the guard's station with her gnarled face. "Who is it?" she asked the guard, who pointed to me. Mary Phinney turned and recognized me immediately. Then she marched toward me with her heavy, thumping tread. I still wondered how such a small person could make so much noise.

"What do you want?" she barked.

I adopted her blunt style. "Dan Doherty was killed yesterday."

"Who?"

"You know who I mean. The designer for Le Jardin."

"What's it to me?" She turned to walk away, but I hadn't even begun with her. I had to hook her and get her back, and I had to do it fast.

I said, "I was just talking to your boyfriend."

Mary Phinney paused in her steps.

"I mean Mr. Lough," I said in mock apology. "He admitted he knew all about Danny's death."

Mary Phinney looked to see if the guard had overheard me. Then she said, "We'd better talk inside." She led me through the mechanized assembly lines, which were cheerfully producing hundreds of bunnies and chicks and eggs from an insidious brown sludge that resembled industrial waste more than chocolate.

She took me to John Lough's office, the glass-enclosed cubicle that overlooked most of the production floor from all four sides. Through the panes of chocolate-speckled glass I could see machinery outside whirling and twirling and wrapping masses of brown Easter creatures that would eventually melt and stain and sicken many unsuspecting buyers.

In the relative quiet of the office she asked, "When did you talk to John?"

"Just now, out in the parking lot. He sure looked guilty when he saw me."

"Maybe the sight of you made him sick."

"Why are you both pretending not to know about Dan Doherty's death? Are you in on it together?"

"That's a good one. Some queer boy gets killed and you try to blame me? Who sent you here?"

"Who else?" I shrugged. "The police."

"What?"

I continued the lie. "Sure. I'm a deputy detective for the Boston Police. They put me on special assignment for this case."

"You?"

"Sure. To use your word, A queer gets killed, they figure maybe a queer can help find the killer. We queers come in handy for that kind of thing."

Through my queer harangue Mary Phinney was stealthily opening one of the drawers in the desk. Then she reached deep inside, snaking her hand furtively around for something familiar. But her search was futile and it vexed her. "Where the hell is it?" she said. She crouched down and peered into the far, dark reaches of the big drawer. Then she jammed her small arm into the drawer, past the elbow, almost to the shoulder. Still nothing. When she sat up again, she opened another drawer and pulled out a crumpled old pack of unfiltered cigarettes. She lit one and puffed nervously—which quickly filled the air with an acrid, yellowish cloud.

"You know," she said through the smoke screen she'd created around herself, "with people like you and that Doherty boy, it's really no loss. Oh, I know the liberals all make a fuss, saying what they think they're supposed to, all trying to sound like they accept it all. But everybody knows in their hearts that the world's a better place without you and your kind."

"That's not a very Christian attitude, Miss Phinney."

"It's Mrs. Phinney. I told you, my husband's dead."

My sympathy went out to him, since to my mind no mortal could have long survived the Mary Phinney conjugal experience.

I said, "But can't you see how Dan Doherty helped the whole company, including you, with all the work he did for Le Jardin?" Was I actually defending a dead fairy for his design talents?

"Don't you talk to me about the company. I've been here all my life, ever since Helen Kingsley ran it herself, the way it should have been run. I know what's good for this place, and it isn't some artiste coming in here and changing the way everything looks. What's so good about it? What was wrong with the way things were? I never got what I was entitled to, and now you people all come in and try to take over. Well we don't need any more niggers and fairies here, so get out."

Mary Phinney gazed over her bifocals with a lizardlike stillness. Part of me wanted to scream at her, even hit her. But then I'd be sinking to her level, wouldn't I? I shook my head sadly.

"You're wrong," I said.

"No, *you're* wrong. That little pansy wormed his way into the family and connived to get some of the money when Mr. Kingsley died. That money should go where it rightfully belongs—to John Lough, Mr. Kingsley's brother."

"Half brother," I corrected.

"They had the same father. That makes them brothers."

"Still, Prentiss Kingsley has a right to divide his estate however he wants."

"Not if his mind is unsound. Don't you know the first words of a will? *Being of sound mind.* You have to be of sound mind when you write your will. And that means you don't leave your company to a conniving young gigolo."

"Gigolo isn't—"

"Why do you think we've been talking with the lawyers all

this time? There was no way we'd let that happen. That boy was evil, I tell you, evil. You all are."

"We are not evil."

"You are, and you deserve everything you get." Mary Phinney got up from her chair. "You get out of here before I have you thrown out. I don't want you in this place again. You poison the air just by being here."

"You should talk about poison, with that sloppy job you did on the truffles last Sunday."

"I'll get a restraining order on you. You and your equal rights. I'm fed up with it. You'll all burn in hell, believe me. I pray for it."

I can tell when I'm not welcome, so I left her office. I headed back to the shop, but the ride back on the MTA's Orange Line only got me more depressed. Mary Phinney's irrational words and hatred echoed the horrible rantings and abuses of my youth. I thought I'd finally emerged from that dark, doubtful period of my life—somewhat scarred, to be sure, but free of all the guilt that had been electroplated onto me by church and state. Now, though, someone was again accusing me of crimes against Nature and God, and all the old fires were being stoked again. I said my mantra, but it had little effect. All I wanted to do was throw my so-called crimes and perversions directly into Mary Phinney's face. It's no wonder that the art produced by a repressed culture is often so angry.

And I was still left with the same questions I'd started out with: Who killed Dan Doherty? Was Trek Delorean's death at the reception really meant for Dan, or for Prentiss Kingsley? Why did the killer switch from poison to a gun? Could John Lough kill a person the way Danny had been killed? Could anyone? Would he have done something like that just to reinstate his claim to the Kingsley estate? It didn't seem a sufficient motive for that kind of killing. Mary Phinney's religious vehemence almost seemed a more believable one, at least for the moment, while I was still hot for revenge.

16

MY HEART BELONGS
TO DADDY

When I got back to the shop, Nicole and Tobias had long since returned from lunch.

"Where were you?" she asked, slightly vexed.

"I took a break, doll."

"You had a visitor, a very sexy Mediterranean."

"Branco?"

"No, the other one—Lance Leather, with his big red machine."

"You mean Rafik?"

"Uh-huh."

"He's not Mediterranean. He's Armenian."

"Aren't they the same thing?"

"No, doll, but you'd still approve. His family owns an export business in Paris. It's your kind of stuff, too—caviar, foie gras, pâté, truffles."

"Then marry him, Stanley. He sounds delicious." Nicole smiled lasciviously. "And to think he's a world-class lover to boot."

"Boots? We haven't tried that scene yet."

"You will. I can feel it under my fingernails."

"Is *that* where a woman's intuition is?"

Nicole's response was an enigmatic smile.

I wondered why Rafik had returned to the shop though, since he'd seen me earlier.

"Did he leave a message, doll?"

"He asked if you were involved with anyone."

"And you said?"

Nicole cocked her head slightly and replied, "I told him that you and the lieutenant were an item."

As if on cue, Branco's familiar tall, dark, and handsome figure entered through the shop's front door. He gave Nicole a warm hello, but when he greeted me, it was cold air.

"I just received copies of the police reports from Abigail. The bullets that killed Dan Doherty match the ones we pried out of the walls at the Kingsley house in Chestnut Hill."

"So it was the same gun."

Branco smirked. "You've seen too much TV. We know it's the same type of weapon, but we haven't been able to narrow it down to exactly the same gun."

"It's still good news though, since it proves Laurett wasn't involved in either shooting."

Reluctantly he conceded. "You're right about that."

"So when are you releasing her?"

"Within the hour."

"You finally saw the light."

Branco's face didn't move. "No. We completed our investigation on her, and given the recent evidence, the original charges have been dropped. She's been advised to remain in town."

"What finally convinced you to let her go?" I was hopeful that I, and not Charles, had ultimately been responsible for Laurett's release.

"Look, Kraychik, I don't have to tell you any of this. I thought you'd want to know so you can tell her boy, since you're taking care of him."

Nicole interjected, "Why don't you tell him yourself, Lieutenant? He's playing in the waiting area."

"It's this way," I said, and led Branco to where Tobias was playing—only he'd fallen asleep on one of the big, comfortable chairs. "He's all yours, Lieutenant," I said coyly. I doubted that relating the news to a young boy about his mother's incarceration was part of Branco's civil-code repertoire. I glanced at Nicole and caught her switching her attention between me and the cop as he approached Tobias.

"Son," Branco said softly, and I felt my throat tighten. Then he knelt down and put his big hand gently on Tobias's shoulder. "Tobias, wake up, boy. It's good news." Tobias stirred and opened his sleepy eyes. Branco said, "It's about your mother. She's coming home today."

Tobias rubbed his eyes, then threw his arms around Branco's neck. I expected Branco to be embarrassed and awkward about it, but instead he picked the boy up and held him close in a sustained embrace.

Standing beside me, Nicole sighed deeply and murmured, "Quite a scene."

I muttered back, "Damn lucky little shit."

"Jealous?"

"Yes."

Branco put Tobias down, then stood up and faced Nicole and me. "If you want, I'll take him back with me. It'll probably be easier for his mother that way."

"That's fine, Lieutenant," I replied, my own voice a little raspy with inexpressible emotion.

Branco nodded and said, "Good." Then, seeing that the shop's customers had been watching the touching moment between him and Tobias, he asked, "Is there a place we can talk privately?"

"Sure, Lieutenant. There's the notorious back room."

As I led him away, he turned to Nicole. "I'd like you to come along too, Miss Albright."

"Gladly, Lieutenant," she said, and stepped briskly up alongside him. I wondered, Does Branco want a witness? Or a chaperone?

Once in the quiet confines of the storage room, he asked us, "Either one of you seen Rafik Panossian today?"

Simultaneously Nikki and I replied, "When today?"

Branco aimed at me. "Since you and him spent the night together."

"Well, yes. . . ." I stalled. Make 'em beg for the awful truth, especially when their grammar's faulty.

"Where?"

"Here, at the shop. Out front, on the street. In fact, if you'd been here, Lieutenant, you could have arrested us in flagrante."

"When was that?" exclaimed Nicole.

"Just after you took Tobias out for lunch."

"So you were out with Rafik?" she demanded.

"No, doll. He just gave me a ride. I went alone to the chocolate factory." But her look implied doubt. I turned to Branco. "Lieutenant, I still think you're going after the wrong person."

"Just tell me where I can find Panossian."

I was tempted to suggest the Epicure Shop at Neiman-Marcus, where Rafik's family name appeared on the most exclusive imported items. Instead, I said, "I honestly don't know, but it doesn't matter, Lieutenant. He's not the one. You'd do better to question those two people from the Gladys Gardner factory, John Lough and Mary Phinney."

"On what grounds?"

"On the grounds that they were both relieved that Dan Doherty was dead and, if I may quote them, 'out of the way.' Those are the words both of them used." I knew they hadn't said it exactly like that, but I had to convince Branco to go after them.

Branco said, "Thanks for the tip, but we have our suspect, and he's the man you insist on protecting. I hope I don't have to haul you in too, for withholding evidence or for aiding and abetting a criminal."

"Are you using a script, Lieutenant?"

With Rafik I'd finally found someone who was vaguely compatible, someone I might be able to spend a romantic Valentine's Day with, and now it turned out he was wanted by the police. Oh, I know I was suspecting him too, at first. But it's one thing to imagine your newfound love-thing harboring a dark, secret life during your time apart, but it's another thing to have the cops after his butt, and yours, as an accomplice. Was I so lonely that I'd date a felon? As the French say, I was in deep honey.

"Lieutenant, I'm telling you everything I know. If you want, I can make up some stuff that you'd rather hear me say."

Branco grumbled, "Never mind." He turned to leave.

"Wait," I said. "There's something else, something that might finally convince you to look in another direction."

Branco's eyes glittered angrily, which only encouraged me to continue my Nancy Drew shtick. If Branco wasn't going to treat me like an equal—like a man—I was perfectly willing to take on another role.

I continued, "I know it's irregular, but is there any way to get a look at Prentiss Kingsley's will?"

Branco shook his head and pulled his lips tight. "We're not the FBI."

"Aren't you kissing cousins?"

"We can't violate peoples' privacy like that."

"Not even with a court order?"

"You don't get a court order just because you're curious about something. You have to convince a judge. You need a good reason for that."

"There is a good reason. I think the key to this whole case lies in Prentiss Kingsley's will, something to do with including Dan Doherty as an heir. Even John Lough and Mary Phinney knew about it."

Branco said, "You've been reading too many mysteries."

"Not so," I replied. "I am my own special creation."

Branco grunted, then walked out of the back room and returned to the shop.

Nicole clucked her tongue at me. "You'll never win his heart that way, Stani."

"Who cares about his heart? It's probably as hard and black as coal anyway."

"Then with time and the right kind of pressure, it could become a diamond."

"Doll, you're going to make me spit up."

But having seen Branco's earlier scene with Tobias, part of

me wanted to believe Nicole's prediction. My optimistic, romantic, trousseau-ridden self thought maybe, just maybe. . . . Then
I snapped myself back to cynical sobriety. "Let's go say good-bye
to Tobias."

We went back into the shop to find Lieutenant Branco
helping Tobias into his overcoat and boots. Sproing! went my
heart again. Branco stood up, then in one strong swift motion, he
lifted Tobias and perched him on his shoulders, straddling the
boy's legs around his strong neck. Daddy! He turned to Nicole
and me and gave a slight upward jerk with his head. That was
Branco's version of a fond farewell. Meanwhile, Tobias giggled
and waved happily from his high vantage point. Glorious steed
and young knight departed the shop through the front door as
customers waved them off. Calm sea and prosperous voyage, I
thought. Tobias's little voice yelled, "Bye, Uncle Stan. Bye,
Uncle Nick."

Nikki gave me a cross-eyed look. "Uncle Nick?"

"He's democratic about gender."

"Then why not Auntie Stan?" she asked, then nudged me.
"Back to work."

The rest of the afternoon flew by, and I was busy every
minute. My friend Francesca, who manages Chez-Chez, a local
cabaret, dropped by to invite me out with a gaggle of gabbers to
a special Valentine's season show that night. I hesitated, then
realized I was no longer a foster parent. I was free again. I would
celebrate. I would even shed the guise of Rafik's forlorn lover
and Branco's misunderstood, self-appointed deputy. I would
have my own good time.

After we closed the shop, Nicole and I settled in the back
room for a quick drink and a cigarette. A cigarette for her, that
is. I'd already tried in vain to smoke. No matter the glamorous
image it was supposed to project, it was too much trouble getting
used to it all—the coughing, the dizziness, and the yucky after-
breath.

Nicole lit a slender, rose-colored cigarette and drew the
smoke in deeply. I did envy that first drag, the obvious pleasure
it gave her. As she let the smoke slip from her lips, she said,

"Now that Laurett and her son are back together, you don't have to be involved with the case anymore, right?"

"You bet, doll. It's back to work and play for me. That, and the dependable love and affection of a Burmese cat. Back to the simple life."

"What about shopping?"

"Are you giving me a raise?"

Nicole ignored that. "What about Rafik? Aren't you going to try to save him now?"

I paused. "Nope."

"Doesn't love call you?"

I shook my head no. "It was just one of those things."

"But he's in trouble."

"He got himself into the mess."

Another drag of cigarette, a sip of cognac, and Nicole continued. "So no more trying to prove to the lieutenant that you're right and he's wrong?"

"No. I don't care anymore. I helped Laurett this time. That's enough." I gulped at my bourbon. "I did help her, didn't I?" I was trying to recall what, if anything, I'd done to help get her released. I came up with a blank.

Nikki shrugged. "Does it matter?"

"Not tonight. I just want everything back to normal. No more cops, no more killers, no more babies. Just fun for me and the moment."

Nicole gave a knowing look. "Well, you should have fun tonight, out with the boys."

"Or the girls."

"Drag?"

"Only for the performers. They're doing scenes from *The Boyfriend*, with an all-male cast for the Valentine's gala. Speaking of which, I'd better get going."

"Have fun, darling. See you in the morning."

We kissed and I left the shop.

It was almost eight P.M. when I got home. As I climbed the stairs, I smelled dinner through my neighbor's door. My stomach grumbled and my head spun from the aroma of fresh garlic being sautéed in olive oil. I was famished, and tonight I'd have time only for some leftover pizza from Tobias's recent encampment. So much for the diet again. And I had yet to undo the ravages of work. It's not the same as, say, a trucker who's been on the road overnight, but chemically speaking, a hair stylist's body can be pretty ripe after a day of bookings and sleuthing.

I opened the door and whistled. "Honey, I'm home!" Sugar Baby greeted me with a wary look, as if expecting more torment from Tobias. "Not to worry, baby," I said. "We're alone again. The place is all yours."

I picked her up, and she licked my cheek with long, rasping strokes. I carried her on my shoulder while I listened to the answering machine. Francesca had called with some vague reason why the theater-party group was running late, which was fine with me. That gave me some extra time to unwind, even heat up the pizza. I put the cold, obtuse slab in the oven—my nuker is broken—and turned on some hot tango music. With Sugar Baby on my lap, I opened my mail: VISA had upped my credit a thousand dollars (the joke's on them); my college gay alumni club was planning a luxury winter cruise (maybe next time, guys); a psychiatrist with whom I'd once worked in a community clinic and with whom I'd shared a brief, supersexed affair was announcing the arrival of his second child with his wife in upstate New York; and a yellow slip identified a package from New Jersey waiting for me at the Back Bay Postal Annex. It was probably an extra Valentine's Day surprise from my mother, the one dependable sweetheart in my life.

My body needed a long, hot shower. First I fed Sugar, then I went into the bathroom, which is off the bedroom, and turned on the water to get it hot. On the top floor, that can sometimes mean a five-minute wait, and with the spicy tangos putting me in a better mood, I got the urge to do something silly, something to purge myself of the past few days. With each gutsy phrase of music I asked myself another question. Who needs Valentine's Day anyway? Who needs romance? Who needs Rafik? Who needs Branco? Who needs parenthood? Who needs clients? Who needs corpses? Who needs anyone? So I put on a little show for myself in front of the large mirror on the bedroom closet door.

Shoes and socks came off first, with seductive grace and timing—a prelude for what was about to happen. I unbuttoned my shirt and twisted my torso so that the front edges of the starched cotton rubbed against my nipples. That was good for quite a while, about one full chorus of music. Then I slid the shirt off my shoulders one sleeve at a time until it was hanging from my waist. I unfastened my pants and let gravity pull them down my legs along with the shirt, while I bumped my hips to the music. I stepped out of the rumpled pile and danced around the bedroom. Sugar Baby watched with a wide-eyed, bewildered look that said, "What's going on in here?" My strip show was weird enough even to pull her attention from her food bowl in the kitchen. It was time for the big moment—the briefs. I teased myself, pulling each side down and up to expose a hip or cheek, then covering it again. Finally I turned my back to the mirror and literally leaped out of my undies. I flung them high and did a pirouette to finish facing the mirror. My stocky body looked okay, even with the extra "winter" pounds it seemed determined to carry throughout the year. The smooth pink skin showed the faintest hint of last summer's tan line. Though not cultivated, the muscles have good tone and definition. I do extra things through-out the day, like holding in my belly whenever I shampoo a client. That helps keep it flat. The legs are good—my best fea-ture, actually—though they're inherited, so I can't really take credit. They're real Slavic limbs with meaty, well-shaped calves springing up from highly arched feet. The thighs are full, and curved and sculpted like a dancer's, not sinewy like a runner's.

I slapped my butt in time to the music and hooted, "Olé!" The cheeks turned red where I'd hit them. And Bruno, my personal pet, stirred to new life between my legs. I looked at my face in the mirror. The newly shorn red hair stood up like a brush, and the green eyes glittered happily. The dopey grin meant I was ready for the steamy heat. Then it all crashed under a wave of Slavic melancholy. Were these antics the reason I was alone? Was I so eccentric that others didn't dare to spend private time with me? Didn't anyone else like my flavor of fun?

I got out of the shower at eight-thirty. The pizza was almost burnt, but I chewed on it anyway while I towel-dried my hair, something I forbid my clients to do. Besides, when it's as short as mine was, almost nothing can hurt it. I finished drying off, put on clean clothes, and headed out to Chez-Chez for a night of fun and frolic.

But it didn't work.

I was with friends I liked, and who liked me, yet I couldn't relax. Even the stellar performance seemed too contrived, too sophisticated, too intent on entertaining, not like my ingenuous, homegrown striptease earlier. I downed drink after drink, but that didn't help either. I was unpleasantly distracted by what had happened during the last several days. Sure, Laurett was free again, but what was going on in Abigail? Someone was after something, and they were willing to kill people to get it. Who was it? Rafik? John Lough? Mary Phinney? Liz Carlini? Prentiss Kingsley? As much as I wanted to, I couldn't shake off the effects of recent events. And yes, perhaps there was that element of wanting to show Branco up again, to prove to him that even a hairdresser is worthy to breathe the same air as the rest of humanity. Perhaps the liquor was kicking in if I could think like that.

I stayed until the end of the show, then went directly home. Francesca was concerned that I was coming down with something and suggested more liquor, but I knew it was simply mental exhaustion, which doesn't take much with me. Within minutes after arriving home and collapsing into bed, I was asleep.

17

IS THAT A GUN
IN YOUR POCKET?

Next morning, Friday, as I was leaving for the shop, I discovered outside my door yet another large, heart-shaped box of chocolate. These velvet-covered behemoths seemed to be turning up everywhere, as though Saint Valentine's theme this year was feast-or-famine, only with chocolate. I figured that Rafik had sneaked into the building again, so I called out his name in the hallway. No answer. I picked up the box—Sugar Baby had already begun her sniffing, chin-rubbing inspection of it—and took it back inside. Attached to the top was a small envelope. I opened it and read the note inside. "I love you," it said, in small, neat printing. No signature. A pleasant, if unoriginal sentiment. If you loved me, pal, you wouldn't try to fatten me up so much. The box seemed extra heavy, which made me extra curious about its contents. Perhaps it was a slab of fine *couverture* for me to gorge on. That's the highest quality chocolate, used only for coating . . . and decadent noshing. As I slipped the ribbon off the box, I promised myself I'd get a fresh start on the diet the first of March, or the first day of spring, or the first of April, or sometime.

Inside the box was a gun.

So much for my cocoa butter fix. I called Nikki and explained that I'd be a little late getting to the shop, since I wanted to take the newfound evidence to Branco. She sounded almost relieved that I was once again embroiled in the case. After all, it would give us something to argue about, which is probably the basis of our friendship.

I took the loaded chocolate box to Lieutenant Branco. When I got in to see him, I told him breathlessly that I had something important for him. He glanced dubiously at the heart-shaped box, then spoke with a cool, condescending smile.

"I already told you once, I can't accept gifts. It's against regulations."

"Lieutenant, it wasn't a gift last time, and it isn't one now." If the notion persisted in his mind, was he secretly hoping for a gift from me? And if I gave it, would he take it, or refuse it? Was I projecting? Maybe it was simply Branco's presumption that *all* people are doomed to worship him.

He clenched his jaw and remained silent.

I continued, "You might want to make an exception to your rules today, Lieutenant."

"Kraychik, your games get tiresome."

Arrogant bastard! I lifted the lid to the box, so that the carefully padded contents showed. Branco saw the gun, but maintained his composure.

"Where'd you get it?"

"It was outside my apartment this morning, just exactly like this, in the box. I thought you might want to know about it."

Branco took the box and studied the gun inside without a word—and without touching it, of course.

I said, "Maybe it's the gun that killed Dan Doherty and fired the shots at Liz Carlini."

Silence. Using a pencil, he lifted the gun out and sniffed at the barrel. A tiny nod. "Strange coincidence," he said. "Someone just called to report a missing gun."

"Who?"

No answer.

"Mary Phinney?" I asked. "John Lough?"

Branco grunted. "Was there anything else with this?"

I reluctantly showed him the love note too. He studied it

carefully, for quite a few moments, then raised his eyebrows and said, "Looks like you have an admirer."

"All my suitors send guns and poison."

Branco called the lab to have someone pick the parcel up, then turned back to me. "Now that you've relinquished the weapon, why don't you tell me where to find him?"

"Who?"

"Your lover."

"I don't have a lover."

"You know whom I mean."

Who, went my tic for proper case. "There's no way to prove Rafik left the gun."

"Who else has been at your apartment recently?"

"Tobias Cole was there, but that's back when I was still a pederast."

"I want facts, not sarcasm."

"If you want my cooperation, Lieutenant, you get all of me."

Branco grunted again. I figured he'd repressed most of his urges to slug people into those rage-laden grunts. He'd not yet mastered the art of verbal jousts.

"For your information, Kraychik . . ." He paused as though savoring a secret. "There's been another victim."

"Who?"

Branco eyed me. "Can't you guess?"

"Sure, let's play twenty questions. Let's see, is it a man or a woman?"

"Cute, real cute, considering who the victim is."

"If you don't like cute, Lieutenant, why don't you talk with the same directness you expect from everyone else?"

"All right, then. Prentiss Kingsley was found by the Gloucester police early this morning."

That stopped me. "Where?"

"In his car at a roadside rest stop, a place known to be frequented by . . ."

Long pause.

I prompted him, "Big burly truckers?"

Branco nodded. "It's the kind of place you guys like to go to."

"Don't assume we all check our dipsticks the same way."

Branco sat back in his chair and crossed his arms behind his head. He grinned sadistically. "Gun was fired right into his mouth." He waited for my reaction, but I sat mute. "Think the killer was trying to tell us something?"

"Like what?"

"Seems to me there's a similar kind of sexual theme operating in both killings."

"You mean because a gun was inserted into a body opening?"

"Sounds like sex to me," he said with a cruel glint in his eye.

"Is that how cops do it?"

He bolted himself straight up and stuck out his jaw—all man, no nonsense. "You know what I mean."

"No, I don't. I thought there was more to sex than putting something in."

He let out a cynical little snort. "Maybe," he said, avoiding my eyes.

"Could the death have been suicide?"

"Funny you should ask. There was a note."

"Which explains your scrutiny of the card that came with this gun."

"You don't miss much, do you?"

"Lieutenant, you obviously didn't have to decipher the message, so it must have been the handwriting."

"What do you think, Kraychik? Suicide?"

"Prentiss Kingsley did seem despondent about Danny's death."

"Enough to kill himself?"

"Maybe he really loved Danny."

Branco shook his head. "Can't imagine it."

"What? Feeling that strongly about someone?"

"No. What it's like to blow your brains out. Whole back of his skull—"

"Why do you relish all the gore, Lieutenant?"

Branco sat forward again and stared coldly at me. "I don't relish it. It's my job. I got used to it. Life isn't all those pretty girls' heads you spend your days playing with."

"They're not all girls, Lieutenant, and they're certainly not all pretty. And for your information, that's *my* work. There's a place for it, and I'm good at it. At least no one gets bullied at Snips." Well, almost no one, I thought, recalling the occasional S/M blow-drying session with certain clients.

"Kraychik, I know you're protecting Rafik Panossian. I'm prepared to detain you on that alone, but right now you're more useful out on the street, where you'll undoubtedly lead us to him. After all, you just handed over what is probably the murder weapon."

"You said you can't make a positive identification on a gun."

Just then, a woman from the lab arrived to take the gun and the parcel down for analysis.

When she left, Branco said with a twisted little grin, "I can't, but the lab will. And just for your information, we have an APB out for your lover, so if you know where he is, you have a responsibility to tell us."

"He is not my lover! We had sex, that's all. You act as though we're married already."

"Isn't it all the same thing?"

"Sounds like your definitions of sex, love, and marriage are a little confused, Lieutenant." Look who was talking.

Branco banged his fists on his desk. "Fool! You think you're smart playing around with a killer, don't you?" He shook his head disdainfully. "Your kind gets feeling a little too cocky once you're out of the closet. Maybe it's time to come out of the clouds, Kraychik."

"I'll remember that, Lieutenant."

"You're playing with a killer."

The phone on his desk rang. Branco grabbed it and listened intently. Then his face lit up into one big gloating smile. He hung up and announced his victory.

"We got him, no thanks to you. You can go now."

"Where is he? Can I see him?"

Branco dismissed me with a brusque wave of his hand. "Go. Now."

"I was just leaving anyway, Lieutenant, to flutter back to the shop and play in the blond hair of some pretty girlie sex object."

Grunt went the cop.

I left Station E and headed back to Snips. With Rafik caught now, I felt a sudden urge to help him. My own confusion of sex and love was fast becoming the confusion of sex and crime. By the time I arrived at the shop my anger had grown to the point that I tromped in and greeted Nicole by yelling, "Goddam Branco and his stupid macho brain!"

Nicole replied quietly, "Seems to be contagious."

"Damn it, Nikki, he drives me crazy. It's as though his brain is cement. He gets these ideas, and once they're set in there, nothing else can get by them into what's left of the soft, grey part of his brain. He doesn't think."

Nicole cooed softly, "There, there, darling. Those manly brutes are all the same. I've always told you to pursue the more sensitive types, but you never listen."

"Like Charles, you mean?"

"Now, Stanley, don't turn on me just because you're upset."

"I'm not turning on you. I'm turning on Charles. His brain can't be calcified—it's made of stainless steel."

Without further comment, Nicole placed her reading glasses back onto the bridge of her artfully remodeled nose, done back in the time of talented surgeons, in the days before you selected your new nose on a computer screen. "You have a client waiting," she said coolly.

I leaned toward her and whispered, "Prentiss Kingsley was killed this morning."

Nicole shrieked. Then just as she had done the day before, she pulled me toward the back room for some privacy. Once inside, she asked what had happened, and I recounted my earlier visit with Branco. I didn't believe Prentiss Kingsley's death was suicide, and I was disturbed by Branco's blasé attitude about the horrors of death.

Nikki remarked, "It's an occupational hazard, darling—just like you with your clients' sense of style."

"The difference is, doll, I *do* know what looks good on them better than they do."

She asked, "Are you going to rescue Rafik now?"

"What else can I do? Branco wants to fry him. I just want to continue our import-export arrangement."

"Sounds like you're in love."

I looked directly at her. "No, doll. I am not."

"Good."

"It's nice to see that you still believe me."

"I want to believe you, Stanley. That's why it's easy to."

That made me wonder if I was using the same logic with Rafik. I *wanted* him to be innocent, which made it easy for me to believe it was so, despite all my suspicions to the contrary.

Nicole seemed to read my confused thoughts. "You know what I think, Stani? I think you should get back to work and concentrate on that. Don't force things. Let matters resolve themselves." Then she added, "And you'll be safer too."

"I thought you wanted me back on the case."

"I changed my mind. Don't resist. Go with the flow."

I smiled at Nicole, then hugged her. "You know, doll, if you keep talking like that, you might want to sell the shop and go to California to start a self-actualization clinic."

"Chaz has mentioned it, actually."

"Oh, no!" I wailed. "Get me to the sinks, quick."

For the rest of the afternoon I was busy, interrupted only by a surprise visit from Liz Carlini, who'd just driven in from Abigail. She tore into the shop, breathless, and insisted on speaking to me. Fortunately, I was in the middle of a cut, not tricky chemical work. I took her to a private corner of the shop, near the changing rooms. I noticed that she looked peaked, with dark circles around her eyes. She related the horrible news of her husband's death, and how she was afraid she was next in line to be killed. She looked and sounded desperate and scared—borderline hysteria.

"Liz, I think you should talk to Lieutenant Branco."

"Vannos, I've already spent hours with the Abigail police. I'm exhausted."

"But listen to me. Branco can help you, get you some protection. Go see him in person. Tell him everything. Got that? Everything."

"What do you mean?"

"I mean all the trouble with Prentiss's will, with Danny and John Lough and Mary Phinney."

"But that's none of his business."

"It is now, Liz. You're in danger. I've tried to tell Branco what I know, but he doesn't believe me. Maybe if he hears it from you, he'll listen."

She looked at me dubiously. "Are you sure?"

"Trust me," I said solemnly. "And insist on a bodyguard too. He can arrange it." I gave her his number.

Then Liz inhaled a quick, shallow breath and lifted her shoulders tensely. She held the position for a few impatient seconds, then she let the air out in an explosive puff. I guess that was her version of deep, relaxed breathing. No inefficient mantra for Liz. She wanted her relaxation fast.

"I feel better already, just talking to you," she said, but I could tell it was just words. She was still sending out gigavolts of nervous energy.

"Don't tell Branco I sent you. Make it sound like it's your idea, that you remembered him from being out in Chestnut Hill the other day."

She smiled, as though recalling something pleasant, which was probably the feeling of Branco's eyes admiring her legs. "Why not mention you, Vannos? Wouldn't that help?"

I paused. "I think not."

She hesitated, then said, "If you're sure."

"I'm sure. And if you want, you can call me too, either here or at home." I gave her my home phone number. "Maybe I should reserve some time for you at Alaine's studio. Sounds like you could use some pampering."

"I could use a week of it."

"I'll book you for the whole weekend. That way you can get some serious rest, and you won't be alone either."

"Vannos, what would I do without you?"

I wanted to say, You'd find another hairdresser. But instead, I said, "You know where Alaine's studio is?"

"Just down the block, isn't it?"

"Right. Get some rest there, Liz. But remember, go see Lieutenant Branco first."

"Thank you, Vannos." Suddenly she lunged at me and hugged me in an awkward embrace. "Oh, thank you!" she said, and then whispered in my ear, "I owe you."

She departed from the shop in the same wild state as when she'd entered. Nicole had overheard the entire conversation.

"She's only a customer, Stanley."

"Sometimes our services have to extend beyond the sink and the styling chair, doll."

Nicole replied, "And since your chair is still occupied, you might want to finish what you started there."

I returned to my station and finished with my customer. She was the last appointment for the day, and I was looking forward to an early cocktail with Nicole in the back room.

We closed up the shop, then went and sat together in back. With lit cigarette in one hand and cognac snifter in the other, Nicole asked, "Now what?"

"Believe it or not, doll, I don't know. Suddenly my time is all mine again."

"What about Rafik?"

"If I had a white horse and shining armor, I'd try to rescue him. But he's in jail, and I'd have to slay the whole legal system to free him." Then I gave her a hopeful look. "I don't suppose Charles would . . ."

Nicole shook her head.

"I didn't think so," I said with a droop in my voice.

"No, darling. The work for Laurett satisfied his pro bono quota."

"Now he can give his pro bono to you."

"Don't be rude."

"Your new vocabulary inspired me."

"Chaz and I do talk, you know, in those rare quiet moments between orgasms."

"Don't rub it in."

"Stanley, sometimes I think you relish your loneliness, and frankly it's becoming tiresome."

"It's out of my control."

"No, it isn't. You expect too much. You have to learn to settle for what's available."

"You should know about that."

"Why do you hate Chaz so much?"

"Because he's taking you from me."

Nicole sat motionless. The only movement in the room was the smoke spiraling upward from her cigarette. "Aren't you being unreasonable?" she asked.

"Oedipal is probably more like it," I replied. "But it seems that ever since you met him, it's been Chaz-this and Chaz-that. You spend every free moment with him. And now you're even spouting legal jargon and bragging about your sex life together. You've got the goddam Prom Queen Syndrome."

"The what?"

"That's when a high-school deb starts dating the hunky quarterback, and suddenly she's lost to the rest of the world, including family and friends. *Incommunicado in todo.*"

"Is that how I seem?" she asked with real concern.

"Forget it, Nikki. I'm just lonely and full of shit."

I gulped the last of my bourbon and got ready to leave.

"At least Liz will be safe at Alaine's studio. Whoever is on this killing spree probably won't be looking for his next victim at an urban New Age beauty clinic. And meanwhile, oblivious to the mortal world, Liz will be pampered with mineral baths and hot mud therapies, full-body massages, horticultured food, European cosmetics, and high-tech spirituality."

"And what will you do?"

"Doll, I'm going to resume my normal routine. I'm going back on the diet, I'm going to get in shape, and I'm going to find me a man."

"Don't forget to come to work tomorrow."

"After ecstasy, the laundry," I replied, and left the shop. With the responsibility of Tobias gone from my life, maybe I really could get back into the dietary regime. No more pizza and calzone, no more chocolate-covered mallowpuff treats, no more nachos and burritos, no more excuses to avoid the veggie sticks and bran crackers. I promised myself after one last gastro-splurge this weekend, I'd be good again.

The next day life resumed its so-called normal pace. I saw clients, I made them beautiful, they thanked me, and I earned some money. There was no Rafik provoking and pursuing me, no Tobias requiring attention and expecting entertainment, no Laurett hoping for release, no Branco saying no-no-no. I even went out with some friends that night. The superb Peter Arden was in town, on tour from San Francisco, along with his personal Stein-way, making a guest appearance at the Copley Plaza. All five nights were sold out, but I have clients in high places, so getting a table near the keyboard was a cinch. One brilliant moment in his program was a deconstructed version of Strauss's famous waltz, "Voices of Spring." The maestro Arden would attempt the little flourish that begins each phrase of the waltz, but he'd purposely trip over his own fingers, then lapse into a completely different number for a few bars. Then it was back to the beginning flourish for another try, only to fumble again, each time more elaborately than before. The musical joke had the audience in mirthful convulsions, especially later in the evening, when the little flourish would appear without warning in the middle of a Gershwin ballad or a Cole Porter tune. It was a night of pleasure and glamor, with martinis and starched collars and cuff links and romantic music—all part of that certain, steady, assured kind of life that most people strive to attain—a normal life.

But within twenty-four hours, I became restive and bored. Recurrent thoughts of Rafik both depressed and agitated me. I yearned for him, but I couldn't bear to go see him. He was probably having wild sex with the inmates anyway.

By Sunday night I was nearly catatonic with indecision and

doubt. That's when Liz Carlini called me at home and begged me for a special appointment early Monday morning. It was my usual day off, but she insisted that it was an emergency. She even promised to "make it worth my while." I reluctantly agreed. At least I'd be in motion and making some money.

18

GOOD-BYE, MR.
CHOCOLATE CHIPS

Early the next morning, before the shop was open for regular business, Liz Carlini arrived direct from her brief retreat at Alaine's studio. She was escorted by a hulk of solid but shapeless muscle that she introduced as her bodyguard. No name, just bodyguard. With opaque brown eyes and a tiny head stuck onto a thick neck that was broader even than his ears, he probably answered to Moose.

Liz, however, looked radiant, especially for a recent widow. It made me wonder if perhaps I shouldn't try coming up with the lordly sums that Alaine charged for the royal treatment at his studios. Yet despite the ultraexclusive services Alaine offered, Liz wanted me to style her hair. I was flattered to be the "touch of home" in her life.

"For Prentiss's memorial service," she said softly, as I led her to the changing room.

"When is it?" I asked.

"Today, this afternoon."

"So soon?"

"I made the arrangements late Friday afternoon, right after I spoke with you here."

"But aren't the police still holding his body?"

"It doesn't matter. There won't be a burial, even later. Prentiss chose cremation, so rather than let it all drag on until then, I want to settle everything as soon as possible."

A perverse thought: Were Danny and Prentiss lying near each other in the morgue?

I said, "Sometimes it's better to let the mourning expend itself, rather than hurry it or repress it."

Liz sighed morosely. "Not for me. I can't bear it. It's a nightmare, and I want to end it now. Then I'm going away for a while, and try and sort things out."

"Take your bodyguard along," I warned.

"It's all been arranged," she said knowingly.

Since we were alone in the shop, I shampooed her myself, a rare privilege usually reserved for special customers or special occasions. For Liz Carlini, the sudden deaths of her husband and her business partner certainly qualified as a special, if bleak, occasion.

She asked, "Have you seen Rafik?"

"Not for a few days," I replied as I worked up a moussy lather in her hair. I wondered why she was asking me about him. "Did you know that the police are holding him for the two killings?" I said.

"He couldn't have done it, Vannos."

"I agree," I replied, but I recalled the potential violence that always seemed to dance around him, kind of like Branco's aura too. "How well do you know him, Liz?"

"Danny's the one who knew him best, obviously. When I needed a driver, Danny brought him in and I hired him. It's too bad they wouldn't commit to each other. They made a nice couple. Rafik would probably like you too."

I smiled shyly. "We already got to first base."

My remark caused a familiar old voice to shriek inside my head, nearly piercing my eardrums from within. "Furdst bayze?" it screamed. It was my Aunt Letta, grilling me as usual in Grand Inquisition style. "Stanislav Krecik, he iss claimink you."

Liz's voice brought me back to the conscious world. "Are you going to help him, then?" she asked.

"I don't know how. It seems all I can offer him is my gut feeling." And I meant that literally.

I rinsed Liz's hair and wrapped it in a towel, then we headed to my station, where she settled herself in the styling chair. I'd already decided to do her hair in a way that would reflect tragic grief with understated flair. While she sat, I pressed my hands onto her shoulders and massaged her gently. That kind of reassuring touch can strengthen the bond between stylist and client. The muscles in her neck and shoulder were pliable and relaxed, so the time at Alaine's had been well spent.

I sectioned her hair and began cutting. At one point I glanced into the reflection of her eyes in the mirror, the strange medium by which stylist and client often communicate best. "You're doing great, Liz," I said, intending to bolster her morale. But my very words of confidence seemed to unhinge her bravery, and she let out a loud gasp.

"I'm so frightened!" I saw her fearful eyes looking back into mine through the mirror. "All this trouble started when I found out I was pregnant," she said. Her words caused me to stall my scissors mid-snip, just short of cutting what we call in the trade a "hole."

"That should make you happy," I said.

"It should have." Her eyes stared directly into the reflection of mine, and she held her head up proudly, refusing to break down. "We were both delighted, of course."

"What's the trouble then?"

"Prentiss's will." She shook her head, as though trying to wake up from a bad dream. Then she began to explain the facts with a chilly clarity that neither grief nor fear could cover. Liz Carlini did, after all, have an MBA.

"Despite my dear husband's limited vision, his board of directors had made some shrewd investments and acquisitions over the years. As a result, and almost without knowing it, Prentiss controlled a multinational fortune with Gladys Gardner Industries." The name alone implied the dregs of smelting rather than delectable food items. Liz continued, "So there's now a whole new level of wealth in the estate."

"At least there's that," I answered, not too sympathetically. "But I still don't see the problem, especially now that you'll have an heir."

Liz Carlini's body responded with such intensity that her hair actually bristled. While I recombed it to relax it, she said, "I miscarried last week." Then for the first time in all the recent horrors, she broke down and sobbed loudly. I stopped working on her hair and put my hands on her shoulders again. She explained through her tears, "It happened right after Danny's death. I was working too hard with Le Jardin, and then his dying just drove me over the edge. I feel as though it's my fault."

"It's nobody's fault, Liz."

"With all this bad luck, I feel like there's an evil spell on me. In the old days they'd probably burn me or chop off my head."

"Not if they saw the artwork I'm creating with it."

Liz giggled softly through her tears, and it helped her stop sobbing. Without further comment, I handed her a tissue. When she regained her composure, I continued with my brilliant creation.

"So now I'm back to square one," she said.

"But as Prentiss's wife, won't you get everything?"

"I'm not the sole heir. That can only be a true Kingsley daughter."

It sounded like a brand name.

Liz continued, "According to an ancient trust that the first Helen Kingsley set up, unless there's a Kingsley heiress, the estate is split between one heir and the trust. Only a direct blood descendant, and a woman, can inherit the entire estate. In the past, there was never a problem."

"So Prentiss wasn't the sole heir to the estate either?"

Liz shook her head imperceptibly—imperceptible except to me, who froze my scissors at attention for a moment. She replied, "Since he was a male, Prentiss had to share the estate with the trust, which was just as well, since the trust is what helped the corporation grow."

"That explains why John Lough didn't inherit from the estate—because he has no Kingsley blood in him."

"Right. The only way he could get at the money would be to marry a Kingsley daughter." Her voice wavered. "Now there can never be a Kingsley daughter, *ever*."

Because Prentiss is dead, I thought.

Liz sniffed. "But John can still inherit a portion of the estate from a previous heir."

"Which *is* possible with Prentiss's will."

"Exactly," said Liz.

No wonder that baby had meant so much. She—or he—was the meal ticket, the guaranteed reservation on the Kingsley gravy train.

"What happens now?" I asked.

"Half the estate remains in trust, and the other half is distributed according to Prentiss's will."

"And that half goes to you."

"No. It goes to John and I together."

I stifled my grammatical reflex for something more important: a potential showdown in Bonbon City.

"But isn't that settled by the terms of the will?"

"It should be, Vannos. A share of millions is fine with me, but John wants my share too. He wants everything. He never got over having a rich brother."

"What can he do, though? The terms of the will are set. There's nothing he can do about it except . . ." I trailed off, not quite able to add the last words, "to kill you."

Liz replied, "It's not too late, Vannos. With an estate this size, the will has to go into probate. The lengthy delay caused by that would give John time to . . . to get rid of me." Had she read my mind? "Then he can inherit it all."

Probate, the very process that was supposed to prevent the bungling of a will, ironically caused more trouble than it prevented. Still, something didn't settle quite right with me. Surely some shrewd lawyer would have spotted the loophole years ago.

Then again, perhaps it was just such loopholes that allowed people to gain vast amounts of wealth from the exercising of mere technicalities—along with murder.

"One thing is certain, though," she said. "You've been a real help to me through all of this. When everything is settled, I'll show my appreciation in a fiscal way."

"There's no need for that, Liz."

"It's nothing. I'll be rich, seriously rich."

"In spite of that, if there's any way I can help . . ."

Within seconds she replied, "There is something."

"Sure," I said, a bit surprised at her quick response. "What is it?"

"Could you come to the memorial service this afternoon, as my escort? You've been such a comfort already. You really validate my feelings."

It sounded like I was good for free parking.

I thought a moment. How far did I want to extend this arrangement? As Nicole had reminded me, Liz was only a client. But now she was also a widow who was asking for my help. Like Branco, I could rescue a hapless maiden. It would be a simple matter too, since it was my day off. Besides, whom else could she ask now? And she'd mentioned the possibility of remuneration for my assistance. I heard myself weighing this personal situation like a business contract. Was I doing a favor, or was I gaining points? Maybe I wasn't so different from an MBA . . . or a cop.

"No trouble at all," I said after a moment. "Tell me where and when." And she did.

I finished my work, then helped her out of the styling chair. As she donned her winter coat, I got a chance to take in the whole picture of her: With the rosy glow courtesy of Alaine's ministerings, and with the sad, watery eyes caused by Prentiss's death, and with the severe, almost sexless hairstyle I'd just created, Elizabeth Anne Carlini-Kingsley looked the perfect yuppy widow in mourning.

Her bodyguard reappeared to take her away, just as Nicole came into the shop. She nodded a polite greeting to Liz and

Moose, then just as quickly bade them farewell as they left the shop.

"Darling," she said brightly, "isn't it your day off?"

"Special appointment, doll."

Nicole said, "I'd be careful with her, Stanley. There's more to that woman than meets the eye."

"That's your female prejudice talking. Liz told me she intends to bestow a tidy honorarium for all my help and comforting words."

"Stanley, you are easy prey to the guiles of attractive women."

"Does that include you?"

"Thank you for the compliment."

The memorial service for Prentiss Kingsley took place at an Episcopal church—it might have been a cathedral, actually—in the South End. The two hundred or so people present barely filled the first few pews of the imposing nave. Apparently a larger attendance had been anticipated, since the show was taking place in the main church, complete with bells and smells, rather than in the smaller chapel. I would have expected a larger crowd too, since Prentiss Kingsley was the last blood of an old Boston line. Maybe the Brahmins were all basking in warmer climes.

Liz and I were led to our places in the front pew. The sickly drone of a funereal pipe organ accompanied our walk down the main aisle of the church. Except for the backs of their heads, I couldn't identify who else was there, not without turning around and staring directly back into the congregation. From all the unfashionable clothing though, I guessed that the Gladys Gardner assembly line had been shut down for the afternoon so that the workers could pay homage to their leader.

Once we were seated, I noticed John Lough and Mary Phinney in the pew opposite the aisle from us. They looked our way and clearly recognized us, but instead of polite acknowledgment, Liz and I received blank stares. Again I wondered, Why are those two always together?

As for the service, there was none of that stand-and-deliver testimonial stuff, where members of the congregation proudly share their personal impressions of the dead person. No sharing here, not for a blood-line Kingsley. The only worthy testimonial could come from the mouth of God's own deputy, the rector of a high Episcopal church. He gave an embarrassing homily about Prentiss Kingsley's heroic life, then ended with some blather about the glories of death. At one point, my attention was absorbed by the meanderings of a small black fly along the intricate handcarved details on the front rail of our pew. What did she care about any of this nonsense, except to find her way out of the mahogany maze and the lingering clouds of incense?

Throughout the service, Liz Carlini maintained her composure and displayed her grief with the same refinement that a beautiful and sophisticated First Lady might show after her husband's assassination. After the church service, we all went to the memorial reception, which was being held in the same Copley Plaza ballroom where Le Jardin's gala celebration—and first killing—had taken place a little more than a week ago. During the brief limousine ride to the hall, Liz told me she was planning to stay at the house in Abigail until the estate was settled.

I commented, "Wouldn't somewhere else be better, considering all that's happened out there recently?"

"The place belongs to me now, and I have my bodyguard," she replied, with a somewhat resentful glance at Moose. "The Abigail police have offered their assistance to protect me, and I've put a restraining order on John Lough. He can't enter the town without my consent. Since the Boston police would do nothing to protect me, I accepted the best offer, which was in Abigail."

The Boston police probably had a lot more serious problems than looking after a rich widow who claimed her brother-in-law wanted to kill her. Besides, they thought they had their killer in Rafik.

When we arrived at the reception hall, Moose, Liz, and I waited inside the limousine and watched the others going in.

When John Lough and Mary Phinney walked by, the sight of them caused Liz to grip my arm with fearful tension.

"She hated Danny so much," Liz said. "I heard her say once that gay people are all sinners and should be punished or be put away." Liz gasped suddenly and paused to catch her breath. "Sorry," she said after a few moments. "I've never said anything like that to a gay person."

I thought, The truth is often breathtaking.

We also saw Laurett Cole and her son, Tobias, going by in the crowd. Once everyone had gone inside, Liz and I joined them.

There was plenty of food and liquor, and most of the crowd was eating hungrily. Their jobs at the factory probably didn't provide much in the way of personal satisfaction or fringe benefits, so this event was their chance to gorge and guzzle at company expense. So what if the boss was dead? For her part, Liz wanted nothing but a glass of water, no ice.

Various people lined up to offer Liz their condolences. Among those in line was Laurett Cole, with Tobias along beside her. I hadn't seen or spoken to Laurett since her release, and I was looking forward to a friendly hello. But before the line got up to Liz and me, I saw Mary Phinney nab Laurett and begin talking sharply and insistently. Laurett looked down at the older woman defiantly, but remained silent. Mary Phinney persisted in her attack until John Lough finally arrived to halt the barrage of insults and lead her away from the line. He made no apology to Laurett, who'd remained stoic through it all. When it was Laurett's turn to speak to Liz, she was surprisingly cool to me, treating me almost like a stranger who'd been hired as Liz's escort. I suppose in a way I was. Laurett addressed Liz plainly, without emotion and without the usual and intentional misnomer.

"Ms. Carlini, I am sorry. Your husband and young Danny were both fine people."

Meanwhile, Tobias tugged at my trousers.

"Uncle Stan, that lady said Ma was a poisoner." He pointed

to Mary Phinney, far away from the line now, but still standing with John Lough, always with John Lough.

"You mean a prisoner, Tobias."

I looked askance at him. Had Mary Phinney really said "poisoner," or had he imagined it? I wondered if all the horrible talk regarding Laurett's murder charge had branded its impression on his young little brain. Or was it something simpler and more familiar, something that Tobias and I seemed to have in common?—the tendency to imagine things that happened that really hadn't.

Tobias turned to Laurett. "Ma? Ma, didn't she say you killed him?"

In one swift, smooth motion Laurett knelt down and grabbed Tobias's little arm. She shook it firmly and said, "Don't ever say those things, young man."

Liz looked down at them, then back at me. "Vannos, can you take me out, please?" she asked.

"Now? You want to go already?"

"Yes."

I took Liz's arm and quickly led her back outside to the waiting limousine. Moose tagged right along with us. I let Liz into the car first, then held the door open for Moose. I was about to close the door on them when she asked with big, moist eyes, "Aren't you coming too?"

"Would you mind if I stayed? I want to talk to Laurett."

"That's fine," she said, but her face looked sad.

"If you need anything, Liz, call me."

"Thank you for everything, Vannos."

I closed the heavy door, and the limo pulled away with a quiet whoosh. The loudest sound was its spongy rubber tires crunching through the crusty snow along the edge of the street.

I ran back inside to find Laurett and Tobias. I wanted to know what was troubling her and why she was being so cool to me. But they'd both vanished from the place. I tore outside again, just in time to see them getting into a cab.

"Laurett, wait!" I called out. But the cab took off and they were gone.

Again I went back inside, this time in search of Mary Phinney and John Lough. In my meanderings through the guests, I overheard two people talking, apparently a married couple, who'd met at Gladys Gardner years ago. They'd remained faithful to the old guard and to each other ever since. To them, Prentiss Kingsley had represented the ideal corporate benefactor, doggedly following in the footsteps set by the Kingsley matriarchs, all women of godlike vision. So this was the kind of pure and holy sentiment felt by the workers of a candy company that nowadays used mostly cheap chemicals in their products.

I finally found Mary Phinney standing with John Lough. Like Tweedledum and Tweedledee, the two seemed inseparable, like partners of a peculiar marriage. I approached them from the side, where they couldn't see me. Mary was devouring a large piece of ham. John was holding onto a big glass full of amber liquid with ice. I noticed that Mary had put on special makeup for the occasion. She'd painted herself like a grotesque porcelain doll, with a near-white foundation accented by red rouge and lipstick. But she'd neglected her neck and under her chin, so her ghastly, wrinkled face seemed to hover, disconnected from the rest of her body.

I addressed them both loudly. "They say a killer always returns to the scene of the crime."

Mary faced me with her powdery mask. "What are you doing here?" she asked.

Instead of answering her, I asked John Lough, "Who took your gun?"

"Who told you that?"

"I recall Mary looking for it in your desk when we were in your office. I figure you used it to kill Dan Doherty and then your brother. You sent it to me like a gift, but it wasn't very convincing, Mr. Lough."

John Lough spluttered, "How dare you!"

"It's called freedom of speech."

"You can't accuse someone just like that."

"The question is, are you planning to kill Liz too, so you won't have to contest your brother's will?"

"Is that what she's been telling you?" John Lough's eyes brightened suddenly, and he chuckled, then broke into merry laughter. "My sister-in-law is a compulsive liar. She'll say anything. And you believe her like a fool. Hah!"

Mary added, "You don't know what you're getting into. Just mind your own damn business."

"All I know is that if anything happens to Liz Carlini, both your asses are automatically fried. Mr. Lough, you really ought to take your share of the estate and shut up."

"Young man, you need psychiatric help."

"Hey, I was a certified counselor."

John Lough said to Mary Phinney, "Let's go." And they left me standing in the big hall of happy, hungry mourners. Before leaving, I ate something too. Why not? Liz Carlini had spared no expense to supply grand cuisine to the minions, in memory of her rich, dead husband.

I left the Copley Plaza and headed home, but I was distracted and bothered by a recurrent vision in my mind of John Lough and Mary Phinney and their chronic togetherness. It was the quality of that togetherness that nagged at me, the "marriedness" of it, as though they were two parts of a synergistic whole. Yet they weren't married, at least as far as I knew. Then I thought about Prentiss Kingsley's will. How could I find out about that? Where could I go for more information? When a fool flounders, the solution appears—and I found myself facing the old facade of the venerable Boston Public Library. I was in luck too, since they were still open.

I bounded up the the Dartmouth Street stairs past two majestic granite lions and went into the building. I always use that entrance because it takes you into the old library, the real one, with its dark halls and misty gray light and the lingering odor of ancient, deteriorating paper. Once inside the building, I was happily overcome by the sight of one of the grandest marble staircases ever designed and built by mortal man. Exquisite proportions, graceful lines and curves, varied textures of wood and marble, vast colored murals, and lively window light that changed dramatically in angle and hue according to the season and time of day—all these were facets of a singular gem of architectural detail in the old library. Whenever I'm in there, no matter where else I'm headed, I always make one trip up and down that staircase. It's a brief and pleasant detour into another place and time.

I'd heard that the library had access to one of those general data bases of periodical information where anything that has ever appeared in a magazine or newspaper was catalogued and available through a computer. Perhaps a computer would help me where human efforts had failed. I found my way to the office where the computer searches were requested. I pushed open the door to the small room, and was greeted by the smell of stale cigarette smoke inside. Seated at a computer terminal behind the counter was the librarian, a burly, blond lumberjack of a man in his early forties. Numerous half-filled paper coffee cups littered his desk, along with a large earthenware bowl mounded high with cigarette butts and ash. He looked up from his computer screen with a disappointed frown. "I'm about to go on break," he said.

"It's important," I replied.

Annoyed huff. "Fill in the form," he said, and pointed to a stack of preprinted computer requests on the countertop.

I examined the form, which resembled a complex twelve-step program in computer queries. I said, "Can't you just ask it to look up something for me?"

He answered, "You have to formulate your search strategy."

I paused and studied the form again. Too many words. I gave him my helpless-but-eager look and said, "I'm sure you're better at it than I am." But the ploy to soften him up didn't work.

"You fill in the form," he said, "and I'll run your search after my break." He pushed himself away from his computer and stood up.

"Wait," I said. "I need this information in a hurry. If you can help me, I'll return the favor."

He eyed me suspiciously with his big Nordic blues. "How?"

"I'm a hair stylist at Snips Salon near the Ritz. I'll give you a free cut and style."

He approached me where I was standing at the counter. The name on his employee tag said Thor. "If you're willing to barter," he said, "you must really need the data."

"I do." Did I dare tell him it might be a matter of life and death?

He took a blank form from the pile. "What do you need?"

"I need to find out what's in Prentiss Kingsley's will."

He rolled his blue eyes up at me. "We're not a legal data base, and that would be confidential information anyway."

"I thought they printed that stuff in the newspaper after someone dies."

"Only after a will goes through probate."

I thought a moment. "Then what about finding anything else published about the Kingsley family?"

He nodded, then printed the word "Kingsley" in compulsively neat letters on the search form, a sharp contrast to the pigpen he'd created on his computer desk.

"What else?" he asked.

"Just Kingsley. Isn't that enough?"

"You have to narrow it down, or you'll get too much information."

I replied, "How can you have too much? I want it all."

"Then you'll have to wait a couple of days. A set that large would have to be printed off-site and sent here."

"I can't wait that long."

"Then you have to streamline your search. Give me more criteria."

"I thought *streamline* meant less, not more."

"Not with computers."

I thought another minute. I was already discovering that my internal Slavic data bank and the real-world electronic ones had little in common. "Can you add John Lough and Mary Phinney to the search?"

"L–O–U–G–H?" he asked, spelling out the name. "Like *rough*?"

I nodded. "Good guess."

"Not a guess. I'm a search librarian. We're good with names."

He added the two names to the search form, which now said:

KINGSLEY AND (LOUGH/JOHN OR PHINNEY/MARY)

"Dates?" he asked.

"Pardon me?" I replied. Were my personal needs so obvious?

"You have to specify a range of dates. Otherwise you'll get results from the beginning of time until today."

"That would be fine," I said eagerly. "I need the historical stuff too."

He reluctantly x-ed out some boxes on the form, then turned it around toward me. "Sign here, please," he said, and offered me the pen.

"Why?"

"It's a rule. Can't do a search without a signature."

"Do you need an ID, too?"

"Only if you're a student. Otherwise, just a signature."

So I signed the name Dan Doherty.

Thor took the form and sat at the computer terminal. He typed in the request, scrutinized the line he'd typed, then gave a sadistic whack to the "Enter" key.

"Give it a minute or so," he said.

"That's all?"

He nodded proudly. "They got five SuperBank X-3's networked on this data base. Makes an IBM look like a vending machine."

"What else is on there?"

Thor said, "You name it, I'll find it. Ran a search on Yma Sumac this morning. The results put the guy in ecstasy." Thor chuckled. "Amazing what can give someone a kick."

Just then his computer screen filled up with amber-colored text.

"Here we go," he said. "Got a couple of good ones here, but mostly short stuff. It's all pretty old. Don't know how much it'll help you."

"How old?"

Thor studied the screen. "Thirty, forty years."

Shit, I thought. I wasn't even an egg or a sperm then.

"Still want it?" he asked.

"Sure."

He punched another button on his keyboard, and a small printer sprang to noisy life, buzzing and zinging the lines of text onto paper. When it finished, Thor removed and folded the paper into a neat pile and brought it to the counter.

"These are just abstracts of the original articles. The publications are quite old, so if you need the complete text, you'll have to try the microfilm archives."

"This will be a good start for me," I replied.

"There's usually a charge for nonstudents," he said, as he handed me the little stack of computer printout. "But this one's on the house." A lonesome little smile appeared on Thor's solemn face.

"Thanks," I said. I took out one of my business cards, scribbled the words "cut & style by Vannos" on the back, and handed it to him. "Best to make an appointment first," I said.

He took the card in his tobacco-stained fingers, read it, and said, "This isn't necessary. I'm just doing my job. Besides, it was kind of fun."

"Suit yourself," I said. "But I may need your help again sometime."

Thor pushed my business card into his shirt pocket amongst the collection of pens and pencils crammed in there. I gathered the printouts, said good-bye, and departed from the little office. No sooner was I out of there than I found a place to sit down and devour the new clues. I unfolded the sheets and placed the thin stack of paper in front of me. I could feel my heart pounding in anticipation, so I put both my hands on the papers, palms down, and said my mantra. When my heartbeat and breathing had returned to normal, I said quietly, "Please, please, please, give me an answer." Then I turned over the first page.

As Thor had mentioned, most of the clips were from about forty years ago. As I pored over the lines, I thought perhaps there was a great data base god somewhere, since the first few abstracts gave me more answers than I'd expected.

> KINGSLEY WILL CONTESTED — The will of deceased Helen Kingsley, most recent matriarch of the Gladys Gardner Chocolate Company, has Boston attorneys testing and battling each other's wits. Kingsley's husband, Jack Lough, the flamboyant, handsome Brahmin son, contested his wife's will on the grounds that their daughter, Mary Kingsley-Lough, who stands to inherit the entire estate according to the terms of the will, is not a bloodline descendant at all, but was adopted as an infant. A thorough investigation is under way.

The facts tumbled around in my tired brain. All kinds of notions I'd had were being disproved in one small paragraph. Helen Kingsley hadn't died giving birth to her son Prentiss, as Danny had told me in Abigail. Not only that, she had an adopted daughter as well. Branco had been right about one thing—I believed too readily the lies people told me. I continued on to the next abstract.

> ADOPTION REVEALED — Federal Court investigators declared Kingsley heiress Mary Kingsley-Lough (née Phinney) ineligible to inherit the multimillion-dollar Kingsley estate from the late Helen Kingsley. Mary Phinney was adopted in infancy by Helen Kingsley and her husband, society playboy Jack Lough. According to the terms of the original Gladys Kingsley Trust, set up three generations ago, only a bloodline Kingsley daughter may inherit the estate in total.

That information confirmed the first abstract with an additional, incredible detail: Mary Phinney was the adopted daughter of Helen Kingsley. My heart was racing again as I read onward.

KINGSLEY ESTATE DISTRIBUTED — The distribution terms of the multimillion-dollar estate of the late Helen Kingsley were released today by executors of the Gladys Kingsley Trust. Sixteen-year-old Prentiss Kingsley, natural son of Helen Kingsley and Jack Lough, receives a monthly allocation from the trust and, when he comes of age, acquires senior management privileges for the Gladys Gardner Chocolate Company. In a turnaround decision, the courts determined that Helen Kingsley's widower Jack Lough, who contested his wife's original will, and Kingsley's adopted daughter, Mary, who stood to inherit the entire estate according to Helen Kingsley's will, should both be denied any portion of the estate, according to the terms of the Gladys Kingsley Trust. Jack Lough is appealing the decision.

No wonder Mary Phinney had despised Dan Doherty. She'd been denied her inheritance, and now it was about to go to something less than human, at least in her dim vision—a gay man. I continued on.

SON BORN TO KINGSLEY WIDOWER — A strapping eleven-pound boy, John, was born last week to Jack Lough, Boston society gentleman and former husband of the late Helen Kingsley, and to his wife Myra (née Gorbitch).

LOUGH APPOINTED VICE-PRESIDENT — John Lough was recently appointed a Senior Vice-President of the Gladys Gardner Chocolate Company. His brother,

Prentiss Kingsley, is President and Chairman of the Board.

It was enough for now. I was armed with new facts and ready to act. I could barely wait to share the treasures I'd unearthed. Snips was close by, and it wasn't quite closing time, so Nikki would still be there. I jogged down Newbury Street all the way to the shop, clutching the computer paper like the Dead Sea Scrolls. I rushed into the shop breathing heavily from my short run. Nicole was surprised to see me there, and in such a state.

"How was the funeral?" she asked.

I hurried by her toward the back room, not even pausing as I exclaimed, "You won't believe what I just found. Come back as soon as you lock up." I zoomed into the back room and plopped heavily into a chair, not even bothering to take off my jacket. There was too much to do. I quickly called an old beau at the telephone company to get the street addresses for Mary Phinney and John Lough. My friend gave me the information, and I offered him a free style in exchange. So much for Ma Bell's confidentiality clause.

When Nicole joined me back there, I showed her what I'd discovered at the library. She seemed blasé.

"What's the point?" she asked.

"Nikki, don't you realize what all this means?"

"No, darling."

"It means Mary Phinney and John Lough planned this whole thing together."

"Stanley," she said, after taking a deep pull of smoke, "you sound like a fool."

"That's seems to be my nickname lately." I poured us both a drink. "At least now I understand the source of Mary Phinney's foul disposition better. She was abandoned twice by two sets of parents and then again by the legal system."

"You're not forgiving her, are you? You almost sound like one of those born-again people."

"No, doll. She's still despicable, but at least I know the

reason now." I downed my bourbon in one gulp, like a real man. "I'd better call my friend Ruiko and see if I can borrow her car."

"Why do you need a car?"

"Mary Phinney lives in Dorchester, and John Lough lives in Forest Hills. There's no way I'm taking public transportation out there."

"Where are you going?"

"To confront them both and make them confess."

Sensing potential danger in my expedition, she said, "Do you know what you're doing?"

"As usual, no."

I called Ruiko and happily discovered that she didn't need her car that night, so my plans could proceed immediately. Then I asked Nicole, "Can you drop by my place tonight and feed Sugar Baby?" I paused. "In case I don't get home."

"What do you mean, don't get home?"

"There might be complications."

"Meaning?"

I shrugged. "I don't know. Delays. Trouble."

Nicole became stern. "Stanley, if you really believe those people are killers, then why are *you* going after them?"

"What else can I do? Branco won't help. He's got one idea in his head, and he refuses to see any other solution. He's right, the rest of us are wrong."

"Sounds like you."

"We all have stubborn moments, doll."

"You and the lieutenant fight for an entirely different reason, not stubbornness. If you haven't figured that out, you're simply being . . . stubborn."

"Nikki, I got no time for theoretical debate."

Nicole growled in a low, mocking rendition of machismo, "A man's gotta do what a man's gotta do." Then she extinguished her cigarette. "I will feed the cat, Stanley. Then I will remain at your apartment until you call me there or arrive in person. How long will you be?"

"I don't know."

"You have to give me a time, Stanley."

"Why?"

"So that I can call the lieutenant to go and save you if you're not home by then."

"Let's hope it doesn't come to that. I'll call him if I need his help."

"It may be too late."

"Then let it be on his conscience. I'd better get going."

I stood up to leave, and Nicole got up and gave me a long hug. "Why must you indulge in these heroics?" she asked.

I thought a few moments. "I don't really know. Maybe it's just to free Rafik for a repeat performance on Valentine's Day. Who knows? Without the edge of danger to his lovemaking, perhaps he'll be just another ordinary mortal."

"What about the lieutenant? Are you trying to prove something to him too?"

"Maybe a little."

"What you do in the name of love."

"I'm not alone."

I kissed her and left the shop. On the quiet walk uptown to Ruiko's place I had some time to wonder why, in fact, I was so damn stubborn. People have often accused me of compulsive behavior, a neurotic need to have my life ordered into discrete bundles of tidiness and logic, kind of like a computer. All I can say is, those people obviously haven't seen my housekeeping habits or analyzed my thought processes. I believe my stubbornness is part of my healthy Slavic tenacity, the ability to stand my ground in the face of adversity, or to hang onto any passing flotsam and ride out the storm.

If Branco thought the matter closed and I didn't, what was left for me to do but to pursue things in my own way, wantonly provoking people, stirring up the stew of lies and facts and events until the truth finally rose to the surface like the scum that must be skimmed off?

19

A LEAP OF FAITH

My friend Ruiko lives in the Fenway Studios in a spacious, skylit duplex where she paints impressionist watercolor scenes from her summertime travels around the world. Her excellent work has won her prizes and exhibits and fame. Our connection goes back before her days of great celebrity, and the give-and-take arrangement we have with her car—I contribute to the expenses, so I get to use it whenever it's available—still exists without question. Ruiko remains a true friend despite her recent elevation to artist's Valhalla.

I have a set of car keys, so after brushing the accumulated snow from the hood and the windows of the old station wagon, I climbed inside, ready to begin my night's sortie. Ah, the convenience of a private carriage without the hassles of ownership, I thought, with the naivete of someone who never drives during wintertime. Inside, attached to the dashboard, was one of those yellow "stickies" onto which Ruiko had penned in one of her many distinctive calligraphics the word OIL. It was typical of her to render so artistically a political reminder about fossil fuel.

I pushed the key into the ignition switch and turned it. The frozen lock required extra force to twist it to the Start position. The starter groaned painfully and barely turned the engine over. The sluggish battery seemed to resent my intrusion on its hibernation. Was there enough juice to get the engine going? After a few worrisome minutes of pathetic sounds from under the hood, the engine stumbled to unsteady life. Puffs of black smoke trailing behind, I maneuvered the car out of the parking lot and onto

Massachusetts Avenue, heading south towards Dorchester and Forest Hills, where Mary Phinney and John Lough lived.

I went to Mary Phinney's place first, since it was closer; but no one was home there, so I continued on to Forest Hills. By then the car was warm and running more smoothly, and I was feeling more confident too. Once in Forest Hills, I saw that some parts of the neighborhood had retained their prim white-middle-class aura with well-kept houses and sidewalks cleared of snow. Some of the charming cottages even had long icicles hanging down from the roof in perfect complement to shuttered windows and snow-covered hedges. I found John Lough's house easily on the wide, well-lit street. Instead of his staid maroon sedan in the driveway though, another car was parked there—a boxy, generic thing. I guessed whose car that had to be. The house lights were on. I parked Ruiko's wagon on the street and walked to the front door. I rang the bell, waited, rang it again, waited some more, then finally banged directly on the door. I sensed someone moving behind it, then heard the sharp clack of the peephole being opened and shut.

"I know you're in there," I shouted, then realized what a fool I was being. If John Lough and Mary Phinney had purposefully killed two people and had inadvertently killed another, why did I think myself immune from harm? What was to stop them from shooting me dead on the spot, then claiming that I'd been intruding on their property? Like Liz Carlini, I seemed to have lost my survival instinct.

Then the door opened slowly. I prepared myself to avert the barrel of a gun if it emerged through the crack, but instead, the face of Mary Phinney appeared with its usual disapproving scowl. Now, at least, I knew the origin of that anger: It was mostly disappointment.

"What do you want here?" she barked.

That seemed to be her opening line with me no matter where we met.

"I want to talk to you and John."

"He's not here, and I have nothing to say to you."

"Mary, I know why you and John did what you did, but you should both give yourselves up. Don't make it worse."

"Get away from here before I call the police."

"Go ahead. Then you can hear me tell them what I found out today, about you and Helen Kingsley, and your stepbrother Prentiss, and how you lost everything, and—"

"Quiet!" she snapped. "Get away from me. I don't want you near me."

"But even when the police arrest you and John, they can't force you to testify against each other, since you're married."

She glared at me. "Where'd you hear that?"

"It's true, isn't it?"

"It's none of your damn business."

"I figure it's all part of your plan to take over the company. If you're married to your business partner, chances are you won't get double-crossed."

"That's not why we got married."

"Don't tell me it was for sex, or something sordid like that."

"You shut your dirty mouth."

"Maybe it's an Oedipal kind of marriage. You're the mommy and he's the naughty boy."

Mary Phinney's face became livid as I continued to provoke her.

"It sure is a neat arrangement though, with the two of you trying to swipe half the estate from Prentiss Kingsley and Liz Carlini and Dan Doherty. Too bad you didn't check out the legal complications before you started killing people. You didn't get anything from the estate before, and you won't get anything now, and you certainly won't get away with the deaths of three people, not if I have anything to say about it."

"You don't know anything about the estate. This all started long before you were even born, so what do you know?"

"I did a little research, Mary, and I know about you and the Kingsley family, and I know that three people are dead and the killer is still free. The question is, who's at the bottom of it all? Is it you or is it John?"

"I had nothing to do with the killings."

"Then it's John."

Mary stared at me. The opaque pupils of her eyes seemed to block any part of her real self from coming out. "Maybe it's true," she said. "Maybe he's finally taking care of old business that was never settled right."

"So he's out to get Liz Carlini?"

"You'd better get away from here before he comes back, before he has a real reason to shoot someone—for trespassing!"

Her threat gave me exactly the information I needed. Now I was certain that John Lough had gone to Abigail to kill Liz Carlini. I left Mary Phinney standing at the door, looking slightly bewildered. Perhaps she couldn't believe she'd actually scared me off. Well, she hadn't. I had more important things to do. I drove away quickly and looked for a pay phone, which was not easy to find in that part of town, especially one that worked. Oh, for a car phone now! When I found a public phone, I first tried calling Liz Carlini in Abigail to warn her of John Lough's arrival. All I got was the answering machine with Prentiss Kingsley's message. It was strange to hear a dead man's voice asking you to leave a message. I left a rather frenetic one telling Liz that John Lough was on his way out there. Then, mid-sentence, I wondered, Was I too late? Had he already done the deed? Was he standing there at that very moment, screening the call, listening to me blabber away everything I knew?

I hung up fast and called Lieutenant Branco at the station. He wasn't there, so I called his private number, the one he'd given me for emergency use only, in case I had urgent information for him. Hell, this was urgent. Branco answered on the second ring. I quickly explained what had happened, but as usual he didn't want to believe me. He actually accused me of having a Dick Tracy complex. That was the last straw for my patience, since my true hero is Perry Mason. I heard myself screaming at him over the phone, "Goddammit, Vito, just get someone out there!" Then I slammed the receiver down, feeling like a real he-man, one who is on a first-name swearing basis with a big-shot cop.

I got back in Ruiko's car and headed onto the expressway

going north. I broke the speed limit all the way to Abigail. That was just another of many mistakes I made that night. The aged station wagon couldn't bear the strain of high-speed driving. There on Route 128, when I was nearing my destination, without warning the dashboard lit up like a Christmas tree. All shapes of colored icons were blinking and beeping at me, telling me to stop the engine and abandon ship. One of the lighted panels said CHECK GAGES, and at that critical moment, my first response was to question the spelling. There's no predicting how your mind will focus in an emergency. I pulled the car onto the shoulder and turned off the engine. I waited five minutes, thinking maybe if it cooled down, I could drive it again. But it took fifteen precious minutes before I could start the engine without a repeat performance of the dashboard's special effects. Once I got the car going again, I found if I kept the speedometer under forty—Is such a thing possible on Route 128?—the lights only glowed instead of blinking brightly, and the buzzers and beepers remained silent. Along with everything else after tonight, I'd probably have to spring for an engine overhaul, or perhaps even replace Ruiko's car.

I finally got to Abigail. I drove the car at a crawl through the center of town and noticed a snarl of police cruisers and people clustered around one part of the marina. Had John Lough already killed Liz Carlini down here near the water, not up at the house? I stopped and asked an observer what had happened. As it turned out, it was a bomb scare on one of the large yachts. Then I wondered if Liz had planned to leave Abigail by boat, to escape from John Lough that way. Perhaps he'd foreseen her scheme and prevented it. Even if there were no bomb, the mere threat of one could disrupt her escape plans.

I got back in the car and drove up the hill to the Kingsley house. On the incline, the dashboard began to glow again, more brightly the higher I climbed, until finally, with nary a clank or a pop, the engine just stopped, completely dead. I got out and witnessed a colorful cocktail of steaming viscous fluids dripping out from under the chassis. Ruiko's poor car had apparently gasped its last, but I had no time to mourn its demise. I said a quiet thank-you to it, then trotted the rest of the way up the hill.

On the crest, I jogged along the curving road until I finally saw the Kingsley house ahead. Then my stomach lurched. There in the driveway was John Lough's staid sedan alongside Liz Carlini's glitzy touring car. The house lights were on, and all seemed quiet and peaceful. Had he killed her already? I moved stealthily around to the back of the house, to the dramatic expanse of sea, sky, and land. The heavens were clear and dense with stars—a sight rarely seen in the city—and the moon's bluish light cast sparkles on the ocean water. How could cold-blooded murders happen in a setting like this? But that same moonlight also gave the wet grassy land an eery glow. I heard the surf bashing and pounding against the jagged rocks lying beneath the high bluff at the edge of the property.

I turned my eyes toward the house. The solarium glowed with a hospitable warmth from within that seemed to say, Welcome to murderland. Through the glass walls I could see John Lough and Liz Carlini inside. She was seated and still very much alive, but John was standing over her with a gun aimed at her neck. On my cat-quiet feet, I slipped silently into the house through one of the side doors. Once inside, I crept soundlessly toward the solarium until I could overhear their words. John Lough was trying to force Liz to sign something.

"Why should I sign it?" she asked smartly. "Go ahead, John, shoot me. What will you get then?"

"I told you, it's not for me. It's for her. There was supposed to be a trust for Mary when Helen Kingsley died."

"Where is it then, John? Maybe there never was a trust. Maybe it was all in Mary's mind. Or maybe it's all a lie, and Helen Kingsley never intended to provide for her the way Mary claims."

"Then it's up to you to do it now."

"I don't owe Mary Phinney anything. Besides, I'm helpless. The estate is in probate."

"I don't believe you."

"So what are you going to do about it? You've already killed

Danny and Prentiss. Are you going to shoot me just to find out that I'm telling you the truth?"

"I don't care about them. Mary is right, they were perverts anyway. It's no loss that they're gone."

"So now there's just one more person to remove. Is that what you're thinking, John? Then you and Mary can have the whole company in your fat little hands. Is that what you want?"

"We deserve it. Prentiss had everything handed to him, while I had to work and work."

"He was a Kingsley. He had every right to his mother's money. He was her flesh and blood."

"But I'm blood too. I'm his half brother. You're just his wife. I have more right than you."

Liz was about to counter that remark when I rushed in behind John and put my Slavic limbs to their magic work. My legs, at least, are still full of young kick. It took just one swift boot under his arm, the one that was holding the gun, to set it off and send it flying through the air. The bullet hit one of the huge glass panels in the solarium roof high overhead. The tempered glass shattered and showered us with pebbly crystalline pellets. The next second, I knocked John Lough behind his knees, and he fell to the floor. I straddled him from behind and pinned him down.

Liz exclaimed, "Thank God you've come!"

"Where the hell's your bodyguard?" I asked. Liz positioned herself behind me. I said, "What are you waiting for, Liz? Call the police."

"There's an emergency at the marina," she said calmly. "All police personnel are there."

"Bad timing. We need help here."

"That all depends," she said, her voice now strangely untroubled.

From his facedown position on the floor, John Lough was struggling against my weight. "Let me go," he said. "You've got it all wrong." He twisted his head backwards and was looking up at me. Then his eyes shifted to something going on behind me. I turned my head.

Liz was holding John Lough's gun and aiming it directly at the two of us on the floor.

"You meddlesome little twit," she said to me. "I arranged that false alarm down at the marina just to keep the local police occupied tonight. I wasn't taking any chances. A bomb scare is the most exciting event that's happened out here in fifty years. I invited John here for a little conference, a final settling of accounts, but I certainly didn't expect him to arrive armed." She shifted her eyes toward me. "Now, thanks to you and your fumbling intrusion, I'm back in charge of the situation. The rest of this ought to be easy."

"She'll kill me," said John, from under me.

"That's right," said Liz.

Finally, stupidly, I realized the truth. "It's you, Liz. You're the one."

"Who else? Who else could have had such lousy luck right from the very beginning?"

"At the gala reception?"

"That stranger ate the truffle I'd prepared for Dan Doherty. God, what confusion."

"Why did you want to poison Dan?"

"To save my marriage. My husband was losing his senses. He'd named Dan Doherty as an heir. Imagine that? A whole corporate fortune was about to be redistributed because of a young man's charms."

"It wouldn't be the first time," I replied, and recalled that I had ascribed the same motive for Dan's killing to Mary Phinney, except that she hadn't acted on it.

John Lough said, "He was going to get my share."

Without acknowledging him, Liz continued. "I tried logic, I tried emotion, I even tried lying—but nothing would change Prentiss's mind. He was smitten with Danny, blinded by his feelings for him. So killing Danny was the simplest answer."

"You could have given up the money."

Liz ignored me. "And there'd be two ideal suspects—Rafik, that charming gold digger who expected Dan to give him whatever he wanted, and John here, whose fundamentalist beliefs and insane jealousy of Prentiss might drive him to kill a young homosexual."

"I didn't do any of it!" screamed John Lough. "I wanted to, but I didn't." He seemed on the verge of crying, which surprised me, given his appearance of strength. Liz ordered me to get off him and let him up, so I did. But John remained crouched on the floor, trembling in fear. I stood up and faced Liz.

"But that first attempt to kill Danny failed," I said.

"Yes, and the truffle flavors got confused too. Prentiss could have been poisoned by accident. Fortunately the police believed the most obvious thing—that Laurett Cole had clumsily killed her boyfriend." She smiled slyly. "You see? There are advantages to being educated, professional, and white."

"But you still wanted to kill Danny."

"Yes, and it was simply a matter of timing. I knew he was staying here in Abigail with Prentiss, and I knew that Prentiss went for a run every morning. It was his only addiction, bless his boring purity. He ran every morning between seven-thirty and eight-thirty, like clockwork."

"So if you came here within that hour, you'd be pretty sure that Prentiss would be gone."

"Yes. And if by chance Prentiss *was* here, well, I do have a right to come to my own house in Abigail, don't I? Besides, I might simply have wanted to warn him of John's threats."

"I never threatened you," John Lough wailed.

"But Prentiss wouldn't know that," replied Liz smugly.

John went on, "You have no right. The money is ours."

I was concerned more with Liz Carlini and the gun she held than with John Lough's pleas about money. "How did you get Danny alone?" I asked.

"That was tricky, since now I intended the blame for Danny's death to fall on Rafik. The timing was crucial. So, when I got to the center of town, I called the house on my mobile phone.

"That's why Ben remembered your arriving earlier."

"Yes. He seems to remember everything but my name. The engine was stalling terribly that morning, and I had to stop for help. While Ben adjusted something under the hood, I used the car phone to tell Rafik that the Immigration and Naturalization Service had come to the factory looking for him. And since he'd been working without proper papers, he wouldn't want to be found."

"So your phone call scared him away from the house long enough for you to go in and kill Danny."

"Yes, it really was that simple. You see, Vannos, like any shrewd business person, I know how to adapt to changing circumstances, how to exploit an opportunity."

"But how did you manage to kill Danny so intimately?"

"Another lucky break. He was asleep. The room smelled of sex. I imagined Prentiss mounting him, and the idea that he would choose a young man instead of me—it made me furious."

"But you didn't know for sure that it was Prentiss."

"I suspected it, and that was enough. When I saw Danny lying facedown on the bed, his body was still glistening with sweat. It was so easy. The muzzle of the gun almost slipped right in."

"That's disgusting."

"Don't you judge me! You don't know what I've been through. My marriage was a sham. My life had no meaning. The new business was my only hope. Then Danny showed up and Prentiss lost his reason." Liz sneered. "What a fool I was, thinking that once Danny was dead, Prentiss would reinstate me in the will."

"He didn't?"

"No. In fact, he wanted to name this brain-dead creature"—she pointed the gun at John Lough—"as his heir."

John interjected, "It is mine by right."

"Not if you're dead," replied Liz.

I asked, "Why did Prentiss cut you out of the will?"

Liz snickered. "He discovered something that made me unworthy of the sacred Kingsley money."

"Not another man?"

She laughed. "You are so simple, Vannos."

John Lough remained crouched on the floor. He had covered his ears and was shaking his head. Apparently the facts were too difficult for him to bear.

Liz said, "Poor thing. It's almost not worth killing him."

"Why do it then?"

"You both know too much."

"It has to stop sometime, Liz. You'll surely be caught for killing us."

"Then it won't matter if I do it."

I obviously had to stall her until . . . when? Hadn't Branco alerted the local police yet?

"But why did you kill Prentiss, Liz?"

She smiled coyly. "You're trying to buy time, aren't you?" She shrugged. "Why not tell you then? At that point it was the only way I could still get anything from the estate. See, even though Prentiss had explicitly cut me out as his wife, I still stood to inherit what he'd intended for Danny until he named another heir."

"But I thought you said John Lough was the next heir."

"Prentiss hadn't made the change yet, which is why I had to act quickly."

"But then you'd be the prime suspect."

"Not really. I wasn't in the will. Technically I had no motive for killing my husband."

"But wouldn't Dan Doherty's inheritance go to his heirs?"

Liz let out a sly giggle. "Dan Doherty, with typical youthful arrogance, assumed that he would live forever, or at least longer than Prentiss. He left his entire estate to Prentiss in a gesture of false gratitude. Everything kind of canceled itself out."

"So then you killed Prentiss."

"Yes, but now the time and place were a challenge. I decided to do it at that rest area on the highway near Dykes Pond. I'd heard it's a place where men meet for sex."

"How did you arrange to meet him?"

"I got a Boston taxi driver to call and leave a message on the phone machine here in Abigail, saying that he wanted to meet Danny at the rest stop. It's amazing what people will do for money. The taxi driver thought it was a kinky joke."

"But Danny was already dead."

"Yes, and I knew that would arouse Prentiss's curiosity. Even if his relationship to Danny was platonic, there was still jealousy. That's one thing Prentiss was quite good at . . . being jealous. So I dressed the way a gay man does when he's out for sex—blue jeans, T-shirt, leather jacket, boots—and went to meet him there."

"We don't all use the same drag, Liz. But it was still dangerous. You could have been seen."

"The risks are high when the stakes are high. I waited until Prentiss's car was the only one at the rest stop. Then it was simply a matter of getting him to lower the window and then putting the gun in his mouth."

"Didn't he resist?"

"It's strange," she said, and a pensive look passed over her face. "Not at all. He seemed almost to want it to happen."

"Did he know it was you?"

"I don't see how he couldn't. Our eyes met."

Who knows what drives people to act out their death wish?

"And the shots fired at your house? How did you manage to do that undetected?"

Liz smiled. "It was another opportunity that begged to be exploited. All three neighbors with a limited view of our property were on vacation. It was still risky, but no one saw or heard. And it put suspicion on John."

"Why me?" cried John Lough.

"Because it served my purpose," replied Liz.

"Liz, where does all this get you in the end?"

She laughed. "I'll have the satisfaction of knowing that I didn't just sit idly by, hoping for things to change, bemoaning my lot in life. I did something about it. I took action. I showed strength."

"Even if it meant killing people."

She shrugged. "This time, that's what it meant."

I shook my head. "I actually feel sorry for you."

"Go tell it to the village priest. Now let's get going. We're taking a little walk, the three of us. I hope you'll enjoy your last stroll by the water."

She kept the gun on John and me and directed us out of the solarium toward the bluff. I tried to keep her talking, hoping to reason my way out of this jam, at least until the local police arrived. What was taking them so damn long? Then I had an unsettling thought: What if Branco hadn't even called them?

Out on the bluff overlooking the private beach I asked Liz, "What was it that Prentiss found out to make him cut you off in his will? Was it that you'd had an abortion?"

"Clever of you to guess. Yes, I got rid of it. I wasn't about to share anything with my offspring."

"Even a possible Kingsley heiress?"

"I was sick of hearing about the Kingsley bloodline. I wanted my share free and clear of anything or anybody."

"But you killed three innocent people. You took matters into your hands that you had no right to."

"I'm surprised you're not accusing me of murdering the fetus too, with your self-righteous piety."

"That choice should be the woman's."

"Hah! You liberal sons of bitches really get me. It's easy for you to talk—you're a man. But I've had to struggle. I've had to sacrifice. I've given up the pleasure of my life for what I have, and no old ghost of a mother or two-timing young designer was going to ruin my chances."

"So Prentiss and Danny *were* lovers."

Liz shook her head. "Never," she said. "There was never a sexual thing between them. It was a simple father-son thing. It had to be. Prentiss simply wanted Dan to have some security."

"It was so simple you had to kill them both."

John Lough spluttered, "You're all a bunch of perverts. You'll all burn in hell."

"Dear, sad John," said Liz Carlini. "If there is such a place, we'll all be meeting there. At least we'll confirm its existence. That ought to satisfy at least one question of your faith."

She pressed us onward to the edge of the bluff. We stopped short of the precipice, and she said, "Now I'd like you both to embrace each other before you throw yourselves over the edge."

"Oh, no!" wailed John Lough, as he peered down into the craggy surf well over a hundred feet below. "She's really going to kill me."

"We're in this together, pal," I said.

John pleaded with her. "Maybe we could work something out. I'd give up any claim to the estate. I'll forget about the trust for Mary. Anything. I promise. Just please let me go."

"You silly man. You have nothing to give up. Now just hold on to each other. I want it to look like a pathetic lover's pact. Think of the tragedy. The world has turned its back on you. Danny and Prentiss are gone now. There's nothing left to live for. Just embrace and jump. It's very simple."

Simple, simple, simple.

"Find another word," I muttered, and I rammed John Lough's heavy body into her. She fired the gun and he went down. His falling seemed to surprise her. Before she could take good aim at me, I shoved her hard and knocked her to the ground. We wrestled for the gun. I struggled to get it from her while she tried to aim it at me. She was strong and wily, but my beautician's hands are strong and clever too. Finally I wrangled the gun from her. Then I stood up and heaved it over the bluff onto the rocks far below.

When I turned back, Liz was already running away. I raced after her on my springy Slavic limbs. I caught up to her and tackled. Me, who'd never played football in my life—now I was chasing women and knocking them down. I pinned her to the ground. She bit and clawed and kicked at me. She was lively and wriggly, and worse, dangerous. But that extra weight I carry around with me finally came in handy. I pressed myself onto her heavily and pinned her to the ground. Then I removed my belt. After a lengthy and breathy struggle, I succeeded in binding her wrists to her ankles behind her. S/M bondage came to mind, and I mumbled an apology for taking a step backwards for women's rights.

One thing I was never much good at, though, was tying knots, especially with leather belts. Almost as soon as I released

the pressure of my body, Liz squirmed her way out of the belt.
She got up and fled to the edge of the bluff.

"You come near me, I'll jump."

"Don't, Liz."

"I've botched it all. I've failed."

"It's not the end."

"What's left for me now?"

"There's paying for your actions."

"That's worse than death."

"So you bail out instead of facing the consequences?"

"Don't preach to me."

"I'm not preaching. I'm talking karma."

"You take your cosmic consciousness and shove it."

"Liz—"

But my voice was taken by the wind, unheard by Elizabeth
Anne Carlini-Kingsley. She had thrown herself over the bluff
onto the craggy rocks below. I moaned and shook my head. Then
I started to cry.

Some moments later, through the sound of the wind I heard
John Lough calling out weakly. He'd only been wounded and
was playing dead to save himself. "You'd better call me an
ambulance," he said.

I resisted the obvious retort.

That's when the Abigail police finally came running across
the moonlit lawn in response to Branco's call from Boston.

20
COMB-OUT

The next morning I was back in the shop working again, as if the events of the past week had been an extended television series, instead of so-called real life. Nicole had offered me some time off, but I refused. My clients always come first . . . sometimes.

Laurett was in my styling chair, where I was finishing her hair for a special memorial service that afternoon for Dan Doherty, one that she'd personally organized.

"Will you come later?" she asked.

"I think I've had enough church for a while."

"It won't be like that other one, Vannos."

I shook my head no. "Thanks anyway."

Lying on the top of my station, amidst the tools and bottles of my trade, was yet another, and I hoped the last, heart-shaped box of Le Jardin truffles. It had arrived by special courier, but I hadn't opened it yet. I wasn't worried about poison, since all the other chocolate that had mysteriously appeared during the past week had been fine. I just wasn't interested. In fact, I was almost nauseated by the thought of chocolate. Perhaps my lifelong addiction to the stuff had finally been cured, and those extra pounds would now melt away easily.

Tobias, however, was eyeing the box, and I saw his little fingers twitching in anticipation of squishing each and every piece inside.

"Vannos," said Laurett, "I apologize for being mad with

you. I thought you were being too friendly with Miss Lisa. I never knew you were going after her."

"It's all right," I replied. I couldn't confess the truth to her—that I had naively befriended Liz Carlini, and had honestly tried to help her, though more out of propriety than real concern. I wondered if my hands would ever regain their purity after working on a murderess and one of her victims. They felt genetically altered.

Nicole strutted jauntily toward my station, leading the handsome Rafik, who'd been released from jail that morning.

"Look who's back," said Nicole.

"You can lower your bosom, doll."

Rafik smiled broadly at me. "You are hero, eh?" he said with a wink.

"And you are ex-con, eh?" I said, imitating his accent and returning the gesture.

As I was removing the protective cape from Laurett's shoulders, Rafik noticed the unopened box of chocolates sitting on top of my station.

"You don't open my gift?"

"I'm trying to become slender and attractive."

"I don't care about your figure." He said it "fig-*goor*." "I care that you are brave." He put his arm around me and pulled me toward him. He fondled the extra weight around my waist, and I wished I were sleek, like him. He seemed to be enjoying it though.

I said, "Brave isn't quite right, Rafik. It was all kind of an accident."

Nicole interceded. "How can you say that, Stanley? It was all your chasing and prodding and hunting that finally got the mystery solved and got these two released from jail."

"Sure-you're-right," said Laurett as she got up from the chair.

"*Merci*," said Rafik. He gave one more squeeze, then let go of me.

To all of them I replied, "But it was John Lough's statement that cleared everything up with the Abigail police last night. They sure didn't want to believe my story."

"Darling, it did all sound rather melodramatic," said Nicole. "Especially the finale, with that leap from the cliff."

I shook my head sadly. "Liz Carlini was a sick woman. At least she's not tormented anymore."

Laurett was admiring my fabulous work on her hair—a high-fashion updo and twist—while Tobias had already pulled the chocolate down from my station and was opening the box.

Nicole said, "You were lucky John Lough witnessed it all. At least he's the kind of person the police listen to and believe."

"But I wonder if he'll ever recover from touching me. On top of that, he had to tell them the whole truth, which absolved me of any suspicion. He ended up saving a fairy, poor man."

"Hardly poor," said a familiar baritone voice behind me. It was Branco. He'd just come in from outside and had brought the scent of clean, cold winter air along with him. After some strained hellos with us ex-suspects and ex-prisoners, he said, "We got a hold of Prentiss Kingsley's will this morning."

"Finally had a good enough reason, eh, Lieutenant?"

Grunt. "According to the terms stated there, John Lough inherits Prentiss Kingsley's share of the estate. The remainder stays in trust with the corporation."

I clucked my tongue. "All of Liz Carlini's intrigues were in vain."

Laurett said, "What she was fearing the most, that's what happened anyway."

"Lieutenant," I asked, "what was the deal with the Mary Phinney Trust? Was that in the will too?"

"It wasn't, but it came out in John Lough's story. Apparently the most recent Kingsley woman who owned the company had wanted a daughter. It took a long time, but when she finally had a child, it was a boy."

"That was Prentiss Kingsley," I interjected.

"Right," said Branco with a little frown—a little frown that told me to keep quiet. "So she decided to adopt a daughter, and that was Mary Phinney."

Since I already knew the facts, I felt compelled to finish the story Branco had started. "So when Helen Kingsley died, Mary Phinney was supposed to inherit everything, according to the tradition of the Kingsley daughter. But since she wasn't a bloodline Kingsley, she got nothing, not even half." I paused. "Right?"

Grunt. An approving one at least.

I continued, "So when Prentiss died, Mary hoped to get some of the estate back from Liz Carlini, since there was no more Kingsley bloodline business to contend with."

"That was her theory," said Branco. "But as I said, it went to John Lough."

"And to his wife, Mary Phinney," I added.

"What!" exclaimed Nicole.

Branco nodded. "He's right."

Laurett nodded. "I always knew there was something."

Rafik nodded. "Americans."

Tobias squashed a raspberry parfait truffle.

I said, "From John Lough's perspective as a Good Samaritan, if he was a second-class Kingsley, then Mary Phinney was traveling in steerage. He probably married her out of guilt."

Nicole asked, "But no one knew?"

Branco replied. "Who's to say?"

I shook my head in wonderment. "Prentiss Kingsley never acknowledged his adopted sister, so his half brother married her. It gives new dimension to dysfunctional families."

"What a mess," said Nicole.

I added, "And with John Lough and Mary Phinney now at the helm, Gladys Gardner can return to her stodgy old ways, a reactionary's dream come true. Maybe the time for ultrachic boutiques like Le Jardin is coming to an end."

"Like me and my boy in Boston," said Laurett. "We be leaving here soon to go to Baltimore. My sister is coming from Jamaica, so we all have a new beginning there."

Rafik said, "Mebbee we go away too, Stani, *en vacances*, so I say thank-you. Yes?"

Gulp.

"I don't know if I can get the time off, Rafik."

Nicole piped in, "I'm sure it can be arranged."

Rafik's eyes twinkled with desire, and I wondered what new tricks he'd learned in prison.

Laurett whispered to me, "Honey, the man loves you."

Stupidly, I looked at Branco for a cue. With that curious curl of his lip, he said, "Sounds like a good offer to me, especially someplace warm."

I faced Rafik, who was still waiting for my answer.

"Sure," I said.

"Bien."

Then, after much hugging and good wishes, Laurett and Tobias left the shop. Even Branco gave Tobias a last farewell kiss on the cheek. Don't ever wash there, boy.

Branco prepared to leave too, and I walked with him to the door.

"Lieutenant, there's one thing I haven't figured out."

Branco turned. "What's that?"

"Whose gun was in the candy box?"

"It was unregistered, but it was the same gun that killed Dan Doherty and Prentiss Kingsley and fired the shots at Liz Carlini's house."

"So it was the weapon Liz used for everything."

Branco nodded. "And John Lough admitted last night that he was using his own gun."

"The one from his desk at the factory?"

"Right. The same one we found down in the rocks near the Abigail house last night."

I shook my head. "It's still unbelievable to me that Liz Carlini did it all, the lengths she went to, just for money."

With a knowing look, Branco said, "Her behavior had little to do with money. The woman was unbalanced."

"Lieutenant, I think we finally agree on something."

Branco put on his hat and waved good-bye to Nicole and Rafik. Then leaned close to me and said three words, waggling a warning finger at each syllable.

"You play safe."

"Yes, sir."

And he walked out the door.

I went back to my station, where Nicole and Rafik were chatting. When I arrived, their conversation halted and they both looked at me with wide, guilty eyes. They'd obviously been exchanging notes on me. Nicole spoke quickly, as if to cover the lapse of sound, "What about Ruiko's car?"

"My karma is working there, doll. Turns out she was going to have an engine overhaul anyway, but she couldn't find a good mechanic in town. I actually did her a favor by driving the car out to Abigail, where Ben, the last trustworthy mechanic in New England, is going to do the work. Her insurance even covered the towing."

"How nice," she said. "Everything is settled. Now we can get back to a normal life around here."

"To normal?" I said, then added a grunt, like Branco.

Nicole walked back to the front desk, leaving Rafik and me alone at my station. After a long gaze at each other, after our heartbeats had quickened and the background of the shop had receded, and there were just two people in the world, I heard myself say, "Let's make plans."